Acknowledgement of Country

The RMIT students, teachers and contributors
acknowledge this anthology was produced on the
lands of the Wurundjeri people of the Kulin nation.
We pay our respects to Elders past and present.
We recognise that sovereignty was never ceded.
We acknowledge the Aboriginal peoples' rich
tradition of storytelling, which continues in spite
of colonisers' attempts to silence and erase
First Nations people.

Always was, always will be. Aboriginal land.

Rise is published by Clover Press, an imprint of the
Associate Degree in Professional Writing and Editing at
RMIT University, 23–27 Cardigan St, Carlton, 3053.

ISBN: 978-0-6487056-2-8

Printing: IngramSpark

Cover design: Design by Committee

 A catalogue record for this
book is available from the
National Library of Australia

ABOUT CLOVER PRESS

Clover Press publishes work from the RMIT Professional Writing
and Editing programs. The clover, a humble, charming, resilient little
plant, spreads far and nourishes many. Its distinctive three-lobed eaves
perfectly capture the strength of these programs, integrating the three
key areas of writing, editing and publishing.

This name is also inspired by Arthur Clover, a longstanding teacher
who retired in 2015. Arthur had two influential mantras: Always Put
Students First; and always, always, Drink It While It's Fizzy!

Our Clover Press illustration has been created by PWE graduate
Ella Dyson.

Rise

an anthology

Contents

Introduction

Graeme Simsion

As a writer, I'm a little envious. Just a little, in the spirit of being careful about what you wish for. Because the opportunity to write what you want, without regard to theme, style or even audience, is both rare and confronting. *Show us what you've got, what you want published against your name, what you're prepared to be judged by.*

The contributors to this anthology have risen to that challenge, giving us an extraordinary variety of writing, from the conventional to the experimental, from memoir to fantasy, from standalone stories to slices of something bigger.

As a reader, it's exciting to encounter a collection which has not been curated according to an overarching vision or even somebody's idea of merit, but which represents the best work of emerging writers whose novels and short stories we will likely be reading and discussing in a few years. Absent a gatekeeper, or some sort of competitive ranking, we are seeing the stories that might not have made the cut as well as those that could have been prize-winners. We are invited to engage more critically, perhaps to reflect on our own tastes and prejudices.

We are accustomed to being able to decide after a few pages whether we want to read further. No such indulgence here: there's every chance that a piece we struggle to relate to will be followed by one which will be unforgettable. And perhaps that unforgettable piece will be one we'd never have read had we stayed within our literary bubble.

The job I didn't envy was that of coming up with a title: finding a theme that unifies a collection deliberately created without one. But these pieces do have something in common: they are the work of people who have chosen to devote significant time and effort to the craft of writing. That requires a certain optimism, a belief in the power of words and of writers to wield them to good effect. It seems to me that all of these stories, even the darkest, embody something of that optimism.

Rise is an inspired choice.

A Diary Entry

Joshua Dabelstein

Unlike the small, white 100 mg sertraline pills, the 50 mg ones that I've weaned down to are not scored. Having administered these Selective Serotonin Reuptake Inhibitors (SSRIs) every day for eleven years, I am fully aware of the ramifications of a mis-dose.

I stand over my desk guillotining pills with the switchblade that Albert, a family friend, gifted me for my ninth birthday. Albert died of leukaemia soon after, and I got the day off school to watch his casket move slowly along a conveyor belt and into a furnace. My father took the switchblade, blunted it, and gave it back to me. But blunt or not, I have always felt warm and safe with it handy. Now I need it to perform the opposite function: I'm using it to cut pills in half in order to encourage vulnerability, not fend it off. Dr Eli says that I need to learn how to engage with my emotions. I must gauge whether or not I truly have the chemical imbalance that I was diagnosed with as a teenager. The experiment piggybacks off another: I'm an alcoholic drug addict who has just reached thirty days sober, smashing the decade's previous record of forty-eight hours. This is no ordinary oil change. I've got a whole new engine. I'm learning how to drive manual in heavy traffic. And I'm playing chicken with an empty fuel tank on an open road.

But it's not all about chemicals and diagnoses and the buckets full of bodily fluids I clean out as I arrive back home from the hospital. The wean is an existential exercise too. I want to know if I can—left chemically unadulterated, and out on that open road—idle, rev and brake like a normal person. I am weak, I am compromised, I am not a man. I live in split cognition: on an intellectual level knowing these things I tell myself about myself to be untrue, but feeling their weight all the same.

* * *

I'm yelling for my mother from the toilet, age two or three. I eventually stand up and waddle across the bathroom with my pants down, opening the door to call out again. I've tried taking myself to the toilet but I can't seem to manage the folding and wiping situation. I know I can safely expel what needs expelling, but have failed to consider the rest of the routine. I'm distressed and red-cheeked, overwhelmed, standing in the bathroom doorway, penis out and pants down, with my father sitting at the other side of the room watching.

My father teases: 'Mummy's boy can't wipe his bum. Mummy's boy can't even take a shit without having his hand held.'

Mum walks into the room, puts her brick-sized Nokia down, and just when I think I'm being rescued the yelling starts. I shuffle back into the bathroom and close the door behind me. I'm sure he's going to kill her and then he's going to kill me for making him kill her, if not tonight, tomorrow night or next week maybe, because it is my fault they are fighting.

* * *

I chop another few tablets in half.

Eleven years ago, when I first started on sertraline, I had Mum promise not to tell Dad. Late that evening I hear the lurching of the stairs, and feel the familiar pang of dread as my bedroom door opens.

'Your mother says you're taking some sort of medication. Is that so?'

'Yes.'

'Why's that?'

'The doctor said I needed it.'

'I see.'

I hear the sneer in his voice as he walks out the door. Mummy's boy still can't even take a shit without having his hand held. Dad doesn't believe in 'the whole mental health thing'. Only when I imagine what it might have been like for him to have walked in on his own father's suicide attempt, at age eleven, do my fists unclench and melt from anger to deep, unspeakable pity.

* * *

The switchblade has been folded closed for weeks and I have been taking the half-pills. Then one Monday morning, it comes time for me to wake up and take none. I go to university that day, and everything is fine and normal, in fact everything is better than normal because I am so, so proud of myself. Monday evening, I'm elated.

The next morning I head to work and I feel free.

On Wednesday, I wake up a bit restless. Throughout the day I experience brain-zaps—which feel like someone ripping a bit of velcro off your skull from the inside. They're not painful, just disorienting. I find that the floorboards at work appear to be wobbling, despite the fact that I know that they are not. I decide that I should definitely not be riding a bike around Melbourne, just until I straighten out.

Thursday is rough. But sometimes things are a bit rough, and something that Alcoholics Anonymous has taught me is that as long as I go to bed sober, without having caused any damage or pain to others, everything is fine. Tomorrow is a new day.

And oh baby, it is. Friday, I am insane. I wake up manic, and begin commenting innocuously on people's social media posts because I am incredibly lonely. By lunch I am crying because people don't walk their dogs as often as I think they should.

Saturday is day six. I notice that the three assignments that I have due have all been half-written by someone who was up all night researching 'drones'. 'What about drones?', you ask. Cost, range, battery life, how much they can carry, whether they can send and receive encrypted information or whether it is *safer* to have your drone store the information it collects to its own solid state memory. Do I want to buy a drone? No, but I want to know what that man in the park was doing and why.

On Sunday morning I stare into the mirror for a very long time. 'The experiment has failed,' I announce to nobody, swallowing a 50 mg pill, because by this stage I'm narrating my own life out loud more than I realise. I call my grandmother. She tells me that she loves me and that diabetics take insulin every day.

* * *

I watch the man-child with the drone fiddle with his toy in the park, undisturbed. I wonder if every man on their fortieth birthday is presented with the option: a stand-up paddle board OR a drone. You can only choose one! A wry smile creeps up on me as I remember studying him from behind a tree only a few months ago. Lacey thinks it's a bird, and she does not like birds. Or rather, she feels very strongly about birds, and because she is a kelpie she is unable to express whether her incessant hounding of all birds is an expression of love or hate.

Perhaps it is both, perhaps it is neither. Perhaps the delineation between such strong feelings isn't so clear when those feelings can't be boiled down to their elements and poured across a page. Perhaps dogs just feel things differently, too.

We walk home and I consider my own feelings. The whitening of my knuckles when the bus is late; the swelling of my eyes every single time I read Tim Winton telling us that 'not all of Fish Lamb had come back'; the warmth in my chest when my grandmother excites herself into a description of the weather outside her window, as I picture her sitting on her couch with Noushka the dachshund draped across her lap. The quiet moment of peace when I regard myself in the mirror before I walk out the door.

I am right-sized, idling brightly in the front door; gratefully glacial, thawing in the morning sun.

JOSHUA DABELSTEIN is a Melbourne-based writer, cartoonist and musician. Having spent his formative years as a young journalist in Canberra's senate press gallery, Joshua's writing has since appeared in *The Sydney Morning Herald*, *The Age* and *New Matilda*. His current project can be accessed at uncooking.net or via Instagram @captain.cookd.

If We Go Down

Grace Costello

Middle Seat

The two glasses of white I had before boarding loosened me up, and when the plane left the ground, some lid inside me popped open and I started spilling out. As we rise through the clouds, and the pink sky darkens to purple, tears fall onto my tightly fastened seat belt. The men on either side of me sit like well-behaved schoolboys, Window Seat's length and Aisle Seat's bulk awkwardly contained in economy seats. Neither seems to notice me, which is fine. I'm used to being with people yet utterly alone.

The Game

It was an unspoken and unavoidable fact that Eric and I were playing a game. The winner was the person who cared the least: about anything, but especially about the other. He proposed to me after a fight; it doesn't matter what about specifically because, as always, we were fighting over the game and not acknowledging it.

'Hey, actually,' Eric said, breaking his brooding silence. 'Let's get married. Fuck it.'

'Ha, okay.' I said, waiting for the punchline. 'My family would *love* that.'

'Fuck your family.' He looked me in the eyes, a rare occurrence. 'I'm serious. Fuck them. My family too, and our friends. Let's do it.'

'Ha!' I said. 'Totally.'

Ghost

Looking past Window Seat at the black outside, I wonder if I'm invisible or fading away. I picture the engine stopping. Everything quiet, still. The plane dropping, everyone screaming, crying, but mute; the rush of the fall louder than anything, even our despair. I like the thought.

BYO

I expected never to hear about marriage again after the proposal, but Eric brought it up the next day, and we started planning a wedding. A cheap one in a rec hall, BYO, and yes, we are accepting gifts.

I kept waiting for him to laugh at me for not realising it was a joke, but he didn't. Sometimes we would even laugh together when we imagined how his mother, who hated me almost as much as he hated her, would look when we said, 'I do'.

Window Seat

I took a photo of myself smiling on the tarmac and posted it before take-off so Eric and everyone would see it and know I was fine. Pictures of me in LA with sunlight bouncing off my shoulders would confirm that everything is fine. Alternatively, if we go down, it will be official that nothing is fine. Eric will sob over the tarmac picture, regretting everything.

I catch myself smiling in the window reflection and glance at Window Seat to see if he's noticed me. He's watching something on the screen in front of him, so I look a little longer. His shirt is buttoned up to the neck. He has broad features and sombre eyes. His pink lips look dry but soft.

Winning

So, I knew the wedding *was* a big joke, but I thought we were in on it together. I got my dress—an 80s prom dress, I think—from an op shop. It was too big on me and bright white with a low waist and lots of swirling polyester. But I thought it was perfect for the joke.

When a brand-new navy suit and shiny dress shoes appeared in our house, I considered getting a different, prettier dress but decided against it; I couldn't let go of my lead.

Oh

I'm staring at my empty screen in front of me when I feel fingers gently tap my shoulder, and I turn to see Window Seat looking at me like he's been trying to get my attention for a while. Like he regrets that he had to touch me. I wonder how many smiles and frowns have passed over my face since I ceased being invisible. I try to look normal.

His mouth moves but I can't hear anything. Or maybe I can, but I'm too busy still trying to arrange my face. Then, his eyes dart to the front of the plane.

'Bathroom?' he says, enunciating with flaking lips.

'Oh!' I gulp, aware of my cheeks, puffy and warm from crying.

I unbuckle my seatbelt, stand up, lean back. Eric stopped touching me months before the proposal; I haven't felt a body this close to me in a long time.

Cheers

My heart raced throughout the ceremony, a whooshing in my ears made it difficult to hear anything, and I was so focused on hiding my nerves that I only glanced at Eric furtively, confirming that he was avoiding looking at me too.

After Dad's insistent clinking of silverware against his Corona to signify speech-time, Eric snuck outside, and everyone watched him go. They turned back to me, and I felt my face grow hot.

I said, 'He hates to have a fuss made over him,' and smiled and kept smiling until my face froze into a horrible thing.

Dad lifted his beer and said, slurring, 'We know she must have a good reason for this, and we look forward to seeing what it is.'

Everyone laughed uncomfortably.

It might have been okay if Eric had returned after the speech, stinking of cigarettes. But he didn't.

Sorry

As Window Seat squeezes back past me, the plane lurches and we're shaken together like two spoons in a sticky cutlery drawer.

'Sorry,' he says.

'No!' I say, which isn't the right response.

'We're flying into a storm,' he says, sitting. 'I heard flight attendants talking.'

'Oh no.'

He keeps looking at me.

'I'm sorry about the crying before,' I say.

He smiles, his dry lips cracking. 'I'm Charlie,' he says.

I imagine marrying Charlie and inviting Eric. Picture him skulking in the corner wearing the navy suit and shiny shoes.

'Nice to meet you, Charlie. I'm Lydia.'

The plane starts shaking.

Cake

The bright rec hall lights illuminated the guests slumped in their suits and strappy dresses, on chairs and some even on the floor, chatting or on their phones. The music had stopped, but with Eric gone, no one had bothered to fix it. I could hear the jangling of phone games.

Mum said Gran needed to go but wouldn't leave until after the cake. No one would. So, though I had been looking from the front to the backdoor, to my phone, hoping to see Eric in the hall, or 'Eric' on the screen, I didn't call or text him. Instead, I cut and served the cake.

Once everyone had a slice, I grabbed a chunk of what was left on the tray with my fingers and shoved the sticky mess into my mouth. The sponge was dry, but the icing curled over my tongue all sweet and satiny, and the cream was pleasantly milky.

My parents waved as they helped Gran out the door with her cake to go.

Don't Worry

The plane's shaking is okay if I imagine that I'm in a car driving down a cobblestone alleyway. It's a very long alleyway, though, and I'm starting to regret the wine from the airport. And the coffee, and the pie. Finally, an announcement comes over the speakers to remind us to fasten our seatbelts.

I turn and look at Aisle Seat, who's sound asleep, despite the turbulence, neck bent like it were snapped.

'Don't worry, Lydia,' Charlie says, leaning towards me with a smile. His breath smells like off milk.

I try to smile back, but the plane lurches, and I feel my stomach slosh and my mouth droop.

Clean Up

It was a warm night, and though I couldn't see the beach, I could smell the salty air mixing with rot when I threw the rubbish bags in the bin around the side.

I packed the presents into the boot, smoked three cigarettes in the car, and wondered if I should leave the country, win for good. But instead, I headed back to the place I had rented, which also didn't have a view of the ocean.

Eric was there. Still dressed, splayed on the bed, watching tv.

Confession

'I have a confession.' Charlie yells over the rumble of the shaking plane. 'I'm worried.' He's still smiling but I see now that his smile doesn't go beyond his lips, and his pupils are huge. 'What if we go down?'

'Don't,' I yell. 'Worry—I mean.'

'I don't want to die alone.'

I hear a deep scraping sound from my other side and turn to see Aisle Seat throwing up. I feel burning in my own throat and swallow it. For a moment, panic sits where the bile was, but I picture Eric crying again and feel calm.

'Lydia, will you tell me something?' Charlie yells.

The air reeks of vomit.

'Like what?'

'I don't know, something about you. Like—do you have any regrets?'

I almost laugh. 'I do.'

'Tell me?'

'Well, okay,' I yell. 'I regret getting married.'

Charlie cocks his head like a curious dog.

'Our relationship was a game.' Tears spill out of me again. 'The wedding was no different.'

'Why did you marry him?' Charlie shouts.

'I wanted to end the game.'

Charlie takes my hand in his. His palm is cold and clammy, but it feels wonderful.

I wish Eric could see me now. Moving on. But if we crash, no one will know about Charlie and me—unless our bodies are found entangled. How terrible. I squeeze his fingers tighter, *tighter*.

Losing

Maybe the wedding night could have been a draw if I'd made a cup of tea and a comment about my ex hitting on me in the toilets or just gone to bed without saying anything. But I didn't.

'I don't care that you left,' I screamed through fast-falling tears. 'But to leave me to clean up alone?'

Eric shrugged and told me he had come back to the house to take a shit.

Looking at him with his shirt untucked, fly undone, and his shiny black shoes on the bed, I wanted to run into the ocean and swim until I was swallowed by the salty water in one big wet gulp. Maybe I said that out loud. But I didn't say it was because my heart was breaking in the same place it had already broken a hundred times, rather, I said it was because I was embarrassed in front of everyone.

A mistake. He looked at me like I was sick.

'The whole reason we did this was to show those fucking plebs we don't care what they think,' he said. 'It seems like you care, though. Seems like you *really* care.'

Okay

Like a vacuum sucked all the commotion out, the plane steadies, and the roaring is replaced with the old dull rumble. The lights come back on, and a voice over the speakers announces that we're through the rough weather and the flight should be smooth from here on out. I turn and see Aisle Seat shaking his head with a relieved smile.

Honeymoon

I went to sleep on the couch and woke to find evidence of my caring everywhere. All over me and my try-hard-ironic outfit. In the neatly stacked home goods in the car. In my rotten breath.

When we arrived back home, me with blisters and a hangover, him *still* in the suit and shoes, he said: 'This isn't working, obviously. Might as well annul it, don't you think? Forget the whole thing?'

Fine

Charlie's hand slips from my sweaty grip. I turn back to him.

'See, Charlie,' I say louder than I need to, feeling inexplicably desperate. 'We're okay!'

'I think I need a rest,' he says quietly, smiling his non-smile. 'That was … a lot.'

'Totally,' I say.

The seatbelt sound dings off.

Charlie turns away and rests his head by the window. I look at him, curled up like a scared bug, and turn to face the other way. I close my eyes. He'll wake up before I do and will have to wait for me. That'll even things out. Not that I care. It's all fine.

GRACE COSTELLO is a writer and editor living on Wurundjeri land. Her writing explores love and loss, with a sprinkle of doom. She's had a story published in *Visible Ink* and is currently working on a novel about a girl and a ghost.

The Rats

Anthea Gannon

The glossy red SUV was fancier than any car I'd owned. I yanked at the chrome door handle and slid into the driver's seat. It was more comfortable than my couch. I ran my fingers over the faux wood steering wheel and pressed some buttons on the console. Music came out of speakers that belonged in a Toorak lounge room. I should have been looking at the base model cars at the back of the showroom. I'd never be able to afford this even with my big promotion, but I didn't want to get out.

A well-dressed woman appeared at the window. I'd need to move. I was sure she'd suss me out and send me away, but she opened the door, introduced herself as Lauren and smiled. 'It feels good, right?'

I tried for nonchalance. 'Yeah, I guess.' But I couldn't hide how much I wanted this car and I felt a stupid grin spread across my face.

'It's an RPV. It has the lowest emissions out of all the 2025 vehicles,' she told me.

'Is it electric?' I asked, getting out of the car.

'No. It's an RPV,' she repeated.

A what?

Before I had a chance to ask, she added, 'Rat Powered Vehicle. Rat emissions are very low. Not as low as solar, of course, but we can't guarantee that EPVs aren't charged using fossil fuel generated electricity—'

'What?'

She repeated some of the facts about solar, but she had to know that it was the rats I was confused about.

She lifted the bonnet and in place of the engine was a steel wheel. At the base of the wheel was a rat. A large, sleeping rat.

Lauren left me staring at the rodent inside the car engine. She went to the driver's seat and started the car. A projection of cheese appeared in front of the little guy. His body shivered and he jumped up. He looked straight at me, nose twitching, beady eyes shining. He was adorable. I wanted to reach in and pat him, but Lauren must have revved the engine and the little fella started to run. The spinning wheel turned cogs and the engine hummed to life. I could barely see his little legs. The faster he ran, the louder the engine sang.

How had I never heard of these before? I had been looking for a more efficient car than the old bomb I'd been driving since uni, but mostly I wanted one that would read out my text messages. This was both.

Lauren answered my questions about what to do with the rat poo and how fast we could go on the open road. I beat her down on price to just a little more than I could afford, and she threw in my first rat and a bag of rat pellets. She assured me that RPVs were the cheapest cars to run. It would only cost me a bag of pellets a month. I could do this. It would save me money in the long run.

Before I drove out with my new car, Lauren offered me a final piece of advice: 'Don't name the rat. It's not a pet; it's an engine.'

I drove off with Norman running frantically on his wheel.

As I drove into the work parking lot on Monday morning, a clear voice rang out of the speakers. 'It'll be an unseasonably hot twenty-seven degrees today, before a cool change in the early evening.'

What was I going to do with my little engine? I didn't want Norman to overheat sitting in his wheel all day. I looked around for something to carry him into the office with me. There hadn't been time for me to accumulate any clutter. I only had my laptop bag and my lunch box. That would have to do. I pocketed my sandwich to make room for Norman in my lunch box and kept the lid ajar so he could breathe.

We stopped at Petbarn on the way home to buy a cage. It could get cold where I lived and I didn't want to leave Norman in the car overnight. That would be cruel. I picked up a toy for him, so he wouldn't get bored waiting around for me, and bought some rat treats. That weekend I would be heading to the coast. Why hadn't I asked how far he could go? I decided to get a back-up rat. Just in case.

Two weeks later, the drive to work was slow. I pulled over to swap out Norman for Frank. When I picked up Norman to put him in the cage, he was looking a bit thick around the middle. I looked into his shiny black eyes. 'We'll have to ease up on the treats, Normie.' Was I fat shaming a rat?

The next week, as I reached in to pick up Norman, I found eight tiny rat babies in the cage. Suckling from him. Her.

What was I going to do with eight more rats? And then I realised: more back-up rats!

Two months later, the babies took turns on the wheel. The car felt zippier. My fuel cost was now ten bags of pellets per month: still cheaper than petrol.

Six months later, my alarm woke me before dawn. In the cage next to my bed my little friend was cleaning her paws. 'Morning Normie.'

I got out of bed, careful to step over the network of cages that was taking over the house, and set to work cleaning them out, replacing the straw, and feeding and watering my brood. I got through the process in under an hour. A record.

The sky was grey. I checked the forecast to find that storms were on their way. I couldn't let my little buddies get wet. When I left for work, I said goodbye to Normie, Frank and their progeny and walked past my glossy red car, umbrella in hand, to the bus stop.

ANTHEA GANNON is a writer and editor living and working in Melbourne on Wurundjeri country. She writes technical content for a big corporation during the day and in her time off enjoys writing short fiction, freelance articles and working on her first novel.

Inside Track Learner

Amanda Johnson

Staring at the black wrist guards, ignorant of how to correctly strap them to my wrists, I inhale that particular scent of sweat that is produced by nerves rather than physical exertion. Now that my brain has acknowledged its presence, it will only intensify.

I want to be invisible, but I recall my sister asking me how long it had been since I last rollerskated and warning me that I would probably break a wrist.

In preparation to speak I try to swallow, but I have no saliva and the gravelly feeling makes me want to cough. I breathe hard, like an Olympic gymnast in competition, and finally force the words out. 'Oh hey, can I just check … am I doing this right?'

I am not. My cheeks are hot, but my wrists are thankful.

I don the rest of my borrowed safety gear. The knee pads are too tight, but I'm exhausted by my previous interaction, so I tell myself they are fine. I put my skates on last and the moment I finish lacing up and rolling my feet across the floor from the safety of my seated position, something feels wrong. Surely these are a bit *rollier* than regular rollerskates. Panic washes over me as I realise I will never be able to peel my body from the low plastic bench without falling.

One of the roller derby coaches, Lauren, rolls by, and I aim for a cool and casual tone. 'Hi, I'm feeling a bit nervous and think I might die getting off this bench. Are you able to give me a hand?'

'Of course,' Lauren says, smiling. She holds me, and then I am standing.

The roller derby *Rainbow Rollers Learn to Sk8* classes are not filled with tattoo-clad bodies wearing strategically ripped-up schoolgirl uniforms, fishnet stockings and 'fuck you' printed on frilly underwear—as I had imagined. Everyone has opted for a modest black legging and singlet combo (disappointing) but the space is filled with warmth and comradery just as Drew Barrymore led me to believe it would be.

Even without an understanding of the rules or the point of derby, I knew I liked it. Yet neither the costumes nor the comradery were my reason for enrolling in the nine-week beginners (or fresh meat) program. My almost four-year-old son, Elliot, was.

One day as I hung adorably small t-shirts and undies on a clothes horse to dry, I noticed little brown marks coating each item of clothing. Assuming the marks were from a chocolatey serviette trapped inside a tiny pocket, I continued hanging the wet clothes … until the real source of the marks revealed itself.

There, in the washing basket trapped in a pair of twisted *Teenage mutant ninja turtle* undies, was a rogue poo I had accidently put through the washing machine.

My instinct was to be discouraged by the lack of toilet training progress we had made in the previous five months (also known as infinity). But after I threw away the undies and re-washed the poo-stained clothes, I decided I would try to better understand my kid's fear and frustration. And until *Bluey* makes a 'what to do when your kid is socially withdrawn, jealous of his twin sister's quick skill acquisition and shits anywhere but the toilet' episode, I decided to do what I ask my son Elliot to do every single day: learn something new.

For years I have thought of my son as living in a delightful dreamland of his own creation. He is cool and calm and doesn't need me in the way his sister does. But a child's dreamland can also be described as 'developmentally delayed or a reluctance to engage in or learn new things.' And once someone says it out loud, the 'dreamland' can quickly become feared rather than revered.

I never thought I'd be the kind of mum who wants their kid to 'just be like all the other children.' I mean, I'm a cool mum. I'm a social worker—we don't want to change the person; we want to change the world. I understand communication and empathy and diverse feelings … in theory. In reality, I don't want my son to be left behind because he refuses to learn. I don't want him to continue thinking that his pants are the only place to defecate. And I don't want him begging to stay home and watch telly because, 'there's other kids at the park'.

On the Sunday morning before my first class, I experience my first epiphany as I behave just like my kid. I want to stay in my pyjamas, watch telly, not speak to anyone new, and just be comfortable. Because honestly, watching telly and not speaking to people is freakin' awesome. But instead, I force myself into my car and down Bell Street as my inner monologue tells me I will be the worst one there. I am ridiculous, too old and not cool enough. I doubt my ability to skate and am reluctant to even try. I picture my kid walking away from me as I try to talk to him about keeping his undies clean.

By the time I arrive I am awkward and lonely. There is no clear signage, so I inch towards a dark brick building. I am greeted by a woman in a wheelchair who looks at my wide and uncertain eyes and tells me I am in exactly the right place. Her name is Pi Sexual, and I momentarily fall in love with the kindness of her gesture. I am safe. This is what I want for my son.

After Pi Sexual welcomes me—and after Lauren helps me stand—Curley Burley, another coach, meets me out on track. They take my hand without hesitation. Curley tells me my body just needs a minute, but that I can do this. I want to look into Curley's eyes and genuinely thank them, but my eyes refuse to shift their gaze from my feet. I thank the floor.

The track fills with about twenty-five learners and four coaches. At the beginning of class, Lauren gathers us together and says that Derby is like no other sport. 'We are here for each other, and we pick each other up. When we fall, we congratulate each other. We "woo" and we high five because we are trying, and we are brave.' I want to give myself over to the sentiment, but my fear consumes me.

I picture my mum strapping a couch cushion to my bum with a belt—the way she did when I skated as a child—and have a sudden urge to hold my little boy.

The Derby coaches are kind and nurturing and encouraging. Pi Sexual talks about Derby being grounded in trust. To be somewhere scary, to be brave, to be intimate, you need to trust those around you. By the end of my first class, I am gliding around the rink. We are asked to high five the person next to us. I high five a young woman and we both fall on our bums. Everyone cheers. And it feels fine.

Each Sunday class is still nerve-racking, but my nervous sweat becomes less potent. I stop arriving extra early, because I no longer need to gear up with no one else around (in case I do something foolish).

They still seem impossibly cool, but the Derby coaches have made a safe space for learning. They have made a safe space for us to make mistakes. At home, I read books to my son that affirm that mistakes are important, mistakes mean we are brave, and mistakes are how we learn.

By week five of the nine-week course, the other newbies aren't quite as shy either. There are still no ripped-up schoolgirl uniforms or fishnets, but their black leggings/black singlet combo of week one has evolved into short shorts with band or feminist slogan t-shirts paired with rainbow or tube socks.

This slow entry into Derby attire (as we know it from the movies) reminds me of my son trying to join in dancing with his older cousins. He desperately wants to be a part of the fun, to join the cool kids, but every time he launches his body towards the dance floor, his fear sends him back to that safe place behind my legs.

I stick with black leggings throughout the course, but I find my rollerskating rhythm. I wobble at the beginning of class, then remember how to glide. Each week we are shown new skills, then we practice. More confident skaters go on the outside track and those who require extra support from coaches stay on the inside.

I am an inside track learner.

I have trouble building on the skills from the week before because I don't remember, or couldn't master, them. Every class feels like I am starting from scratch, yet I watch the outside track skaters confidently rocket past me. The young woman with whom I shared a high five and fall with on week one speeds past me and jumps the *big* witches hats.

The pang I feel is not from jealousy but recognition. This is how my son feels when he watches his twin sister just 'get stuff'. I continue to glide and stick to the safety of the small witches hats. The small ones are for me.

After class one Sunday, I notice the referral for a developmental paediatrician I had stuck to my fridge. I am supposed to follow up with a phone call to get an appointment, but instead I consider that maybe my son is like me, an inside track learner. I postpone the phone call to the paediatrician in favour of emulating Derby Coach, Pi, on my first day—I reassure my kid he is in exactly the right place.

I try to ignore the nuisance of stepping in urine barefoot and I continue reading books about bravery and mistakes. I accept that watching TV *is* more fun than talking about keeping undies poo-free. I buy a potty that looks like a small toilet and decorate it with a picture of a pirate, colourful stickers and my son's name. I tell him it's just for him, no one else ... and, slowly, he begins using it.

AMANDA JOHNSON is a Melbourne-based writer, social worker and community services teacher. She has written for *Overland Literary Journal*, *The Big Issue* and *Visible Ink*. Find her published essays, profiles and short stories at amandajohnson.com.au or wait for her first tweet @amanda_jane81.

No Place for a Woman

Ysabel Kershaw

The storm was her fault, of course. The first six days of the voyage had been blessedly calm as the ship crept across the bay, the land never out of sight. White gulls circled lazily around the masts, squawking noisily as the ship cut through the waves. It was cold when the wind was blowing, but there was something bracing about the salt smell in the air. With clear-blue skies and open sea before them, it was hard to think anything could go wrong. The men joked that having a woman on board didn't seem so unlucky after all.

Jossey had never been on a ship before, and she could hardly eat. When she did force down the gruel that sailors substituted for food, it never stayed there for long, but aside from that, she wasn't handling the sea too badly. Some of the crewmen had been kind enough to give her tips on how to keep her legs under her when the hull swayed. But the majority of them still disliked her presence.

'A kennel for a bitch,' Slick Symon had said as Jossey climbed onto the deck of *Blackbird* for the first time and been shown to her cabin. He was a thin, sinewy man, and used a mix of spit and sea spray to keep his black hair back from his face. His goons beside him—Hal and Little Jack, as well as many of the other men—had laughed, but it was Symon's eyes that had lingered on her longest, and his two-toothed smile that always followed her. She had shot him a mean look and spoke to the captain, but Gibbs had just shrugged his shoulders and told her it was the way of a sailor to talk as such. And so, the nickname stuck. Though some of the men were courteous enough to not take part in it—at least not in her presence.

On the seventh day, the rains began and didn't stop. As the ship broke into open sea, Jossey spent most of her time below deck in her cabin. Cabin was a generous word. It barely fit the small cot pushed against the wall. An oil lamp dangled from a stuck nail in the wall. Light from the day rarely filtered in, and at night it was pitch-black. The noise from the heavy rain was muffled down there, but the crewmen more than made up for it with their grunts and snores.

Only an old rickety dressing screen stood between her cot and the rest of the crewmen's quarters. Each night, Jossey had to tug it into place and use spare rope to tie it to the nail. It meant she couldn't have a lamp lest there be a fire, and if one of the men tried, they could easily break through.

But still, she was glad for the semblance of protection and privacy.

On the ninth night, Jossey had to force the screen back with a bang and run up to the deck to retch. The men in their bunks had laughed and howled at her as she clambered up the steps, calling after her with words that made '*kennel bitch*' seem tame.

The sea and sky were as black as pitch. At the oars, the men rested. Jossey had run to the wrong side of the deck and the wind had blown bits of vomit back onto her.

The ocean is rough, her father had told her with a frown, *and no place for a woman.* He'd barely looked up from the papers he had been reading when she barged into his office, firm on the idea that she was due an adventure. Even if that adventure was only a short visit to see her aunt. Jossey could clearly remember the way his shoulders had dropped as he tugged his white moustache. He knew he couldn't dissuade her. Better he organise her trip than she run off by herself. Within the night Jossey had been packed and ready to go.

Maybe he was right, Jossey thought miserably.

'There there, miss.' Robert the Red came up beside her, and with shaking fingers she took the offered blanket. It was coarse and rough, scratching at the neck and catching in her hair, but it was a lesser evil to the bitter wind.

Robert the Red was named for the angry rash of boils that dotted his face and neck. Where there weren't boils there were pox scars. He was frightful to look at—probably the ugliest man Jossey had ever seen—but he was the kindest of the sailors, and the one who had given her the rope for her screen and shown her how to tie it.

'This may be the worst of it,' he said.

'I hope so,' Jossey replied.

No sooner had she spoken than lightning cut across the sky, sudden and blinding. Distant clouds were only illuminated for half a beat, but it was long enough to see their size. Dread made itself known with a chill. There was mountain upon mountain of clouds, purple and crimson and black, seemingly taller than the world. Thunder cracked an instant later, so loud she felt it echo in her bones.

The men hated her for that storm, and the storm hated everything.

The men cursed her as bad luck when she walked past—Symon, Hal and Little Jack the loudest of them all. Soon, all the men had caught on. They spat in every bowl of stew and cup of ale she was given and shoved her back into the kennel every time she tried to go up deck.

The storm clawed at the ship with relentless currents and slapped it with waves as cold as ice.

It raged at them with winds and thunder and hail.

She got no sleep, and the days began to bleed into one another.

Her father was right; she never should have come here.

The crew's hate was a hot poker on her skin; it branded her as cursed. Even Captain Gibbs and Robert the Red refused to speak to her now, muttering about urgent jobs to do whenever she approached to talk to them.

Each day was worse than the one before, and the storm continued to wage war against them.

It was only a matter of time until something happens, Jossey thought with dread. She hadn't left her cabin in three days, fearful of what the crew would do to her. Her stomach soon ached with hunger and her clothes stunk of old fish. Maybe if she stayed in her kennel, they would forget about her completely.

On the twelfth day, the time has finally come.

'Storm isn't stopping,' Gibbs says, standing before her in the rain. Lightning flashes and illuminates the men crowded around her.

'Please, don't do this,' Jossey's voice comes out hoarse. Her cheeks are wet with tears and sea. Hal and Little Jack had ripped her flimsy screen down and tugged her up the deck kicking and screaming. They had not done so gently, and her skull aches from where it banged on the wooden door. The taste of blood is hot in her mouth.

They drag her onto the deck and hold her down, tying her legs and hands with rope. Jossey struggles to free herself but it is useless. They force her to stand before their judgement. All around her, the men stare with cold eyes. Robert the Red is nowhere to be seen.

'Told your father a ship is no place for a girl,' Captain Gibbs says. 'Told 'im to keep you home. A girl like you, too stubb'n for your own good. But did he listen? If you want to blame; blame 'im. The sea is cold. Cold and cruel. She ain't gonna let us live without something for h'rself.' The harsh wind blows his grey hair from his face, and he nods at Slick Symon.

Symon comes forwards and jabs at Jossey with a paddle. She cries out, even though she would rather scream. Scream and curse them all to a watery grave and watch while they drown. She tries to move, but the ropes binding her legs and ankles are too well tied. Symon jabs at her again and she spits at him. The glob hits him just below his left eye. His face darkens. He steps forward and strikes her with the paddle so hard she careens off the gangplank and plummets to the restless water below.

The captain was right: the sea is cold.

Murky darkness obscures all hope of finding the surface as the sea drags her deeper and deeper. Salt stings her nose like a thousand needles and red splotches dance across her eyes. She can't remember if they're open or shut. The pressure on her chest is an anvil. It feels like Jossey's ribs will shatter and her lungs will explode. Despite the coldness of the ocean, colder than any hell that she could have ever imagined, her lungs are on fire and heat rips through her body all the way down to the toes. Jossey kicks and thrashes in the water, helpless against the ropes that tie her legs and the colossal strength of the sea. There is a booming echoing in the water like drums. Maybe it is her heart.

Boom, boom, boom.

There is no peace in drowning. Let that be known.

Boom, boom, boom.

Drowning is like having a pistol held to your head and being told not to breathe. And you must breathe.

Jossey opens her mouth, gasps for air.

Icy water thrusts up her nostrils as salt burns her throat. Despair fills Jossey with every struggling gulp that she can't stop. In the moment that the coolness rushes in she knows that she is already dead. In seconds she will float like the seaweed, nothing more than flesh and bones ready to decay in the currents.

The sea is cold, the captain had said.

Yes, she thinks, *but I am colder.*

And the ocean? The ocean is her mother.

It fills her up, enveloping her where it once beat her, caressing her where it had pulled her apart at the seams. No longer was the ocean killing her; it was cradling her. The current came to comb her hair, to soothe the wailing child, to kiss all the hurt away. The water was no longer cold, but cool against her skin, bracing and fresh and alive like it had been that first day on the ship.

The waves gently tug her dress away, embracing her nakedness. Her mother is angry as she tears the ropes from Jossey's legs, and her rage brightens the sea with lightning. Yet her touch is soft, cradling, soothing, even as thunder cracks above the crashing waves. When the ropes are gone, the current carries them swiftly down into the darkness. Jossey has never felt more natural, more strong. The soft scales are the same shade as the ocean in storm.

When she opens her mouth to sing, her voice is husky from the salt water that had once burned her throat. Now, the liquid flows through her veins. In the distance, her sisters answer her melody. They rejoice for her in their songs, and the current gives her a gentle nudge.

Walk, her human mother had once said to her.

Swim, the ocean sang.

The captain and her father and all the men were right; a ship is no place for a woman.

This is the place for a woman.

I have salt in my veins, she thinks as she begins to swim after the ship, *and I will show them how cold these waters can be.*

YSABEL KERSHAW is a writer, editor and an artist. She has a keen interest in feminist literature, particularly when it's entwined with mythology. Between taking art commissions and studying at RMIT, she is writing her secret debut novel. See more from Ysabel creatively via Instagram @ysabel_claire_ or professionally at ysabelkershaw.wixsite. com/my-site.

Indoor Playground

Dakota Stafford

The first week is uncomfortable; I fidget in my seat.
With make-up and my hair done, I smile through my teeth.
This is nothing like a sick day where I've had to work from home!
Because now I hear my partner greeting his boss on the phone.
My workmates share my nerves while my boss just tries to laugh,
But I can see that she knows too, that this is all a farce.
Is this what work from home will be until we're all let out?
Staring at a screen while we ignore our social drought.

The second week feels better as I sip my third green tea,
My cat has grown to love me here and all the treats I feed.
My partner has settled in at home just fine with all his farts,
If he didn't cut it out, I said I'd complain to house HR.
He said he'd stop but just in case I moved into the kitchen,
His sounds still reach my benchtop like they're cast by a magician.
At least here when I swear at work, I know I won't get sacked,
A blanket and a snack supply are what my workplace lacked.

The third week feels more normal as I admire my pyjamas
(I bought them in a meeting because I liked the patterned llamas).
My boss has quit her make-up, but still straightens her hair,
I applaud her for her efforts because I've lost the will to care.
I think I've gone five days without a shower before work?
It's hard to track the things I do, but I guess that that's a perk.
My clothes might not smell the best but at least I have some candles,
And since I'm trapped inside I can't be blamed for my love handles.
I've reached the stage where I've lost track of how long we've been here,
My partner and I now end the day with a glass of wine or beer.
I wonder about the length of time we'll have to stay inside,
My home has all the comforts that my workplace can't provide.
Here at home, it can be cramped but at least we have AC—
I know that's such a small thing, but it means a lot to me.
I don't know how we'll cope when the horn of freedom sounds,
I think we'll want to stay inside our own indoor playgrounds.

DAKOTA STAFFORD is a budding writer who delights in crafting lively stories that will have readers flaunting their pearly whites. She is currently pursuing her passion for fiction writing and hopes that earlier high school articles do not remain as her only published works. Check out Dakota's website at dakotastafford.com.

Matters of the Fart

Jasmine Alavuk

An inch from humiliation, I feel my stomach tighten in that familiar, gut-twisting way. I am in Grade 3, in a classroom full of nine and ten-year-old students. We're having an indoor lunch due to the heavy rain pelting the windows, and I'm distracting my friends with what I believe is a very funny joke.

'Hey guys, check this out.'

BUUUUUUURRRRRRGGHHHHeeeee

I lean my left bum cheek to the right, lifting a vibrant fart into the stale atmosphere. Inevitably, as with all uncontrollable bodily functions, I misjudge the execution of my release and the pressure evaporates at a thunderous volume. The classroom, which only seconds ago was full of noisy chatter and laughter, abruptly turns quiet.

'Who was that?' My teacher, Mrs Strickland, stands from her desk at the front of the room. Her lips are pressed into a thin line as she moves her eagle-like gaze from student to student. Her hands are on her hips. Not good.

'*Who was that?*' she commands again, shaking her head like

a pissed-off parent. Her bushy blonde ponytail swings fero-ciously from side to side. '*So rude!*' Her voice penetrates the silence.

I'm in the back corner of the room, cowering quietly, hoping that she'll let it slide and everyone will resume their banter until the bell rings, but the room stays nauseatingly still. My cheeks burn. I make awkward eye contact with the others at my table, silently pleading with them not to out me. Their heads lower and my heart shivers. No one has spoken for thirty seconds. The room will stay hushed unless I confess.

'Sorry,' I hear myself whimpering. I look over to Mrs Strickland and bite my lip. My breaths are short and as I inhale through my nose, I can smell the faintest scent of poo particles still lingering around the table—the stench of guilt.

'I'm sorry,' I say again, louder to the silent room. Her eyes pierce directly at mine. I am a puddle. Tears prick lightly under my cheeks and my mouth turns downwards, quivering.

'That's atrocious. How *disgusting.*' I feel everyone's eyes on my hot face. Mrs Strickland turns away, satisfied to have repri-manded the culprit for a loud, stinky fart. The tears roll down my cheeks and I hang my head to hide them, looking down at my feet under the table.

In a roundtable of embarrassing stories, often drunkenly un-folded at parties, I share this memento to warn others not to fart in public. My mum has a joke about my farts, because I do them so often at the dinner table and because I have no shame in letting one rip around familiar and forgiving faces. When the wind relaxes in my abdomen and the noise and smell permeates the room, she'll tsk and say, 'Jasmine, one day you'll be having dinner with the Queen and you'll forget!' I laugh it off and my dad calls me a 'prase' which in Serbian means pig.

·

In Isabel Allende's *The House of the Spirits*, 'Juan of the Fart' experiences a similarly embarrassing fate, much like the archived misfortune of my childhood memory. In Allende's story, Juan is desperately in love with the Harvest Queen, Costanza Andrade, and, vying for her attention and affection, he lets out a burst of wind as he completes a somersault from a tree branch. Costanza laughs uncontrollably, and Juan is so humiliated that he disappears, never to be heard from again.

I read this chapter recently, guffawing at the printed page in my hand, reminiscing about the traumatic embarrassment I faced in a room full of my peers, the terror of being called out for my blatant lack of self-awareness. In that room, all those years ago, as the rain drizzled down the windows in front of my hunched spine, I was determined to shrink until I disappeared. I trembled in the face of unwanted attention, despite calling for it in the first place like Juan. What I had not accounted for when I lifted my bottom, was that the butt of the joke was not the fart; it was me, and no one laughed.

Despite the momentary trauma of it all, my little shame spiral passed. The smell faded and almost everyone forgot about it. In retrospect, while I could've been more discreet, I do believe that sometimes, it really is better out than in. The aching pressure of meals past, bubbling in one's gut, will only continue to build until it is freed. Why should we hold in something just to make others more comfortable?

Farts have long been stigmatised in the lore of society; hold it in or you'll be shunned. I suppose much can be said about a multitude of other things that cause shame in Western culture. A fart is just a nugget of air, a vapour of stink, escaping into the atmosphere. How can something so normal, albeit fragrant, cause so much embarrassment or repulsion?

'Our taboo against farting is part of our taboo against shit,' says Jim Dawson in his book *Who Cut The Cheese: A Cultural History of The Fart*. 'Everything we eat turns to shit or internal gas, yet we act as if turds and farts don't exist.'

If I could go back in time, to being the nervous girl in the corner of the classroom, perhaps I would tell Mrs Strickland this: you are, quite literally, full of shit, which also means that you fart too—anywhere from five to twenty-three times a day on average—and I bet if you could let one rip right now, you'd probably feel really good.

I guess farts are a vulnerable thing to share. They command attention, unwanted or otherwise, and to give them attention means sitting in your stink while your teacher and two dozen pairs of eyes glare at you. Maybe if Juan's pride hadn't been compromised by the Harvest Queen's laughter, he could've owned the untimely burst of air, like some kind of intended 'fartistry'. Farts are a part of life. And I also think they're a bit funny. I hope that when your stomach tightens in that familiar gut-twisting way, whoever is around you at the time can cop a whiff without making you cry.

'Perhaps the notion of proud, feel-good farting is not in the best interests of society,' says Dawson. 'After all, who wants to smell your farts—besides you?'

To that I say—'smell me' for I am just a girl with a cramp in her heart trying not to obliterate her insides by holding it in.

JASMINE ALAVUK is an arts educator in the youth community media sector. When not producing radio shows with teenagers, she writes very personal essays, which can be found in *Refinery29* and *Fashion Journal*. You can see pictures of her cat on Instagram at @b_loated.

A Modern-Day Laika

Theresa Tully

The Pomeranian stood at the mantel in his prized smoking jacket—an Ascot Chang number he'd had tailored during his last business trip to Hong Kong. Despite the quality of the garment and the healthy flicker of the fire, the dog just couldn't get warm.

Oh, how he would've done things differently if he had the chance again. If only he'd tapped a phone call. Propped a hidden camera on the lapel of his coat. Stayed back late to rummage through Mr Bilbo's shredder. All that evidence, now just kibble-coated strips, splattered in sardine oil, garbage-bagged and sent to the tip, waiting to decompose long after he had gone. He whistled under his breath. What a waste. He should've known. After the inquest. And Doug, the poor turkey. Eight years.

They were looking for a scapegoat. Who better than some loyal bastard like himself? A Pomeranian.

But there was Tess, the bitch—his bitch—what would become of her? And the pups? He hunkered down and gnawed at his left paw. Eczema. It always flared up with stress.

Tonight, he'd have a colloidal oatmeal bath. He'd tenderly lick the top of Max and Daisy's heads. And then for god knows how long until the next time—if there would be a next time—he'd curl up beside Tess.

Tomorrow they'd be coming for him. Charge him with tax evasion. Lead him away with his tail between his legs. He laughed now at the thought—a modern-day Laika. Expendable in the end.

THERESA TULLY is a writer, editor and publicist. She's currently working on her first novel, a middle-grade fantasy/sci-fi about a nine-year-old physicist who traverses the multiverse.

When Ariel Came Back

Renée Cahill

When Ariel Came Back is an extract from a larger work.

When Elena gets home from work—a long, success-ful day of bullshitting people out of their money and into some of the worst properties in regional Victoria—she returns to a property no better than the ones she's been embellishing all day. The trick was to sell an idea rather a house. More often than not, that idea was family—home. Just imagine it, she would say, over and over until soon enough the clients, often young couples, would look around some draughty rundown house and see bright walls and sunlight, despite the lack of windows. Soon enough it was clear to them: portraits in place of asbestos and tiny, perfect children running around.

Elena's house is too big for her now. It's just her and Noah, who's fifteen and sure to be gone soon too. The house is much too big, but sometimes it's suffocating. When Elena sells the idea of family she might as well be renting out her own memo-ries. When she talks of perfect, tiny children she is talking about her own. Now Ariel is twenty-six and imperfect—imperfect like a living child always is. Ariel is back after being gone for eight years and she's not half as well as Elena always liked to believe all those years she was gone. July would be twenty-eight. July is still perfect and beautiful, as a dead child always will be to her mother. Perfect and gone.

Elena, so accustomed to quiet, is surprised to find signs of life. She can hear chatter, easy, comfortable, coming from the dining room, Ariel and Noah, siblings and strangers. She almost tiptoes around it, careful not disturb them. She hears something like a laugh. *Ariel.* It's a sound she hasn't heard since Ariel came back. Not for the eight years she was gone. Maybe not since before July died.

Elena cracks something like a smile—however pained—and pours hot tea from the still-steaming pot in the kitchen. Chamomile from the garden. She wanders to the front balcony. Wonders at the view. She has spent half her life looking at that view, but it never gets old. Even though she has, or will. When Elena came to Maldona she was in her twenties, a young woman, now she is ... a less-young woman.

It had been Rob's house really. He'd grown up in Maldona and convinced Elena that the place was paradise. More likely, she had conceded years later, the place was all Rob could afford. Not that she could afford any better, not when they met—met on those long train ride commutes to the city. At first, they didn't notice each other. Then after months of the same journey, they did. Elena noticed Rob and he noticed her noticing him or maybe it was the other way around. It was the kind of story that if they were still together, she reflected, their children might know off by heart. The kind of story Elena and Rob would have turned into a routine for every family occasion. It was the kind of story that through retelling might have become something else, a rom-com instead of a tragedy.

It became Elena's sanctuary, her haven, that train, the conversations they would share. The moments of connections. On either end of the trainline she was in hell. There was the house she'd grown up in, without either of her parents in it, then, in Melbourne, there was her father in hospital.

Every day Elena visited—and she did visit most days—her dad was just a little bit less living. An inch closer to death, as the cancer took more and more of him from her. Took him from the realm of the living. Wiped out more easily on painkillers towards the end, Elena would find him barely lucid. It came to the point where all she could do was put her head in her hands and watch her father, try to breathe in sync with him, like she used to as a child. His breaths raspy, hers somewhere adjacent to sobs. It was a time of urgency. Elena would sit with her sleeping father, praying for him to wake up. She always had the sense she had something to tell him, or something she needed him to tell her. But when he woke, he'd only ask for more pain pills, speak of the weather, or request mashed potatoes. Or some exotic dish he wouldn't be able to swallow, but that Elena would dutifully deliver all the same. Sometimes he'd apologise but he wouldn't say what for.

Now when Elena thinks of her father, decades later, she still cannot disentangle him from his death, from the decay. She tries to picture him as a young man, maybe pushing her on the swings at the park—Elena is sure that he *had* pushed her on the swings and read bedtime stories and shared Christmas lunches, but she can't see it. Her childhood is in fragments, glinting in dim lights like stray treasure. Irretrievable. All she can see is her father, gaunt and hooked up to the oxygen machine.

After her father took his last shaky breath, after the quiet funeral—too loud still for Elena—she found herself back on that commute, travelling for hours and hours, going nowhere. Elena needed the habit of it, needed some normalcy. Once she got to the city, she would walk around for hours and hours. Absorbing none of the atmosphere of it, instead—it was absorbing her. She went to the hospital, sometimes, still. Sat out the front on the steps. Imagining some other man or woman, some other parent perhaps, occupying the bed in the palliative care unit that her father had died in.

And so, in those first weeks, months, when everything was dark and maybe even the view might not have saved her, Elena fell in love on the train with a man named Rob. When he moved her into that house in Maldona it really felt like paradise for a while. The way the house with its quaint airs and mulberry curtains felt brand new, the way it hadn't known her grief. Had not yet seen her cry.

As a young woman, she watched the sun set and rise and set again. So reliable, comforting, she looked out at the vast expanse of forest, the eucalyptus tall and reaching toward the heavens, and imagined her father at the other end. She spied the cracks of blue ocean through the bush and felt as if the whole world were hers.

She had babies, as one does. A pair of beautiful little girls, just two years apart. July named for winter and Ariel for a mermaid or maybe—she smiles wryly as she remembers it—she'd been reading too much Sylvia Plath. The problem was that while Elena raised her babies into girls, Rob still took that damn train every day. Fell in love with other women on other commutes, and slowly, but surely, the forest began to close in on Elena.

Rob came back and left and came back again. They had Noah. Her sweet Noah. They were almost a picture-perfect family again. The kind on adverts for camping gear or ice-cream. But if Noah had brought Elena's family back together, July destroyed it.

After July died, Elena felt this same sense again, worse still, as though the forest were intent on trapping her. The blue behind it, so out of reach, no longer any miracle. She glared at the eucalyptus, no longer a gateway to heaven. If it were, she could only resent heaven for taking her daughter away. And so, the house learned grief. Learned her tears and her screams. Learned dysfunction. It grew from Elena into all the corners of every room. Grew into all the edges of Elena's surviving children. The house learned their grief too.

Rob left, and then Ariel. Fairweather family. Elena stayed in that large trembling house with her relics and wilting flowers and kept all the windows locked for years. She had Noah, the quiet child with a habit of sinking into corners, barely noticed by his mother—the liquor was too strong and July was everywhere.

Now when Elena stares at that view from the balcony, she knows she is not free. The whole world is not hers, nothing is certain, nothing is promised. Inch by inch she has learned to enjoy the view again, all the same. She has learned to enjoy it not as a delusion or some saviour but as it really is, a beautiful vision. Like how you might gaze into a painting, or somebody's eyes. Like how you might look up at the stars and make no wishes. Like how you might look in the mirror and feel no discontentment, asking nothing of your reflection. Like how you might learn to stop asking empty rooms for help. Elena loves the view again, not with passion, not with fire. She loves it steadily and reliably, but she has long abandoned any notion that it might be able to save her.

Maybe this is how Elena has learnt to love her living children—or how she should have learnt by now. Ariel and Noah's voices dance into her consciousness. Easy, lilting laughter. She smiles but she doesn't see the view anymore. She's staring into the future.

RENÉE CAHILL is a writer with a particular love for fiction and poetry. Her writing has featured in *Beyond Words International Literary Magazine*. Renée is currently working on her first novel. Find her work at reneecahillauthoreditor.com.

Her Skin

Isabella Liistro

It cranes its neck at an impossible angle to see its shoulder torn, flesh dangling from the tear like shredded meat. The inside looking at the outside, a near invisible hexagonal layer of mesh, lit only by the blinking traffic signal over the road. Beneath the honeycomb-like web of skin is a ceramic masquerade of bone and vein twirled together. Over the shoulder, above the chin, a motionless, human face of a girl. A nude, factual, anatomical picture of femininity. To call her plain would be inaccurate—she could be attractive if she put the effort into it. Her eyes roll with a strange, deadened vacancy. Her fingers splay, then stiffen, tightening a poorly sewn twine of dental floss through the wound and up to her clavicle. Her eyes travel over the healing flesh.

Suspended from a queue of pipes on the concrete underpass, she pulls her angular limbs into a simple summer dress, the price tag still hanging from its spaghetti straps. A wig tickles her chin, the fringe is uneven, chopped with a child-like crookedness and black with a synthetic gloss, but the effect is striking.

'A ... A ...
B ... B ... B ...
C ... C ...
D ...
F ... F ... F ...'
She speaks with a clipped, digital inflection. There is a slight, imperceptible blankness in her stare which stays pinned to the dips in the pavement.
'G ... G ...
H ... H ... H ...'
She adopts a more playful crescendo.
'I ... I ...
J ... J ... J ... Jaaay'

* * *

Car fumes bite the air as she walks the boulevard, following hundreds of boozed echoes to a nightclub—a shifting view of human life. The girl moves through a melee of people in line against the building wall; women swishing their faux totes between their legs, the skunky, burnt sting of hash on their clothes and men staining their cheap cuffs with philtrum sweat. Some look at her with suppressed desire, one licking his tongue. A boy—so thin a light breeze could blow him over—fishes a cigarette out of his pocket then lights it, sheltering the flame from the wind before blowing a thick cloud of smoke over his acquaintances—one being a blonde, wasp-waisted woman moving to the pounding, sleazy beat. The girl watches the woman the way someone might look at a blank wall they're thinking of painting or knocking down. She could be anywhere from sixteen to thirty, with one of those rare, painfully beautiful faces.

A knockout. Her black high-heeled pumps shuffle across the concrete. Her handbag whirling side-to-side against her summer dress—similar to the girls, though clung tighter to her bottom. The girl copies, easing the hem of her frock a little higher.

The woman picks the thin boy's cigarette from right between his teeth and pops it against her swollen cherry lips, exhaling a clean and luscious plume of smoke that curdles above their heads. Another puff draws focus to her mouth, nose, cheeks, eyes. The girl emulates, pursing her lips and blowing the air like it were a hot meal.

* * *

The woman writhes against the thin man's pelvis, tasting the smoke-filled dance floor with her tongue. He slides his fingers up her bronze thigh, drawing circles under the fabric of her dress. His hands make their way to her neck and then up through her mermaid locks, sniffing it, tugging at it, pulling her closer to his groin with it. It's like watching sin. The girl fluffs her plastic fringe, swinging her hips offbeat with the music. Arms outstretched, she slowly catches onto the rhythm, beginning to dance like the woman, so precise and exact as though a circuit in her brain captured every toe point, shoulder shimmy and hip-pop before she'd even made it. Against the dead end of the illuminated tiles, the girl cavorts, touching her porcelain shell.

* * *

The woman leans against the bathroom sink and cuts a small, loose thread from her panties—black lace, *La Perla*—with a pair of cuticle scissors pulled from her handbag. The girl peers from the neighbouring sink.

'They're very pretty,' she says, 'The underwear.' Spoken softly, delicate, with the innocence of a prepubescent girl.

The woman bites her lip in reply before closing her legs and setting the shears on the mint-tiled benchtop. The girl sets her hand on the woman's collarbone, then elbows, then knees, then under an armpit, even that tiny crevice between her top lip and nostrils; she presses into it, petting it, rubbing it, slathering her touch. The woman's sensuality hangs in the air as her cheeks are pulled and played with before the girl leans forward and gives the woman a gentle kiss, lingering, learning the language of her warm, supple lips.

The girl holds something in her hand. As the woman pulls away, the scissors jut out of her chin and her entire jaw peels off, spurting blood and bone, the girl is painted with it, her synthetic form dripping red as she removes her wig. The body falls and slumps against the tiles. Expressionless, the girl reaches around the back of her head, to the nape of her neck and begins unzipping the shell around her jaw, removing her face, past her shoulders, breasts, abdomen, pubis then down to her toes, revealing the machine beneath. A porcelain, pristine design. The machine's face is blank, rather, an empty mould of where its features should be. It kneels beside the body and uses the shears to flay the skin, carefully, indefectible, like a textilist separating fabric. It steps into the hull, pulling it on like the perfect pair of jeans. The skin swallows the mesh as if magnetised, sucking itself against the robot parts. The ceramic web vanishes as it applies the last section of skin until nothing of the machine remains. It checks its reflection in the mirror, twisting its body in different angles, trance-like, ethereal. A woman.

ISABELLA LIISTRO is a developmental editor and writer specialising in horror and young adult fiction. She spends most of her time talking about films, nurturing her border collie and working on her first dystopian-western novel about a stubborn scav on the run.

Sunflowers

Kelsie Harford

The nursing home was newly built, smelling of paint and sawdust and sanitiser. Abbey was filling out the volunteer check-in when she heard Lolly's loud voice from the hall.

'Open your eyes, you old fool!'

Abbey grinned as Lolly rounded the corner. Lolly stopped in the doorway with her fists triumphantly on her hips. Today she was wearing a hot-pink tracksuit and tennis shoes she had coloured in with texta to match. Her mop of white fairy floss hair stuck out wildly around her face. Lolly was Abbey's favourite resident; she made work-for-the-dole bearable.

'You're looking very pleased with yourself this morning,' said Abbey.

'It's Wednesday,' said Lolly, as if that were something obvious. 'Wake up!' she barked at the receptionist, who jumped in her seat. Lolly chuckled. 'Keep your wits about you, girl.'

'You still smoking?' she asked Abbey, who shook her head. 'Bugger,' Lolly grumbled. 'Come on, we've got work to do.'

Lolly's room never failed to shock Abbey. Residents were given free rein to decorate however they liked, and Lolly took it as a personal challenge. Every wall, from floor to ceiling, was covered in a hodgepodge collage of sunflowers. Plastic sunflowers, pictures of sunflowers and bits of yellow and brown paper from magazines—all cut up and arranged to look like sunflowers. Lolly had once told Abbey she used to live on a farm with two of every farm animal. She and her son had planted nothing but sunflowers, even though it would have been more practical to plant vegetables.

'Here,' said Lolly, shoving a stack of old gossip magazines and a pair of scissors across the small table at the end of her bed. 'You know the drill.'

When she found something suitable, Abbey held up the page and Lolly would give a thumbs up or down.

'You know ... my son visits on Thursdays,' Lolly said after a while. 'He's very handsome.'

'I have a boyfriend,' laughed Abbey, cutting yellow petals out of the red-carpet dress of some actress.

'So?' Lolly snorted. 'Besides, I've already set you up on a date.'

'I don't need a date, Lolly ... Tav takes care of me.'

Lolly raised an eyebrow.

Abbey cleared her throat. 'He's too old for me anyway,' she said lightly. 'He's got to be in his forties, surely?'

'Thirty-eight,' said Lolly proudly. 'He's a summer baby.' She smiled wistfully at the sunflower walls.

That evening, Abbey stopped by the supermarket. She was strolling through the health-food aisle when she saw a packet of sunflower seeds. She imagined splitting open the packet and spreading the seeds all over Lolly's walls and watching her face erupt into joy at all the real sunflowers sprouting from their paper counterparts. She rolled the kernels between her fingers, careful not to crush them through the plastic.

There was no garden at the nursing home but maybe she could find a bucket and some soil. Was it illegal to take dirt from the park? She certainly couldn't take it from her front yard, a bone-dry wasteland of cracked earth they couldn't get anything to grow in. Even the weeds that cropped up after it rained didn't last long. She'd try the park.

Abbey struggled up the path to the front door, her arms full of groceries. She stopped at the top step and fumbled for her keys. As she pulled them out from her pocket, she lost her grip and the groceries went flying.

'Fuck.' She stood staring down at the smashed jar of passata; glass and tomato sauce covered everything, especially the bag of sunflower seeds that had split open on impact. Frustrated tears burned behind her eyes and she blinked them back. She picked her keys out of the passata and shook them off, wiping her hands on her jeans. Then she scraped as much of the mess as she could off the step with her shoe.

She barely touched her keys to the lock but the door swung open.

'Tav,' she called, closing the door behind her and making her way down the hall. No answer.
There was a layer of litter on the floor—chip packets and cig-arette butts and empty cans. Something crunched under her boot and she looked down at a broken pipe. The glass would be a pain to pull out of the rug.

She nudged open the door to their room. Tav was sprawled across the bed; a boy she didn't recognise was passed out on a bean bag in the corner of the room. She gently kicked one of Tav's dangling legs. He didn't stir. She leant on the mattress and gave him a good shake. Nothing. Abbey studied the gentle rise and fall of his chest.

The night they had met, she'd stormed out of her father's apartment after a particularly nasty fight, freezing air whipping at her arms and legs. As she was storming past a house a few streets away, a loud crash of breaking glass made her jump. The front door burst open, spilling thumping music and a boy her age into the yard.

'Mazel tov!' he shouted back into the house. He dusted himself off and lit a cigarette. 'Hey,' he said, noticing her, 'you okay?'

Abbey rubbed her goose pimpled arms.

'I'm Tav,' he said.

'Abbey.'

'Here for the party?'

She shook her head and Tav narrowed his eyes. 'Do I spy a shiner?'

She turned away.

'Hey, it's okay,' said Tav softly. 'Why don't you come in?'

Now, three years later, she rolled him on his side and lay down beside him, burying her face in his back.

It was dark when she woke. Moonlight faintly illuminated the room. Tav was gone, so was the bean bag guy, and the bean bag.

Louis Armstrong crooned from the kitchen, along with clanging pots and the sizzle of hot oil. Abbey pulled on one of Tav's hoodies and walked cautiously down the hall. The rubbish was gone. Tav had his back to her at the chopping board. The groceries were rinsed clean, dripping in the drying rack. She watched the muscles in his shirtless back tense and roll as he worked.

'Fuck,' he exclaimed, 'fuck, fuck, fuck.' He ripped a tea towel from the oven door handle and wrapped it around his fingers. He moved in sharp, jerking motions. Droplets of blood splashed on the linoleum and he mopped them up with his sock. 'Baby!' he cried, his pupils unnaturally large. He motioned proudly to the salad strewn across the bench, only some of it making it into a bowl, then at the sizzling wok starting to smoke on the stove.

'Shit.'

He unwound the bloodied tea towel and flapped at the smoke. Before Abbey could take it off the heat, the wok went up in flames. The high-pitched screaming of the smoke alarm filled the kitchen. Tav threw the salad bowl into the sink, filling it with water.

'Tav, don't!' she cried.

'Ah!' he shouted as the water hit and flames whooshed towards the ceiling.

She ripped off the hoodie and snuffed out the flames. 'Open a window, for fuck's sake!'

After a few minutes the alarm stopped, though it still rang in Abbey's ears. She slid a few slices of bread in the toaster and dug some peanut butter out of the cupboard. As she worked, Tav wrapped his arms around her waist and buried his face in her neck.

Abbey relayed the kitchen disaster to Lolly the following week. She laughed as she told the story and didn't mention Tav's eyes or jerky movements.

'My husband was the same,' said Lolly. 'Could scarcely wipe his own arse till the day he died.'

'You must have loved him a lot, to have taken care of him all those years.'

'Love? Ha!' snorted Lolly. 'We couldn't just get up and go in those days, no matter how much we wanted to.' Her eyes flashed at Abbey, who stared down at her tea. 'Do you want a cuppa?' she asked abruptly.

'We're having one, Loll,' said Abbey, raising her mug.

Lolly's eyes narrowed. 'That's my tea,' she said.

'No, old girl, look.' Abbey laughed, pointing to the mug of tea in front of Lolly.

Lolly picked it up and took a long drink, though it was almost certainly too hot. She stared absently at her sunflowers. 'You better drink up, love. John will be home soon and there'll be trouble if dinner isn't ready.'

'Lolly?' Abbey said cautiously.

But the old woman was busy rummaging through her chest of drawers. 'Where's the bloody cutlery? I bet that cheeky little devil's gone and chucked them in the pond again.'

Abbey pressed the button for the nurse. 'I'll see you next week, Loll.'

As the weeks passed Lolly was present with Abbey less. She stopped meeting Abbey at reception. Instead, Abbey would knock softly on the door to her bedroom and wait for a wild-looking woman to open it, scraps of yellow and brown paper peppering her arms, pieces stuck to her face, which showed no recognition of Abbey. There were sunflowers on the bed frame now, the bedside table, the lamp.

After a while Lolly stopped talking, and Abbey would just sit for an hour while Lolly worked frantically. The only sounds: the crackling of paper sunflowers on the chair Abbey sat in, and the snipping of Lolly's scissors.

A few weeks later when Abbey got home from one of these

sessions, the house was throbbing, bass rippling through the foundations. Tav was passed out in the lounge room. The house was trashed, again. She stood staring at him for a few minutes, noting how the lines of his face smoothed out as he slept, the shadows under his eyes lightened. She flicked off the stereo and heard her phone ping. She had a missed call from the nursing home and a new voicemail.

As she listened to the kind voice, a coldness spread through her body, filling her up until she felt like she could choke on it. She swallowed hard, grabbed her keys, and left.

Abbey sat in Lolly's empty room for a while. The sun was setting; blue twilight settled on the walls, washing out the yellow.

'Abbey!' a voice called from across the carpark as she was leaving. She attempted a polite smile as she walked over to the shiny black BMW Dr Ravka was getting into. 'I'm so sorry to hear about Lolly,' he said.

Abbey felt a sob rising in her chest. 'She was really looking forward to seeing her son tomorrow.'

Dr Ravka frowned slightly. 'Yes, she became more and more fixated on the son towards the end. It was hard to watch her get so excited only to be disappointed—it was wonderful for her to have you this last year.'

Abbey's heart sank. Lolly never mentioned him not showing up before. What kind of child could abandon their mother in a nursing home, not even bother to visit? 'Did anyone reach out to him?' she asked.

'Ah … Abbey—'

'Surely if he knew she was so unwell he could have made one lousy visit.'

'Abbey,' said Dr Ravka softly, 'Lolly didn't have a son.'

Abbey's brain scrambled to make sense of the words. 'But …
I don't understand … she talked about him all the time—'

'She was very persistent with the delusion,' said Dr Ravka.
'She had a miscarriage almost forty years ago, and never went
on to have more children.'

Abbey felt cold, her body ached like she was getting the flu.
'We were supposed to go on a date,' she said quietly.

'Pardon?'

'Nothing.'

Tav was still passed out when she got home. She walked
through the house, running her hand over the uneven painted
brick walls. She wondered if the walls of Lolly's room had been
stripped yet. A slight smile touched her lips as she imagined the
hours it would take the nurses to pull down all the sunflowers.

She pulled a suitcase out from under the bed, filling it with
the few clothes she had moved in with. She dragged it out to
the front steps and called a taxi. While she waited, sitting in the
open doorway, she lit up a smoke, inhaling deeply. She wondered if Lolly was with her son somewhere. She wasn't religious,
but the idea felt nice. She hoped it was true.

The taxi pulled up to the curb and honked unnecessarily. She
turned to stub out the butt and there, between the old cigarette
butts and crispy weeds, a delicate green sunflower stem poked
out of the dirt, raising two tiny leaves to the sun.

KELSIE HARFORD is a writer and reader of many things and is
currently working on her first novel in the science fiction genre. She is
an aspiring editor and part of a volunteer team working to bring the life
stories of aged care residents to print.

The End

Eden Taylor

You said, 'Let's meet at the place where we first met.'

So now I'm walking towards the gardens around the corner from my apartment. It is a short walk for me and a short drive for you.

I remember that first day. We sat cross-legged on top of that weird brick maze across from those big pretty trees as I took your picture. I thought you were sweet in your orange shirt and misshapen mask. I didn't expect you.

Today my hands are shaking, and my sight is a little blurry. But somehow, I send the message that I'm dreading.

I'm here.

You get out of your car, and I see your eyes are much darker. I think they've lost the light that used to be in them when they saw me. You try to smile but your lips only manage to tug half-way up. I feel a slight shiver.

'Is a hug okay?'

I force a slow nod and extend my arms. You move into them, and I place my head onto your shoulder to the left. Your beard tickles my forehead, and it feels familiar. My face droops.

Your hold lasts a few seconds. I say nothing and neither do you.

The sky is cloudy. It is somehow fitting. *Do you remember the bright sun that first day? I have those photos I took as proof in case you don't.*

We don't get too far, conversation wise. There's a boulder between us and we both know it. I dissociate into the grey clouds. I can't bring myself to look into your sad blue eyes. And you keep your gaze low as you pluck blades of grass from the ground.

We don't really make any movement towards anything. You look at your watch a fourth time and call it. You offer me a lift home. We don't kiss goodbye. Instead, we stare at each other as I leave your car. It's different. We're different. I think I am different.

EDEN TAYLOR is a freelance writer, editor and photographer. She enjoys writing creative nonfiction in her own time. Eden is currently interning for bands Meraki Minds and Glass House where she writes, edits and creates social media content. Find her on Instagram @edentaylor1.

Thou Shalt Not Suffer
a Witch to Live

Emma Beckenham

Between 40,000 and 60,000 people were tried and executed for witchcraft in Europe between the years 1400 and 1782. The politically charged witch-hunts of the Middle Ages and the Renaissance left us with horrific and terrifying mythologies and accounts of witches and witchcraft. During this period the Christian church attempted to stir up anti-witch sentiments and—above all—fear. The church at the time was continuing its spread across the continent, carrying with it the opinions and stories of many famed theologians. These stories contained fantastical accounts of witches who met with demons, made pacts with the devil, sacrificed children and practiced cannibalism. Sorcery, paganism and magic were labelled as witchcraft and were punishable by a very slow and painful death at the stake. The Christian church has a lot to answer for from this period. By furthering and solidifying these chilling stories, the church intentionally built the dark mythology that terrified people at the time, and still shrouds witchcraft to this day.

Since the agreed canon of the Christian Bible was established in AD 325, the Bible has been translated countless times from the original Hebrew, Aramaic and Greek texts. This means the original words have been distorted, time and time again. The translators of the time changed the language so much that the verses came to mean something else entirely—sometimes serving a dangerous purpose.

Exodus 22:18 was translated into English as 'you shall not permit a sorceress to live'. The word 'sorceress' was translated from the original Hebrew word *kasaph*, which comes from the root meaning 'to whisper' or 'to murmur'. In the context of the original text, the passage was probably intended to urge the Jews of the time to keep to their own religious practices. One can easily see how verses such as this were twisted to suit a different purpose.

When King James I authorised a new translation of the Bible, his hatred for witches was expressed in it. American historian Jeffrey Russell said of King James:

> He wanted witches exterminated, and his translators deliberately translated 'kasaph' as 'witch' in order to provide clear biblical sanctions for their execution.

Russell showed that the translators of the King James Bible also altered references to Hebrew 'sorcerers' into the English word 'wizards'. Leviticus 20:27 was translated as:

> A man also or woman that hath a familiar spirit, or that is a *wizard*, shall surely be put to death: they shall stone them with stones: their blood shall be upon them.

Russell describes another mistranslation in the Book of Samuel:

The 'witch' of Endor whom King Solomon consulted was originally a *ba'alath ob*, 'mistress of a talisman' … but in the King James version [of the Bible] she too appears as a sinister 'witch'.

King James I had these verses translated to suit his own purposes. In the time of witch-hunts, torture and execution, fear was the Christian Church's most powerful tool. The church used these far-fetched translations to demonise sorcerers, magicians, diviners and witches, giving the public biblical 'proof' that these people were evil and deserving of punishment according to God.

During the late 15th century, and well into the 16th, Christian theologians were busy creating elaborate witch mythologies that were used to back up the translated verse in Exodus 22. One of these was the concept of the 'Witches' Sabbath'. This was supposed to be a meeting of between ten and twenty witches, where new recruits would bind themselves to the witch cult by promising to kill a child, renounce the Christian faith and defecate on a crucifix. Russell tells us the assembly supposedly included feasting and drinking, and consuming the murdered bodies of children and their blood 'in a ritual parody of the Lord's Supper'. An orgy then took place before the witches departed.

Russell has said there was no evidence of such a meeting ever taking place, but the belief in this myth was so strong at the time that it didn't matter:

What people believe to be true influences their actions more than what is objectively true, and the conviction that this picture was accurate brought about the execution of nearly a hundred thousand people.

The Witches' Sabbath was first laid out by Theologian Martin Delrio in the 16th century, in his work *Disquisitiones Magicae*, translated as *Magical Investigations*. Delrio painted a stark and terrifying picture of the Witches' Sabbath:

> Sometimes they imitate the sacrifice of the Mass (the greatest of all their crimes), as well as purifying with water and similar Catholic ceremonies. After the feast, each evil spirit takes by the hand the disciple of whom he has charge, and so that they may do everything with the most absurd kind of ritual, each person bends over backwards, joins hands in a circle, and tosses his head as frenzied fanatics do. Then they begin to dance. They sing very obscene songs in [Satan's] honour. They behave ridiculously in every way, and in every way contrary to accepted custom. Then their demon-lovers copulate with them in the most repulsive fashion.

This mock sabbath was also depicted in paintings as late as the 19th century, such as *Le Sabbat* by Collin de Plancy. This was a panoramic view illustrating a 'typical witches sabbath' with witches flying around on broomsticks, the Devil on a throne being worshipped, people throwing babies into cauldrons for magical salve, and witches dancing in the backwards fashion described by Delrio. Works such as these put witchcraft and witches in direct opposition to the Church, angering the newly converted public by claiming that witches worshipped Satan and parodied sacred Christian rituals like Mass and Holy Communion. These myths were meant to incite anger and hatred among the public, leading to more witchcraft accusations and more executions of the innocent.

Another text that furthered harmful myths about witches was *Malleus Maleficarum* (Hammer of Witches) written by Catholic clergyman Heinrich Kramer in 1487. Kramer detailed how witches fraternised with demons, and suggested that torture and death were the only cure for witchcraft. He encouraged the method of burning at the stake. He also took a decidedly misogynistic approach, and promoted the idea that witches were mostly women. The spelling choice of *maleficarum,* with an 'a' (feminine) instead of *maleficorum* with an 'o' (male) was a purposeful choice to associate witches with the female gender.

In *The Encyclopedia of Witches, Witchcraft and Wicca*, Rosemary Guiley wrote:

> Kramer in particular exhibited a virulent hatred toward women witches and advocated their extermination. The Malleus devotes an entire chapter to the sinful weakness of women, their lascivious nature, moral and intellectual inferiority and gullibility to guidance from deceiving spirits. In Kramer's view, women witches were out to harm all of Christendom.

But Kramer was not the only theologian making such bold and unfounded claims. In the early 5th century, St Augustine of Hippo, arguably the most influential Christian theologian, asserted that 'pagan magic, religion and sorcery were all invented by the Devil for the purpose of luring humanity away from Christian truth'. Yet at the same time, Augustine claimed that neither Satan nor witches had any supernatural powers at all, and that divine power came through God alone. In which case, rounding up witches to torture and execute them during the Middle Ages doesn't make a whole lot of sense. This, along with the church's tendency to twist scripture to suit their purposes, gives the clear sense that the church was picking and choosing scripture to further their own political agenda.

The dark and sinister myths that surround witchcraft are works of fiction, constructed by a powerful Christian church in a terrifying time in history. These stories were used as a political and religious tool to strike fear and distrust into the general public of the Middle Ages and Renaissance. These elaborate mythologies were created by kings, theologians and clergymen to stir up public feeling to their advantage. This resulted in the horrific torture and deaths of between 40,000 and 60,000 innocent people in Europe alone.

In a time when myths were more powerful than truth, the Christian church crafted theologies from mistranslated verses and the words of theologians past, solidifying these beliefs into Christian theology for hundreds of years to come. Witches are still spoken about with disdain and disgust in modern churches today, with the same verses referenced to back up these sentiments. Remnants of fantastical concepts like demon possession and devil worship continue to be passed on to new generations within the Christian church.

EMMA BECKENHAM is a freelance copywriter and editor, working for clients such as The Splendid Word, Megaphone Marketing and Bloom College. She has also just finished editing a self-help novel, which will be published early next year. Emma blogs regularly about her travels and thoughts on her website, emmabeckenham.com.

Aaaddddaaahhhhhchh! dddddeeeummmm ... ...

Tim Loveday

you look at the silver sheet of pills eyes popped out noticing you've left a whole tab untouched there are 2 more in the row below it constituting a total of 12 pills in a sheet of 100 you wonder if you had your pills yesterday or if you forgot them sometime earlier in the week now it's almost 3 in the afternoon well after the time you're supposed to take your pills and the tab becomes a sort of puzzle that must be sorted should you ask your girlfriend if she's noticed wednesday was a train wreck so there's no point returning if it isn't saturday perhaps it might be possible if you hadn't left this till 3pm things would be different but you had to make tea that you didn't drink and put out garbage that you forgot in the hallway and write an essay that's more likely a poem or a letter to a local elected official or an email to a friend you'd forgot existed until you played that one song between the meeting that didn't happen because you thought it was 2pm when it was 1pm so you made a note on a post it and went looking for your diary and stopped for just a second to read that passage in the book that had got you excited last night and something about the flow of the words got you thinking of sex your partner in the kitchen and she's agreeing why not it's early we never do this first a shower please why not get dirty the kitchen needs a clean you're fixing the screw on the bottom of the bin did you drink that tea where's your diary this screw won't go in you just want to write your essay that is likely a poem and what an asshole your boss is for missing that meeting you should write her an email that tells her just what you think you can't live with this uncertainty it's crippling if she'd been on time you could have written that essay and the screw would bloody fit and you'd be having sex sex sex yes you're on the stairs at the door taking off your clothes she's asking where you were thought you forgot shit you were gonna get you a drink each one second screw the tea it's saturday it's fine at this time you'll write the letter to the politician after a beer the screw you should fix the tea is lukewarm no time for a shower if you reword the essay or the letter to the politician no it's definitely a poem you've always known it's a poem you can probably rework it to impress your boss impress on her just how frustrated you are with this tiny little screw that won't hold the bin open just one drink you're sipping your beer thinking i better find my diary when you hear her voice at the top of the stairs fuck you pour her wine the bin can die you'll buy a new bin ten thousand bins in fact deploy an army of secretaries eliminate clocks burn every diary write everything on your fingers cut them off send them in letters only 10 to go round 1 of them's inside of her so 9 minus thumbs plus 2 to rewrite that letter to the politician who likes your poetry or the essay about the difference between politicians and poems cum thin as screwing in a bin or finding your diary or getting hard and staying hard and trying to pour a drink or not making tea or at least not finishing it or the passage in a book that you put down somewhere that impressed you so much but you can't remember the name and if only you'd had your pills this would be aqua-aerobics that's it a hobby like gardening or painting or making gin you'll never need to be naked again you'll finish the essay about the politician who is also a poet or the poem about the politician who writes fine essays as you scoff down the rice without a shirt and wonder whether it's all worth thinking over tea and a meeting conceding you'll make that decision when you take your pills because it should be that time those emails go out and your boss will be impressed and if luck's on your side the poem about politicians and the essay about poetry will be done and it's no joking matter that before 6pm you'll be sitting in front of the tv not thinking about the pills you didn't take

TIM LOVEDAY is a poet, writer, editor and clown-lark. He is the recipient of a 2020 Wheeler Centre Next Chapter Fellowship and a 2021 Varuna Residential Fellowship. His work has been widely published. He is currently writing a novel and collection. You can find more of his work at timloveday.com.

School Supplies

Sally Ryan

'Give us a pen will ya?' Amelia said to me on a Wednesday morning. She swung back on her plastic chair and grinned. I would have told her she might crack her head on the side of the table behind her, if it wasn't for the fact that the thought of her cracking her head on the table behind her gave me a sick sense of joy. Amelia, Amelia, Amelia. What a shit name—boring and basic. It suited her.

'Don't have any spare pens,' I said, zipping up the multiple compartments of my pencil case so she couldn't take a peek inside. 'None that you can chew on anyway.'

'Ha. Guess I won't be doing any work today then.'

I gave a pointed look to Lily who sat on the other side of her with pencils lined up neatly above her notebook, but Amelia ignored me. She pulled her phone from the inside of her blazer and balanced it on her lap as she typed away, out of sight of Ms O'Brien who sat at the front of the classroom, squinting at her laptop while she stabbed at her salad.

I itched to throw my hand in the air and tell the teacher Amelia was on her phone, but everyone already hated me for reminding Ms O'Brien about the homework the day before. It wasn't my fault people didn't know how to balance Year 12 with their social lives.

Amelia was one of those people who never did any work and still got the top marks. She didn't know what it was like to work hard, to strive for excellence, to earn all the love and success she got for free.

She continued to type and Ms O'Brien continued to remain oblivious to the clear violation of school policy.

The clicking of her pink acrylic nails against her phone screen set my teeth on edge.

'You going to Ollie's party this weekend?' Amelia asked without looking up from her phone.

She tucked a long black strand behind her ear and looked up at me. Her foundation was a shade too dark and her eyebrows were drawn on so thick that she might have used sharpie to colour them in. *Cake face.*

'Well, are you or what?'

'Are you talking to me?'

'Are you thick? Yeah, I'm talking to you.' She shoved her phone back into her blazer then focused on rolling up her already-short skirt. 'I heard you've got a car. I need someone to drive me to get booze.'

'I don't know who Ollie is.'

'Ollie. The ranga from St Peter's.'

I didn't know anyone from St Peter's. I didn't know any boys. 'Wasn't invited.'

'You can be my plus-one then.'

I glanced up at Ms O'Brien, and my body tensed, as I waited for her to tell us off for talking. Amelia had a voice that carried, even when she was whispering. Instead, Ms O'Brien yawned, pulled out a pair of headphones and plugged them into her laptop. Amelia and I froze as she scanned the classroom.

'I have to study,' I said, when I was sure Ms O'Brien couldn't hear me. 'Not that you'd know what that is.'

'If you take me to this party, I'll help you study for the test Monday. You don't even have to stay at Ollie's, just take me there. Isla, come on.'

Would she beg if I waited a while to answer?

I considered the offer. All I had to do was drive her to get alcohol, then to some party, and I got free tutoring. It would be painful to be taught by Amelia, but I had barely scratched the surface of Lazarus' Theory of Stress and I was starting to feel, well, stressed.

'Okay. Fine.'

* * *

'Give us a highlighter,' Amelia said to me on a Thursday afternoon after school. We sat in the library with textbooks and notes spread across the table. She gripped the edge of the table, and her knuckles turned white as she balanced her chair on its two back legs.

I rolled my eyes. 'Use your own highlighters.'

'Yours are nicer.'

'Yeah, cause they were expensive. You're not messing them up.' I snatched my pastel pink highlighter away before Amelia could put her sticky fingers on them. She'd been digging into a paper bag filled to the brim with sour worms, and the tips of her fingers had blue slime on them.

'Fine. Then highlight, here, here and here.' She sucked the sugar off her pointer finger then pressed it into the glossy paper of her textbook. The sound of her skin unsticking from the page filled the quiet. 'Those are gonna be your key terms. Use them in every answer and O'Brien will be chuffed. Guaranteed.'

'Um, okay. Thanks. You don't mind me drawing on your book?'

'Nah. It's second-hand.'

After an hour of studying, Amelia needed to go home. She shoved her books into her bag and walked to the exit. I rushed to catch up with her.

'Wait,' I said, grabbing her arm before she could push the library door open. 'I need more study time.'

'I have to get home.'

'Then I could come to your house.'

Amelia raised a brow, but nodded and opened the door, gesturing with her head for me to go first.

We made our way to the bus stop. Amelia didn't touch on her Myki—her card rested behind her clear phone case. It made my skin prickle and my heart race.

'You're acting like I've murdered someone,' she said as I kept glancing at the front of the bus, shifting in my seat every few seconds.

'You broke the law,' I snapped.

Amelia just laughed. 'Not like I'm going to jail for it. Live a little.'

I balled my hands into my skirt. Right. I was boring, a loser, for not wanting to pay a couple hundred dollar fine for fare evasion.

I forced my shoulders to relax so Amelia wouldn't make any more comments.

I didn't open my mouth again until we arrived at Amelia's apartment. She lived in a dingy little building that didn't know what colour was. The carpet in the loungeroom was a grey that might've once been blue. No photo frames hung from the walls, and there were no house plants to liven up the place—just a moth-eaten couch and a three-legged coffee table holding on for dear life. The place didn't suit her.

Her room, on the other hand, perfectly encompassed the image of Amelia I had spent years cultivating in my mind—vain, basic, lazy. Clothes thrown everywhere. Dirty make-up brushes and opened bottles of lipstick lay abandoned on an old-fashioned vanity. Photos of her and her friends covered the entire wall that her bed was pressed up against. Amelia looked her best and everyone else in the pictures looked like they'd been caught sneezing.

She pulled her books from her bag and threw them onto her bed before jumping down next to them.

She bit her cherry lip. 'You gonna sit or what?'

I pulled my own notes out of my bag and sat at the end of the bed, away from Amelia. She was quick to shuffle closer to me.

'Wanna stay for dinner?' she said after we'd been studying for a while. I pulled my phone out and gasped at the time.

'You can say no,' she said with a scoff when I didn't answer. She hopped off her bed and to her vanity.

She pulled out a thick stack of loose-leaf paper that was tied together with pink string.

'What are those?'

'I don't like typing my novel,' she said as if that explained anything. She flicked open to the middle of the paper and started to circle words with a red pen.

'You're writing a novel?'

'Got a problem?'

'No … what's it about?'

Amelia paused, folding the paper so I couldn't see her messy scrawl.

'It's a romance.'

I didn't get a chance to answer. My phone buzzed with a message from my mate, Eleanor.

Where are you?

Studying at Amelia's house.

Funny

Not a joke

Since when are you and Amelia Xavier friends?

We aren't friends, I typed, but my thumbs hovered above the screen. The words looked false—even to me.

At her vanity, Amelia was still scribbling notes in her novel. Her tongue was poking out the corner of her mouth. This was the hardest I'd ever seen her work.

I smiled, then caught myself.

'You gonna stay for dinner or not?' she said without looking up.

'I … no. I can't.'

* * *

'Got money on ya?' Amelia said to me on a Saturday night. We sat in the carpark of The Bottle-O. Her wavy hair was stick straight. Her lips were dark red and her matching dress climbed dangerously high up her thighs, so she constantly had to tug it down. She looked beautiful in a way that pissed me off.

'You didn't bring money?'

'Not enough,' she said, wrapping her parka tight around her body.

I sighed, throwing my head back against my seat, before

wrestling my way out of the car. I made sure to slam the door behind me. The clicking sound of Amelia's heels told me she was following closely behind as I marched across the carpark. In the artificial lighting of the liquor store, the spot where Amelia's foundation ended was a visible line on her neck. I wanted to reach out and blend it with the tips of my fingers. Or maybe I wanted to reach out and wring her neck because she was eyeing the more expensive vodka.

I ran my hand against the fogging glass of the fridge and wondered what I'd be doing if I wasn't with Amelia right now—probably studying.

The sound of hissing pulled me from my thoughts. Amelia stood, laughing behind her hand as she stared at the can she had dropped.

'Oops ... should we make a break for it?' she said, glancing around for a worker.

'What, no? I'll just pay for it.'

'Boring.' My face fell and Amelia brought her hand to my shoulder. 'Only joking.'

I bought the vodka, then drove Amelia to Ollie's house without saying a word.

'You coming in?' she asked as we pulled up to Ollie's house.

'No. I have to go home and be boring.'

'Ha,' she said, unclicking her seatbelt. She opened the door, but paused before getting out of the car. 'You're plenty interesting, Isla.' And with that, she left.

* * *

Amelia said nothing to me on a Monday morning. She wouldn't say anything to me ever again. She wouldn't ask me to borrow pencils, or pens, or highlighters, or money for alcohol. I pressed my palm against the cold plastic of her seat.

'She addressed it to you,' I was told that afternoon by one of Amelia's friends. 'Her dad found it.'

She handed me a thick pile of paper covered in Amelia's terrible handwriting. I spent the rest of the day reading through those papers: Amelia's novel.

Her novel was about two girls our age—one who was studious and always following the rules and one who was a rebel. I recognised myself in the description of the studious girl—blonde, severe, always with her hair in two braids. I recognised Amelia in the rebel—dark hair, an attitude, always speaking her mind. But there were things I also didn't recognise. It was like seeing myself through a blurred lens—through Amelia's eyes. 'The blonde girl spent her days with her head buried in a book, despite never being the top of the class, and despite being shut off from the rest of the world. She was special for trying. She was special for caring.' That's what Amelia wrote.

I hugged the fraying pages tight against my chest and tilted back in my chair.

Amelia, Amelia, Amelia. If only I hadn't left her that night.

SALLY RYAN is a writer of all things young adult and aims to create characters that are relatable and interesting. She is currently working on an urban fantasy novel and, although she is a fantasy writer at heart, she is constantly experimenting with different genres. Read more at sally-ryan.com.

Couch to Hero

Mikey Pryvt

Generally speaking, a fitness montage doesn't begin with our wannabe hero slumped on the couch, watching a movie promo on their phone. But as they say in all kinds of gyms, 'The hardest thing is walking through the door'. Ergo, whatever it takes to get you there must be okay! For me, it was Bob Odenkirk's words reverberating through my phone's speaker, as he discussed his journey in becoming the latest middle-aged action star for his role as a suburban-dad-style John Wick badass in *Nobody*.

'I'm pretty fit, I could get fitter. I knew that would be very challenging to me ... I wanted to commit completely.'

His words proved to be just the encouragement I needed to get up off the couch and kickstart my own middle-aged wannabe action star training montage. In Odenkirk I'd found someone even more inspiring than mid-fifties Keanu Reeves and his legendary six-month training programs to bring John Wick to life. Keanu has been my role model since the hot summer night I rented a VHS copy of *Bill & Ted*, and he's been doing this kind of shit since the late 90s for *The Matrix*. Whereas

Odenkirk spent twenty-five years slouched in the writer's room, before finally standing up, stretching out and becoming an action hero. It just took him a few years to get there—helped by his breakout role in *Breaking Bad* and taking centre stage in the spinoff, *Better Call Saul*—and that was exactly what I needed to hear, too.

Yeah, I'm pretty fit. I could get fitter too. In my mid-forties, I'd just declared myself to be in the best shape of my life, taking my home workouts to the next level during Melbourne's first series of COVID lockdowns in 2020. After roughly a decade spent stumbling along the winding road of recovery from a series of unfortunate events that left me couch bound for six months in 2010, this was an accomplishment in itself. That had been the bad kind of montage: from a minor shoulder injury to being underweight, over-medicated and with a severe vitamin D deficiency, amongst other things. Four years spent on the medical merry-go-round before finally getting the right diagnosis and beginning the journey back to health.

Now, as Melbourne started to open back up, I wanted to take my fitter, stronger body for a test drive and see just how much further I could take things. And I too was prepared to *commit completely*—just on a more modest, achievable scale. The no-budget version of the Hollywood transformation montage, where I had to play not just the star, but the supporting roles of trainer and dietitian and personal chef. I knew exactly what I was signing up for, continuing to pack muscle back on a withered frame that was near-skeletal in 2016 after a particularly brutal detour that saw me drop to 60 kg and mistaken by paramedics for a heroin addict. Increasing my fitness with every workout, but still very much a 'spoonie', as people with chronic illnesses refer to themselves. My most modest ambition was to

train enough on the good days to make the bad days less oner-
ous; to gradually increase, if not the amount of spoons, then at
least their serving sizes of actionable energy.

I figured if Odenkirk could go from couch to hero at his age,
I could attempt to take it to the next level too. With bad hips
being part of the spoonie package, I tapped down my urge to
leap into the Octagon, and decided to crawl my way there instead. Surely I could take a few boxing classes? Even if it meant
napping half the day to store up enough energy to leave the
house. So, after years of walking past with my dog Phoebe and
wondering what lay inside, I tied her up outside the repur-
posed Scout Hall on an otherwise ordinary residential street
and crossed the threshold into Northside Boxing. It was time to
stop fucking around and find out.

I swung by before the beginner's class and found one of
the fighter/trainers, Koder, standing behind a simple wood-
en foldout table with an old tin beer can on it, along with
the new normal sign-in sheet and no-touch thermometer.
He was more than happy to tell me everything I needed to
know to start training. As Koder gave me the spiel, I saw that
Northside Boxing was the definition of an old-school gym.
Rings at each end of the hall with a range of boxing bags
hanging from the roof in between. Walls decorated with flyers
and photos. Rocky Balboa in his prime, blessing the place. I
was so entranced by the authenticity the space radiated that I
tuned Koder out as I took everything in. *This was just the place
I was looking for!*

Out of nowhere, the word 'Boxercise' snapped me back to
attention, penetrating my guard, hitting me like a fast jab.
Visibly wincing at the word, mentally reeling, my head briefly filled with images from 80s aerobics classes and 90s tae-bo

infomercials. I regained my composure in time to learn that, because of COVID, there weren't spare gloves for casuals anymore, so I'd need to bring cash to buy my own. And that was as complicated as it got. The gym is a place that is, by design, as simple as possible to join and start training. No monthly membership fees or complicated plans. As I'd soon discover, it's just walk in, put $5 in the tin and sign in. Put your wraps on, grab a skipping rope and warm up. Then don't stop for an hour. For a break, hold the push-up position. Or jog on the spot, lightly punching the bag. For a change of pace, run around the block. Then back to boxing around: hitting the heavy bags with jabs and crosses, hooks and body shots. Leave drenched, proud of the puddle of sweat you've left on floor. I was very much into it, and quickly forgot Boxercise and everything it conjured up. Happily learning that there's no training 'like a boxer', only training 'with boxers'. One hour of pushing yourself as hard as you can. Whatever was on your mind, whatever stresses or worries you had before going inside joined that puddle on the floor, replaced with knowing how hard you can push yourself. And how much harder you'll be able to go next time.

My first class, they sent us running around the block after a brutal series of jump squats and burpees. My legs gave out as I lurched past the library and hit the gentle incline that ends with the taste of petrol from the station as you round the corner for the home stretch. A week later, and I don't just make it without stopping, I'm jogging alongside a dude taking his first class, struggling as much I had been. We're both dying, but we make it together and bump our wrapped fists before going back in for another thirty minutes of punishment we've willingly signed up for.

Two weeks into training at the gym and I'm rubbing muscle relief cream into my arms, shoulders and neck while I watch *Creed* with a new found level of appreciation for what it takes to get in the ring. What's also striking me is the difference in physique between Michael B. Jordan and the fighters he's squaring off against. Because they are all real fighters roped in for a movie role, and look nowhere near as swole and cut as the character called Adonis for a reason. As the meme goes, it's the classic *Fiction vs Reality*. The physique of someone shaped by their training versus an idealised Hollywood version of what a fighter should look like. I can't help but appreciate the effort Jordan's put in to play Creed, but I relate more to the now-ancient Rocky who's mentoring him.

It's not until my second or third session that I notice the tractor tyre in the courtyard—that staple of post-*300* CrossFit training. But this is not a gym where people come to pose for their 'gram and compete with each other on the leaderboard. No one's shouting in your face like a drill sergeant if you can't do all five burpees before getting back on the bags. If they're screaming, they're screaming with you, not at you.

'I mightn't have thought this through,' our trainer says, between giant gasping breaths. We're dangling off the fence poles outside the gym, cranking out reps of inverted rows as our training partners sprint up and down the road, waiting for them come back and tag us out. She's struggling just as much as everyone else. I'm proud just to be almost kinda hanging in there with them.

Wonky, as she's known, is a pint-sized, 5 foot and change UK transplant, whose favourite word is 'wicked'. Ten years ago, while I was marooned on the couch, she was one of the first women to train at the gym. Now, we're both in the same position.

Later, she's got us doing dips and decline shoulder taps outside the library. My arms and shoulders are on fire and I fucking love it! Training like this is how I've put on another kilo of muscle as my shoulders, back and chest continue to fill out. I'm eating like a machine and *almost* sleeping through the night again. My body aches, but in a good way for once. And I'm much less tired in general. I'm sinking all my extra energy into training, but the spoons are getting bigger. The payoff is happening. *You get a little bit better in a montage*, plays in my head.

After three weeks at Northside I go see *Nobody* on opening day with my friend Paul. It's as good as I hoped, but no better—it's def no *John Wick*, but then what is? There's no doubt though that Bob Odenkirk has morphed into an action star and become the patron saint of my own montage. The real payoff comes later, as I'm shovelling a burger into my face so it's digested by the time I hit up the gym later.

'You're looking great,' Paul says, 'and seem even better!' Last time I'd seen him, I'd apologetically messaged him afterwards for being even more introverted than usual. The other benefit I was seeing was improved mental health, which had taken a battering during lockdowns. I wasn't just back to my old self, I could feel a new one becoming. It felt amazing to be seen that way too! After a year of rarely turning my camera on, I even started posting selfies again. Okay, they're on my secret locked invite-only fitsona Instagram account, but it's a start.

What I didn't tell Paul is that during the lulls in the movie I'd mentally drafted the next stages of my montage. But first I had to get *fit af*, and I'd found just the place for that. My journey had just begun. And if aging action stars are cool right now, then I'm down with that. As it turned out, the hardest thing *was* walking into the gym. Or, as OG middle-aged action star Danny Glover put it best in *Lethal Weapon*, way way back in the 1980s, *I'm not too old for this shit.*

MIKEY PRYVT made the horrible mistake of starting to write a post-apocalyptic novel and ending up living inside one instead. You can find him taking on more attainable goals in the meantime, like training to be the next Doomslayer. Witness his journey on Instagram and Twitter at @eattrainrevolt.

Cutie Disease

Zach Garry

Of all the bits of medical advice I've absorbed in my lifetime, this one has stuck with me: if you even *suspect* you're having a heart attack, go to the hospital.

The signs of a heart attack are not always obvious (dizziness, indigestion, a sense of impending doom) so it's best not to take any chances. I know this because I googled it in a mild panic when my heart started misbehaving at the age of sixteen. A sixteen-year-old with heart troubles? Seems odd. Shouldn't you be safeguarded by the protective veil of youth? You'd think so, but I wasn't convinced—there was always the possibility that I was an exception to the rule.

For several weeks in 2011 I'd been becoming steadily more aware of my heartbeat—more aware in that I had never really been aware of it before.

My trust in my once-reliable heart was slowly eroding. It was keeping me awake at night, hammering so hard I could hear it puncturing my breath. Occasionally it would tumble over itself, missing a beat; it squirmed in my chest as if it needed to say something. I was losing sleep at night, and during the day I reached regularly for my pulse. It was difficult to concentrate on schoolwork while preoccupied with the possibility of suddenly dropping dead. The thought consumed me.

When I raised this unsettling development with my parents, they took me to a GP. By this point I was fairly nervous, and she was both sympathetic and unhelpful. My heartbeat was 'certainly off', but she couldn't definitively pinpoint the issue. So she referred me to a cardiologist for a more comprehensive exam.

He ran me through a series of tests, the most strenuous of which involved me running at steadily increasing speeds while hooked up to a machine that recorded my heart's activity under different stress levels. Drenched in sweat and sprinting at full bore, I wondered if a 'stress test' was really the most appropriate thing for a person complaining of heart troubles. He also had my heart x-rayed and monitored my blood pressure. I left his office without an answer, because the results would take several days, but I was relieved knowing I was at least being taken seriously. I even slept better that night.

When I returned three days later to discuss my results, my cardiologist told my parents and I that I seemed to be in excellent health. Even though my heart did *seem* to be misbehaving, there was 'nothing structurally wrong with it'.

'It *could* be something called Long QT syndrome,' he proclaimed, then quickly reassured us. 'But his heartbeat isn't presenting in the typical manner for that. Long QT syndrome is characterised by fast, chaotic heartbeats, and Zach's seems to be just a bit atypical.'

He explained the potential treatments involved if it really were Cutie Disease, as a friend called it, but he was confident that I had nothing to worry about. Naturally, I googled Long

QT syndrome when I got home that night and discovered that people who are diagnosed with it often die within the next ten years.

Unsurprisingly, my heartbeat ramped up at that.

I wouldn't discover for another year that I had severe anxiety, which causes your physiology to escalate, which will cause your heart to follow suit. Somehow, anxiety wasn't covered in either of my appointments. Or perhaps it was, and I was too caught in the grip of my sympathetic nervous system to hear it. Either way, this was my adolescent brush with anxiety. I believed it was a brush with death. Naturally, I took what my doctor said next quite seriously.

'Just to be safe: Zach should be careful around drugs and alcohol.'

My friends and I weren't very good at hanging out sober. Most weekends we would end up at a different friend's house, usually the one whose parents weren't home, with someone having scored alcohol off a legal sibling or a boyfriend who was a bit old to be dating someone in Year 11.

This weekend, a week after my appointment, Laura's dad was away, so Laura's house it was. One of my friends had bought me a six-pack and I sipped on a beer apprehensively, not wanting to upset my heart. I was doing as the cardiologist advised. I was being careful—as careful as a closeted sixteen-year-old who was desperate to belong was capable of being.

I already knew it was bad to mix weed and alcohol, but by the time the bong came out my friends had done their best to assure me that my heart troubles were all in my head.

I was apprehensive, but my heart *had* been less troublesome lately. It still kept me up some nights, but others it wasn't so bad.

Maybe I could get away with just a little bit, I thought.

Somewhat uneasily, I took a hit.

'Just a small one!' I'd insisted as Laura packed it for me, like she'd just offered me a slice of birthday cake.

The smoke hit my lungs and I coughed, passing the Gatorade bong to the next person. I started to feel nervous as that familiar THC twinkle edged into my brain and I processed what I'd just done. My hands shook slightly.

Fuck.

My heartbeat quickened. A greyish haze crept in around the edges of my vision and I felt my head start to spin. I was overcome as much with regret as I was with sheer panic.

I grabbed Laura's arm. 'I don't feel good.'

'What?' she asked, jumping at my frantic grip. The others went quiet, watching me stare at the floor.

'I feel dizzy.'

'You might be greening out.'

'I can't be, I only had a tiny bit,' I replied, checking my pulse. 'I need to lie down.'

Since her dad was out, Laura said I could take his room. Guided by another friend, I wobbled in there and fainted on the bed.

I regained consciousness fairly quickly and lay listening to my friends slowly relax again, giggling in nervous disbelief at my sudden episode. Now that the fainting was over, I did feel better. But, lying alone in a quiet room, I had time to think.

If you even suspect you're having a heart attack, go to the hospital.

I had a choice: lie here and wonder if my heart was about to give out or draw the most attention to myself that was humanly possible and have someone call me an ambulance.

If I don't, I might die. If I do, I'll be embarrassed. Both seemed equally intolerable.

I sat up and shuffled blearily back out to the kitchen where my friends were still drinking. Their conversation and laughter simmered down as they turned to see me standing in the doorway, flushed of colour.

Outkast's 'Hey Ya' played from the lounge room speakers, its general liveliness suddenly at odds with what I was about to announce.

'Zach, are you okay?'

'Yeah, what happened?'

I took a breath. 'I think—I think I just had a heart attack.'

Stoned chaos.

Laura stared at me, open-mouthed. Another friend took a deep breath and exhaled, wide-eyed, her lips fluttering like a horse's. Someone else started nervously laughing and another, bong in hand, blustered, 'What? What? Wait, *what?*'

Sara, perhaps the most responsible among us, leapt into action and met me at the doorway.

'Zach, do you want me to call you an ambulance?' she asked.

I nodded.

She dialled 000 while the rest of my friends hid the weed. Fearful, I guess, that the paramedics might storm the house and confiscate it. I sat on the doorstep with Sara and waited for the ambulance to arrive.

I recognise that this must have all seemed deeply melodramatic to my friends, who could coolly smoke and drink at the same time without first fretting about all the ways it could go wrong, or without immediately having what they assumed to be a cardiac episode. They were the Bart to my Milhouse.

I felt my face and neck flush with shame as the ambulance pulled into the driveway.

Whatever I was expecting from my first time in an ambulance, it wasn't for the paramedic to comment on how hairy my forearms were before injecting me with something that felt like cold syrup. I think it was an antiarrhythmic drug called Lignocaine.

My heart slowed and I relaxed a little. Now I was just high in the back of an ambulance, vaguely aware that the other paramedic was quite good-looking.

Sara accompanied me to the hospital and went home after I was carted into the emergency room in a wheelchair. I changed into my hospital gown and had a series of cords hooked up to my chest, connected to a beeping monitor. I sat by myself for a while listening to the beeps and the sound of someone retching a few cubicles down.

My heartbeat was slowly making itself known again.

A young nurse wandered over, smiling. 'How are you feeling?'

'Not bad,' I replied. 'A little shaky.'

She nodded sympathetically before turning to examine my heart rate on the monitor next to me. She had quite a calming presence.

'It does look like your heartbeat is a bit abnormal, but I'm not seeing anything too sinister just yet. You said you've had marijuana tonight?'

'Just a bit,' I assured her.

'Mmhm. Okay, well …' She turned back to me and spoke further, but I barely caught it because I'd noticed that she wasn't looking me in the eye; she was looking somewhere on my forehead. Distracted, I inferred from the general cadence of her voice that she was expecting a reply. I nodded, and she continued while I tried to meet her gaze.

'—so, we'll just keep monitoring you for now, just to be safe.'

'Okay.'

Why won't she look at me? I thought as she walked away. I had never been in an emergency room, but I'd watched enough *House* to know that doctors and nurses need to keep a calm demeanour, even when things don't look good. A horrible thought occurred to me: *Maybe it's some kind of tactic?* I watched her walk over to another nurse and hand her a clipboard. *Maybe people stationed in the emergency room are trained to not get too attached to their patients because they could die at any moment … Maybe she's trying to avoid forming a connection with me.*

I didn't immediately accept this but—to my weed-addled lizard brain—it did seem logical. If the slightest stressor could send my heart into a frenzy, of course they wouldn't tell me how precarious the situation was. On what could have been my deathbed, I took solace, I guess, in the robustness of my theory. Still, it was a lot to process.

I suddenly felt very alone.

It was about half an hour before the nurse came back and told me that, while they still weren't hugely concerned about my heartbeat, they wanted to monitor me overnight. I didn't quite trust her. Her eye was still lingering on my forehead, but at this point I noticed that her other eye was pointed squarely at mine. A wave of shame-tinged realisation washed over me. My nurse had a lazy eye, and I was going to live.

I realised I should probably call my parents.

ZACH GARRY is a former YouTube content creator living on Wurundjeri land. He is now a copywriter by trade and writes creative nonfiction when he can. Curious about the role a writer can play in offsetting the end of the world, he is also an aspiring critic of climate literature. You can find Zach on Twitter: @zachgarry.

A Late Mourning

Paul Sutherland

D iane has the no-nonsense haircut of a parishioner. She's decided that gold matches her skin tone more than silver. It's the right decision. Her earrings sparkle like seashells against her clay-tone face. 'What's your relationship to the occupant?' She's all business. None of the 'sorry for your loss'. I consider turning on the waterworks, just to see if she's got that down pat, too.

By 'occupant' she means dead body or, in the case of the older occupants, skeletal remains. 'He's my grandfather,' I say, adding with shame, 'And I can't remember where he's buried.'

* * *

Nudgee Cemetery is close to where Poppie lived, in Brisbane's northern suburbs, where the streets are lined with poinciana trees, and where verandas wrap all the way around the colonial-era timber homes. It's more than a decade since I've been here. Ten years, ten months and twenty days since Poppie was buried.

I can't rely on 'we weren't close' to explain my absence. We were. Horse races and lunches and lessons in carpentry. And I just can't forget the last thing he said to me, blinking away tears in case I noticed this farmer from the bush showing any kind of emotion when I dropped off a few issues of *Australian Geographic* to the hospital ward his leukaemia had confined him to. 'I just don't want to die in here.'

My mum and aunties haven't been back either, aside from one brief visit on the first anniversary of his death. They all agree that he's not really down there. 'It's just his body,' my grandmother said before she got the dementia that's left her convinced he's still alive. And besides, there are other ways to reflect. 'I prefer to speak to him when I'm driving,' one of my aunties told me. Problem is, I haven't been visiting or reflecting. For years I've been meaning to. Finally, I'm here. Even if it's of no service to the dead, I wonder if, in visiting a loved-one's grave, there's any value for the living.

* * *

It's an entire city in here. There are roads with speed limits: fifteen kilometres per hour. I explore the place on foot, down John Paul II Road, following Diane's hand-drawn map. The religious folk are laid out on my left according to their church, order or nunnery. In the plot dedicated to the Mercy Sisters, the headstones stick out of the earth like a perfect set of teeth. The priests' plot is smaller but far more opulent. The ones who died before the 60s, their graves are something else; you could park a Hyundai Getz on some of them. They all need a blast from a high-pressure hose, but when they were built they would have looked like pavlovas. And now? Not a flower on any of them.

Even the weeds have given up.

Sister Nola Riley (who shares a plot with Sr M Philomena Pohlman) died aged ninety. Hers is the only grave in her row with any offerings. A small statue of a white winged angel, with an inscription on the base that says, 'You are remembered with love and will live in our hearts forever'. A jar holding two bouquets of supermarket flowers has toppled over. Each has the price sticker still attached ($25 and $16 respectively).

The newer graves are where the loot is. There are figurines atop many—cherubs, angels, cats, dogs and Mary (Jesus's Mum). There's a toy train, a ceramic lizard, garden gnomes, alcohol, a lantern containing a lit candle, even a plastic owl with a motion sensor that I think is meant to hoot when somebody walks past, but which, having succumbed to the elements, kind of honk-barks.

And then I find it. A2596. In Loving Memory of Ross Brayley. 8.3.1932–22.4.2010. The white lettering is flaking off; I can barely read the 'R.I.P.' I didn't think I would have this reaction. I didn't think I would drop to a knee and drag my fingers through the grass and rub my eyes to clear them of sweat and stinging tears, reach forward and run my hands across the grey headstone that I now know is grandee granite. Because rationality tells me it's just a marker, this grave. Just one of the dwindling pieces of permanence that remind us that he was ever on Earth at all. And I feel like such an arsehole for not seeing it until now.

* * *

It's not a bad spot. I can see Brisbane Airport from here—the control tower and some hangars. He used to take me there when I was a kid, with a pair of binoculars, to watch the planes taking off and landing.

Poppie's neighbours are Vincent Muscat in A2595 and Colin Jackson in A2597. Across the grassy road is Sylvia Hamilton and her plotmate Nell McDonald in A2638. Over the back are the Kings, Cyril and Beverley, at A2554. I can't help but notice that Colin and Sylvia, and Nell and the Kings, have unassuming yet neatly maintained plots. Judith and Geoffrey Martin down the road at A2618 get a can of Jack Daniel's that's swelled under the belting heat of the Queensland sun. Even a disco ball, for Christ's sake. Poppie didn't drink, and I don't recall him having a view on disco balls, but I start to feel that perhaps he deserves more than two rusting pots of murky water, like green tea, if mosquito larvae swam in tea.

He's not really there. But still I promise him, squatting on the grass, that I'll be back with a bucket of soapy water and flowers and paint. He would have done that for me. I pop across the road to the stonemasons, T Wrafter & Sons, where manager Kim Harvey tells me that ever since they stopped using lead in paint there's no longevity. 'It just flakes right off after five years,' she says, as we sit in her office amongst the headstone samples.

I ask her if I could rejuvenate Poppie's headstone myself, or if it would take a backhoe, a permit and a degree in fine arts. 'You could,' she says sceptically, 'if you have a steady hand.' And a few other essentials, I discover, after searching for headstone cleaning tips on YouTube.

A few weeks later I'm back with a bucket, soap, paint stripper, White Knight Rust Guard, a cuttlefish bone (I'll explain later) and a hat with a brim that wraps all the way around like a northern suburbs verandah.

As I scrub, I pity Sylvia and Nell across the road, copping a real eyeful. 'Sorry ladies,' I say, on all fours, tongue out, manoeuvring the paintbrush into the engraved lettering. The name and dates are fine; a simple sans serif font Kim tells me is called 'Heavy B'. It's the 'In Loving Memory Of' that really trips me up; a complex font called 'Old English'. The first 'M' in 'Memory' is a ridiculous maze of lines and swirls. I'm sure it's elegant, but it's a bloody pain to paint. I try to shove the brush into the grooves, but the paint keeps appearing about a centimetre from where I intended.

I'm onto the 'o' in 'Memory' when I notice the first droplets of rain hitting the back of the King's place. And so, I find myself sitting not only under a wide brimmed hat to keep the sun off, but also a large umbrella to keep the rain off. You never can be too prepared. I remember what Poppie would call to my grandmother when she went to Church:

'Pray for rain!'

'Pray for it yourself,' she'd snap.

I stare at the heavy 'B' of his name. 'Did you send this rain, you bastard?' I say, and I see him red-faced and laughing, wiping tears from under his glasses.

The rain subsides, the paint dries. Each engraved character looks like its bleeding onto the granite around it. Enter the cuttlefish bone. I could write several pages about cuttlefish bones, so taken was I—an amateur headstone renovator who does not, it transpires, have a steady hand—with its incredible functionality and efficacy. But in the interest of brevity, they're the things that hang in cages so birds can get more dietary calcium. I pour water over the letters and vigorously rub the bone across them, scraping the excess away, leaving only the paint within the engraved letter itself. What's left is a painted headstone

Michelangelo himself would be proud of. As I arrange some fake flowers and step back to examine my work, I feel proud that Poppie's piece of granite looks just a bit brighter against the darkening sky.

* * *

As I leave, passing what Diane called the 'higher-end' graves, some blokes in high-vis vests mill around an orange Burder 4WD front end loader. They're putting the finishing touches on a hole that's about to welcome the cemetery's newest occupant. Above, they've erected a maroon tent on retractable poles—the kind you see at school sports carnivals. Snappily dressed but glum mourners trickle in, and I wonder if this is the only time they'll come, whether they'll leave some kind of honk-barking owl, or whether they'll do their reflecting at home or in the car. Because we each mourn and remember in different ways. And while there is value in tending to loved ones' graves, for me at least, the greater connection to Poppie came from saying to my family, 'Remember the time that he …' or 'Remember how he used to say …' We recalled memories we'd almost forgotten. And we remembered him just a little bit longer.

PAUL SUTHERLAND is a former journalist and political adviser with more than ten years writing, editing and public relations experience in Australia and internationally. He now provides media relations advice to professional services firms, and freelance writing and editing support to his own clients around Australia.

The Muse and its Painter

Ruth Ryan-Boakes

Albert dashed up the steps to his studio. Rain the colour of dirty paint water rushed through the gutters as droplets pelted his brown hair and duster coat. It wasn't excitement that made him quicken his pace. No, he ran with the nervous energy of a man hunted.

He pushed open the wooden door, glancing one last time at the street before shutting the door behind him. Little light left the single grimy window. The smell of oil paint made his head throb and he breathed in deep. It blazed its way up his nose and singed his sinuses. Turpentine could make his world spin faster than any brand of spirits, and Albert knew his way around a bottle. Tonight he needed a clear mind and steady hands. He hung his coat on the back of the door, then flipped the light switch. An incandescent globe flickered on and dyed the room with mustard-yellow light.

Canvases drenched with murky hues swamped the room. They leant against every wall, they occupied every easel, and they were piled high on his desk. Even the smallest canvases cast long shadows and, despite the light, pockets of the studio were still dark. Albert cleared his desk and dumped the canvases in a corner. They were paintings of street scenes, still lives and portraits of models from life drawing sittings. Emma would probably like them. They depicted goodness and they would earn him nothing; they were mediocre pieces and held none of the anguish and suffering his paintings were famed for. Albert's happiness never sold.

Behind him, a twisted face made of muddied greys and sombre reds slowly dried. A true work of art, marked with the jagged brushstrokes that had put food on Albert's table, a roof over his head and crammed more blank canvasses into his studio. Canvasses his Muse demanded to be inundated with paint. His twisted forms and shadowy landscapes hung in galleries he'd never visit. These *real* paintings had landed him interviews for articles he'd never read. He'd shaken strangers' hands and now their praise plagued him—*Our next Picasso? A living van Gogh? The drama! The chiaroscuro! He is contemporary-baroque!*

The only label Albert should ever have been given was 'fool'.

The eyes of his Muse watched him too, as haggard and bottomless as its gaping jaws. It lingered in his periphery. Contorting its body, it remained within the shadows. His Muse only revealed enough of itself to remind him of its presence.

It loved to loom.

The wind whistled outside his window as the winter air seeped through the thin walls. Shivers racked his body, whether from fear or the cold was anyone's guess. He pulled out the rickety wooden chair from his equally rickety wooden desk—both worn, comfortable and stained with paint. Above the desk were shelves heavy with paint jars, most close to empty. Painting after painting had been drafted here, but tonight he needed words. He needed forgiveness.

Dear Emma,
I leave my final paintings, all of my unsold works,
and all of my money to you. My family will contest
you—it is their final chance to tear out chunks of
me—but my attorney will fend against them. My will
is very clear. I know she can fend them off better than
I ever could.

Dull eyes, harsh words and harsher hands: that's all family ever was.

I do not leave you, or my work, willingly. This is
my only choice. However, knowing my paintings will
belong to you casts a bright light on this grim affair.
Though you know I am haunted, I have withheld
much of my story. It isn't a story worth hearing—it's
pathetic and, worst of all, sad—but it's a story I owe
you.

Albert's hand shook and he pulled his pen from the paper before the ink bled. The floorboard behind him creaked as his Muse edged closer. Its flesh—scored with so many scars that it resembled the stripes of a tiger—was jaundice yellow under the incandescent globe. Albert's hands drifted to his shoulders, squeezing the places where his own scars lay, inflicted by the short, sharp strokes of a Stanley knife. The drops of blood on the floor of his old family bathroom had been such a brilliant shade of crimson they'd made him cry.

My Muse is real, as real as you and me. You've seen
my paintings—you know its face. That is the face I

*see when I fall asleep and the face that greets me in
the morning.*

*It is the face that watched my beatings, my nights
alone, and my days spent begging strangers for food.
During winter nights, as I slept on ice-cold concrete,
it lay by my side and wrapped an arm around my
middle. Its touch was corpse-like, but its weight was
real, grounding. My Muse. My eternal witness. I
thought it would leave. When my life became gentler
and my family was far behind me, I thought it
would dissipate. After I met you, I thought I'd
be free.*

I was not.

*During our dinners, it turns every bite of food you
cook for me sour. It has joined us at cafes, cinemas,
concerts, hotels and picnics. When we lie together, it
watches us from the foot of your bed. And, every day,
it grows closer.*

To think that twenty years ago his Muse was the size of a
bean, a mere insect peeking from his closet, with sharp little
mandibles and the same red eyes. He'd drawn it the next day
and his father kicked him for ignoring his homework. He'd
thought it was just a nightmare, even after he saw it the following night, scuttling across his nightstand.

*The inevitable is now upon me, a moment that I
have been dreading since long before we met. I did
try to fight it once. I have asked for help before. I
have reached out. But all I received was a slap across
the face and hours in confession where I begged to be*

forgiven for seeking attention. Our parents were alike in this way.

I know you're different. You're softer than velvet. You're bonfire bright. My paintings of you are the most beautiful I've ever painted. But I'm not someone who was meant to be happy. I should have reached out to you, but I was afraid you wouldn't believe me. Or, worse, that you would have tried to talk me out of my stupidity.

Stupid, stupid, stupid …

He dragged his hands down his face, pulling at his skin. He had seen what had been happening and had chosen to ignore it. But now he could ignore it no further.

He left his seat and turned to his easel. It called to him, the half-formed face, urging him to finish it. Albert retrieved his paintbrush and pallet—his sword and shield. He added green to the still-pliant red paint on the canvas and turned it brown. He let the paints run together and smear until a replica of his Muse loomed before him from a gloom so deep that it must emanate from the deepest recesses of Hell.

A gurgle from behind him: his Muse, grunting in pleasure at the sight of itself. Every inch of Albert shook as he took a jar from his shelf and scooped white paint out with his palette knife. He was almost finished. It would all be over soon. Albert should have felt relief but all he felt was fear. He highlighted his Muse's eyes, making them glint as brightly as its teeth.

It was finished.

He could fuss over it forever, layering colour after colour and continuing to delay his fate. He'd been delaying it for years. But tonight there was no time to run.

Tonight he needed a clear mind and steady hands.

He returned to his desk and his hastily scrawled letter, his Muse following him as he darted across his studio. Another creak. And another. No more running.

> But I can't let that happen. All I can do is paint, and I will not stop, even if it is the death of me. It is all I am. It is all I have ever been. It is all I will ever be. I can't let go. I can't forget. Without it, I am nothing.

> Love,
> A.C.

Albert tossed his pen aside as tears slid down his cheeks. He wrapped his arms around his body as his trembling turned to convulsion. Sobs erupted from his dry throat and his eyes smarted.

Every time he put brush to canvas, pencil to paper, or even chalk to sidewalk, it appeared. His Muse was all that took form. Its lines and shapes and colours were all he knew. He knew what he was: a puppet on a string. A vehicle for his Muse's image. Albert had watched the monster continue to grow as he drew it. It relished in being acknowledged. It fed off him. Fed off his soul. His heart. His mind. It would feed off him until there was nothing left.

His Muse lumbered behind him. He squeezed himself tighter, banishing the fear that rose within him and churned up his innards.

He bowed his head. His Muse's breath was hot on his neck, its gnarled hands resting on each of his shoulders. Warm, almost loving, hands. Albert leant into them as they crept towards his neck. A finger nudged his cheek and wiped away his tear—its skin scabbed and rotting, its nails chipped and dirty. He gagged at the sickly-sweet smell. The hands tightened around his throat and he began to choke. Albert's hands flew up but, instead of wrestling with his Muse, he squeezed its grip tighter.

Giddy, he tilted his head back. Above him was his water-stained, cobweb-strewn ceiling and the single incandescent globe. Particles of dust glittered as they trickled through the air. A whimper left his throat. Albert's eyes fell shut.

RUTH RYAN-BOAKES is a lover of sci-fi, fantasy and horror, a dweller of inner-city apartments, and hoarder of antique books and jewellery. She has been published by Cardigan Street on Medium. Before her stint at PW&E she was the most terrifying thing of all: an engineering major. Find her at instagram.com/rarb246/ and ruthr-47267.medium.com.

The Italian Solution

Amy Bullow

I gasp—sitting up abruptly with the sensation of my eyes bulging out of my skull as I look directly into the painfully bright light breaking through the villa. I burrow into my skin to rid my body of the bugs I am certain exist. There's a pounding rushing through my ears to the inside of my fucking brain. I'm still here.

Surrounded by nothing but rubble and memories, the crumbling roof lets in just enough light for me to see the decay around me. Handcuffed to a dirty rundown sofa, I sit alone with no one to blame but myself.

It seemed brilliant at the time—revolutionary, even—but here, now, handcuffed to the wooden leg of an old rotting couch and with no rescuer in sight, I can't help but ask myself, what the fuck for? Sobriety? It had only just begun, but it wasn't anything to brag about—the shivering, sweating, the sensation of being thrown on death's door with nothing more than a can of expired chickpeas, a bucket of hose water and a photograph of home—of Crema.

The town was as I remembered it—traditionally charming, but the villa itself had not stood the age of time. I looked around, but only for a second. My serene childhood home had become riddled with mould and grime. Shards of broken glass were scattered by the old windowsill and piles of rubble lingered around the joint. The upstairs floor was now nothing more than an opened sunroof, reflecting even more light into this withering place.

Part of me knew at the time that my genius plan was nothing more than a moment of stupidity, a hallucinogenic thought, but my impulsive spirit had gotten me this far—a no good junkie with nothing to lose. Why stop now? I hadn't anything to live for except the drug itself and living with it was nothing more than a death sentence. I was screwed and I knew that there was a chance—a good fucking chance—that I wouldn't be making it to the end of my spontaneous journey.

* * *

There's a light. A warm trinkle of dust falling from the ceiling and onto the bar. It's an old bar. It's an old town. Lost in noir and left to fade, but her colour screams through as the lights reflect off her diamond-encrusted necklace. Gleaming, she sits by the bar cradling her drink in her hand and draping her long red fingernails over the glass, leaving nothing more than a warm handprint and a lipstick stain.

She's wrapped in satin and drips of lust. She's a regular day Ava Gardner, if ever I had seen one. Sensual. Sultry. She's a beautiful creature. I watch on as the men begin to flock to her, but she's not interested. She's never interested, leaving them all to ask themselves, each night, 'Am I feeling lucky?'

The testosterone in the room rises as the men in polished suits continue to gather—with hair heavily laced in grease, and with the synchronising click of their fingers, they crowd the beauty, stalking her in all her glory.

There. With the hit of the music, she throws her hands in the air. The music thrills the room as the saxophones begin to sing to the swinging jazz tune, setting the mood as she notices me from the across the bar. She stands with the rhythm, hitting each trumpet and vibrato with her body as she begins to dance up a storm. She's seductive, luscious and she knows I crave her—already. She gets closer, closer, closer. She reaches for me, exposing the palm of her hand and a message.

Heroin. It reads.

Without hesitating I give her my hand and step into a life of technicolour.

We spend hours together—years. Again and again until it no longer feels good, and I no longer want it, but there's still something there. A desire. A need. I didn't even like her anymore, and neither did my family, but she was so hard to quit and so easy to have. Here. Now. There was only one way out—

* * *

It had only been eight hours, but I could feel it all. I tried moving, but I couldn't. I tried crying, but I couldn't. I tried screaming, but there was no noise ... just an involuntary yawn heard only by the rats as they circled around, sniffing and peering at me like an intruder. We are intruders. Intruders of a house lost in time and filled with memories.

There's something they don't tell you when you become an addict, and most of the time you don't even remember how the fuck you became one, but it's the nights that will get you. When you're fast asleep, resting your head on a feathered pillow—you're dreaming about the same thing. The same taste. The same hit. And when you open your pretty little eyes and see the morning light, nothing changes. Except that those wild dreams and fantasies are about to become something much better—reality.

AMY BULLOW is an aspiring fiction writer specialising in romance, drama and short-form story writing. When she's not writing, Amy can be found exploring Melbourne's west, reading classic poetry and haunting local bookstores.

Lost in the Wire

Ben Cumming

Lost in the Wire is an extract from a larger work.

'Liz, that shit'll kill you.'

She took a long drag from her poorly wrapped cigarette. 'This place'll bore me to death long before I gotta worry about that, Chris.'

'Don't change the subject.' I kicked a can lying on the road.

I hate to admit she's right, but you know what they say about broken clocks. Somehow, we'd spent nearly our entire summer slumming around the crater town that is Merton, doing crap that had lost its lustre before we'd even started. Dry grass, overgrown forests and rickety old houses were the specialty here. Some places are famous for their fish or their giant fruit—but Merton? Well, I don't think anyone's even heard of the place.

'Want one?' Liz asked.

'Um …' I hesitated, but boredom won out. 'Screw it, sure.'

She took out the crumpled pack and offered it to me.

I picked the one that looked the least likely to fall apart. 'Put it in your mouth, and—'

'Yeah, yeah, I know how to do it,' I lied. The taste of soggy paper was intense. 'What'd you do, drown these?'

She shrugged, clearly lacking a good answer, before leaning over and lighting it.

I inhaled, which was a mistake because I started coughing right away. Like an ass. 'Wrong pipe ...' I sputtered.

'Mmhm.'

We kept walking down the road. Like the rest of the town, it was cracked and worn. The further out of town we went, the less overwhelmingly bleak it felt. But what Merton has can't be fixed with a new coat of paint; the place felt like someone's bad memory of a town most of the time.

It rained all of last night, and the sky was still a dreary grey. *A storm to last the week*. That's what the weather lady I was crushing on said. That wet smell was still in the air, the clouds above threatening to choke out the last of the light if they fancied. Occasionally the sun broke through, slanted gold light illuminating the grass and the pavement.

I tried the cigarette again and didn't hack my guts out this time. I didn't know whether or not that was a good thing, considering it tasted like bleach. 'How do you like this crap?'

'Who said I liked them?' Liz kicked the can this time, launching it a few metres up the road.

'If you don't like 'em, why do you bother making them?'

'Alan won't let me buy them, the righteous prick, so I *have* to make them. It's like the prohibition.'

'Please don't tell me you're doing it out of spite.'

She gave me her signature shrug. 'I dunno if it's *that* deep. I've just got nothing better to do.'

I didn't have a good response. 'Fair enough.'

We walked in silence for a bit, taking turns kicking the can. No birds, no breeze, just the sound of metal bouncing on the ground and the gentle hum of electricity. The thought that launching garbage along a road was what passed for entertainment here made me want to scream.

I groaned: long and slow.

'Same, buddy,' Liz sighed. 'Same.'

'There's gotta be more to it than this!'

'It?'

'Life, man!' I cried, stomping the cigarette out. 'How the hell does everyone else here do it?'

'Couldn't tell you.' Liz thought for a moment, her hands resting on the back of her head. 'If the boredom got lethal, I reckon I'd just sail the sea until I ran out of gas.'

I deflated. 'Into the Great Blue Unknown.'

'That could be kinda fun. Until the seagulls get you, anyway.'

My brain lagged, trying to make sense of what she said. 'What?'

She looked at me like *I* was the crazy one. 'The … the seagulls. The vultures of the sea, man.'

I was speechless. I opened my mouth to say something but couldn't find the right words: the ones gentle enough to say 'you're a lunatic' without actually saying it.

'Look it up, dude! They circle you like sharks. Or like vultures, I guess …' She was second-guessing herself now. 'Whichever!'

'Hey, they're apex predators if you say they are. Just give me another cigarette.'

She was uncomfortably quiet after that. I felt like I owed it to her to break the silence.

'The ocean creeps me out,' I said after a while.

Liz gave me a weird look. 'Why?'

'I dunno. Something about the whole "vast emptiness" thing just doesn't sit right with me.' I shivered. 'Makes me feel small just thinking about it.'

'Huh.' She sounded amused.

'What's "huh"?'

'Nothing. I'm just the opposite, is all.'

'What about that big blue puddle of nothing is appealing to you?'

'Geez, man, I don't know. It's pretty.'

'There's a lot of pretty things that'll kill you.'

'Hey, don't I know it?' She grinned at me like an idiot.

I ignored her self-flattery. 'Is that it? It's pretty?'

Liz sighed. 'That whole emptiness thing is pretty cool. Like,' she paused, 'we're so insignificant compared to the ocean. *Titanic* was supposed to be a real big bad dude, and the ocean swallowed that bitch up like it was nothing.'

'That's terrifying!'

'It can be more than one thing!'

I groaned in disgust. 'And what if you're alone, stranded at sea? Like, you fall off the side of a boat and it keeps on sailing. Is it still cool then?'

'If that's where the 'verse takes me, brother, then that's where it takes me.'

I glared at her. 'New topic.'

'Alright,' Liz paused. Then she laughed. 'What is it about the weather lady that turns you on?'

'Silence it is!'

Thunder boomed somewhere far away. The first few drops of rain came down and hit me square on the head. They were oddly warm. I looked at Liz. She had her tongue out, trying to catch some.

The sky had gotten dark quick. The air had a faint ozone-y smell, too: the kind that makes your nose flinch. The real storm would be coming soon anyway. I started back.

'What, you don't want to at least see what's over the hill?' Liz called out.

'Mmm … not really.'

Liz sagged. 'Come on, it'll be fun! A bit of excitement for once!' She paused for a second, trying to read my face. 'We both know we have nothin' better to do.'

I was unimpressed. 'Is that your sales pitch?'

'Come on! Come on, come on, come on, come on, come—'

'Alright! Jesus, spare me the puppy eyes.' We started up the road again, clumsily pulling our hoodies on.

'What's the worst that could happen, right? We have to Bear Grylls it up for a night?'

That made me stop. 'Come on, man, don't say that shit out loud.'

'What? Bear Grylls?' She gasped. 'Is that like *Beetlejuice*?'

Unfortunately, Liz was never dumb on purpose. I sighed. 'Sure, Liz. Like *Beetlejuice*.'

The air got denser the further we went. It was oppressive, even for a storm like the one they'd forecast, like the sky was threatening to bury us at any moment. We kept walking, the powerlines to our left still humming.

'Where d'you reckon that power's even going?' I asked.

'Beats me,' she shrugged. 'They probably just never shut off the line.'

The ozone smell was getting stronger, and the thunder more frequent. We kept going, picking up the pace a little, past the puddles, the potholes, the fallen pole that somehow hadn't start-ed a fire. My nose wrinkled at the smell in the air; it was getting more pungent, almost coppery. We were nearly at the hill when something bright shot out ahead of us, lighting up half the sky, so quick I almost missed it. It was gone as soon as it appeared.

I stopped. Liz did too.

'Maybe one of the poles blew?' I offered.

'Maybe.' She didn't believe it either.

That light didn't look right to me, and I think Liz felt it too, but we didn't say anything. We kept going, even as the rain started to pick up. The odd lightning strikes that briefly lit up the sky made me flinch every time; they made me worry a pole would *actually* blow. I couldn't take my eyes off the sky, either; something about the way the clouds moved wasn't right. They looked fast, like breaking waves, but they didn't seem like they were actually getting anywhere. They just tumbled along, al-most in limbo. I did my best to ignore them.

We were getting closer to where that light had gone off. I wouldn't say it, but the further we went, the more creeped out I got. I realised Liz was flicking her lighter on and off; she only did that when she was nervous.

We crested the hill, finally seeing what was waiting for us. But what we saw didn't make any sense. The road stretched so far into the horizon, we couldn't see where it ended. The trees eventually died out and it was smooth sailing, but the road, it … it just kept going. The hum felt louder too, but maybe it was just the smell making it worse. I peered down along the stretch of road, looking for the source of the light, but I couldn't make anything out. All the poles looked like they were still standing, with their lines swaying in the breeze.

'Where does this thing even go?' I asked.

Liz didn't answer.

We made our way down the road. It had to have been lightning, I reasoned. If a pole hadn't blown, what else could it be? Liz was talking to herself now, too. Always a good sign.

Above the hum and the rain, I kept hearing her damn mumbling. I was about to tell her to knock it off, but she beat me to it.

'What'd you say, Chris?'

I met her eyes. 'I didn't say anything …'

There was a moment of realisation. My body went cold, ice in my veins. The mumbling had a source now, just to my left.

I turned and saw it sitting there under the powerlines, lying on the grass: some animal's head. Its horns were as black as the fur that curled around the back of it. Its dark eyes were rolled back in its skull, and it had a muzzle like a goat: one that moved and twisted as it mumbled.

'Liz …'

She said nothing.

It kept … talking. It was saying something I couldn't understand, but I couldn't take my eyes off of it. It was almost rhythmic; it could have been singing. There was nothing around it, no blood, no … no nothing. It was just a head. It was like it was speaking backwards, in some language I didn't understand—something weirdly guttural. The longer I looked, the more sadness I felt; like this was a great loss in ways I couldn't comprehend.

My eyes started to go fuzzy, kind of like static. I crawled forward, getting closer to the thing under the lines. The hum of the wires sounded louder now, like they could fry themselves at any second. The head kept singing its incomprehensible song.

Its eyes rolled forward, meeting mine, with purpose in its gaze. The head spoke in its impossible way, like there was something important it wanted me to know. It sounded sorry. For a long moment my brain tried to make sense of it, to un-scramble itself … but it felt like just listening was enough.

Then its eyes seemed to fade, to lose their colour, and I snapped out of whatever trance I was in. The mouth closed a final time and the head curled backwards, sinking into the ground and out of existence. The hum came to a crescendo, then stopped.

Liz tried to say something, but couldn't seem to get it out.

'What the fuck was in those cigarettes, Liz?'

BEN CUMMING is a writer-for-hire with a penchant for most things fiction, a passion for editing and a love for long sentences. When not writing the great Australian novel, he can be found on Twitter at @thebencumming.

COPYCAT

Ethan Lewis-Granland

Elizabeth tied her long brown hair above her head in a bun. Her heavy laced boots echoed through the empty home as she moved down the stairs into the hallway. The house had been vacated many years before she had purchased it. Whatever stories the walls held were long gone. Late into the sombre hours of the night, in the middle of a restless gin-induced sleep, she could hear clawing behind the walls and wails from the kitchen. She still wondered if they were the house's, or hers.

There was a frantic knock at the door.

Elizabeth hoisted her dress up and drew the pistol from the holster on her leg. Finger curled around the trigger, she moved to the door. The knocking was louder now, open palmed and desperate. A woman's voice called out from the other side, over the wind.

Elizabeth shut her eyes, breathed in, and opened the door.

Ms Miller stood in black cloth cradling her youngest boy in her arms. His eyes and mouth were closed but he was not asleep. Elizabeth could see the pale pigment of his skin, not from the cold, and how the skin clung tight to his bones to keep whatever it could inside. She frowned at Ms Miller, who looked at her with wide eyes and an open mouth. Had she not expected to be answered?

'Ms Harper,' she wheezed, before coughing painfully. 'I need your help. Patrick is not well—not well at all.'

Elizabeth looked at the boy and shook her head at the pair. Ms Miller's foot caught the door as it closed.

'Please. The other doctors down the block are closed at this hour and no one is opening their doors. Patty just needs some medicine for his cold and to help him sleep.'

The women stared at each other for a moment before Elizabeth shivered from the harsh winds and holstered her gun. She opened the door and stepped aside, sighing. Ms Miller muttered her thanks through chattering teeth and a brittle cough, before moving inside. She looked into the kitchen at the dining table and back at Elizabeth. They worked together to clear the table and lay the weak boy down over it.

Elizabeth held her hand against Patrick's neck. There was a faint pulse. His breath was a rasp, slow and deep. She could see how malnourished the boy was and the drying blood that had formed around his mouth. Ms Miller caressed his head slowly and was whistling a tune that Elizabeth didn't recognise, but it helped calm the boy's breathing. She watched them for a moment until Ms Miller looked at her.

The two small chalkboards she kept around the house were held up by a single nail just at head height, one on each floor. The one more often used in the hallway had cracked at the edges when it had been thrown to the floor in a fit of indignation many months ago. Elizabeth could not bring herself to make or buy another. Tracing her finger along the smooth yet sharp grooves brought her back to that night. She breathed deeply to remain calm, recalling the stink of gin and regret.

She took the chalkboard off the wall and wrote with the white chalk she kept in her dress:

Symptoms?

Ms Miller squinted, and Elizabeth brought the chalkboard closer. She opened her mouth to ask a question but decided not to. It was okay, Elizabeth knew how that conversation would have gone. And how much time it would have wasted for Patrick.

'He—he's been coughing nearly every minute for the last few weeks. He was moving around just fine until the last week.' Ms Miller paused and caressed Patrick's hair, slick with sweat. 'It's just a nasty cold. He slept one night with his window open. That's all. Just a little cold.'

Elizabeth cleaned the board with her hand, leaving the white chalk dust on her palm, before writing:

It looks bad.

Ms Miller nodded and sniffed a wet glob deeper into her nose.

Elizabeth clenched her jaw. This mother was too blinded by her concerns to see what Elizabeth saw. It was too often the case. People mistook her tone through her writing, and it led to mistakes. Big mistakes.

She moved into the kitchen and wet one of the cloths by the sink. She walked back to Patrick, placing the cloth on his forehead. His head would have sizzled if it was any hotter.

His chest heaved and he burst into a coughing fit, reeling over to his side, away from his mother. Ms Miller moved with him and pulled a crusty black handkerchief from her pocket. Patrick brought it to his mouth as he gave one final heave before resting his head back onto the table. He took a deep reeling breath before he lay his head back into his mother's hands.

Elizabeth eyed the handkerchief and held out her palm for it. Ms Miller hesitated before she obliged. It was wet in Elizabeth's hand, and she could see it was darkened with a thick liquid. She brushed it with her hand and saw the blood which blended with the chalk dust.

Elizabeth took the cloth into the kitchen and drained it into one of the beakers by the sink. She scrubbed her hands roughly with the soft soap by the sink and watched the crimson water flush down in a gentle spiral. It was not the first time her sink had been stained red like this, but this was the first time it was a child's blood.

'Ms Harper?' Ms Miller called. 'Can you help us?'

Elizabeth looked through the kitchen window and out to the delicate oak tree that loomed over her house, swaying heavily in the wind. The moon shone through the clouds and cast wicked shadows over the house. She took her pistol from the holster and held it tightly, until her knuckles turned white.

There were only a few options for the boy. And none of them were palatable.

She wrote across the chalkboard one final time:

It is consumption. There is nothing I can do.

Her eyes caught her reflection in the mirror. The clean bun of hair had become partially undone into messy strands and no amount of make-up could cover the darkness under her eyes. Elizabeth was convinced there was no other way.

It is always better not to suffer before the end.

ETHAN LEWIS-GRANLAND is a Melbourne-based writer, editor and game designer. He is currently working on expanding his brand, focusing on working with tabletop games and designers. With a mix of creative storytelling and editing, he enjoys all aspects of the publishing process. Find him on all social media: @Ethananddragons.

A Myriad of Overcomings

Jess Di Giacomo

I remember the first time I thought I had overcome. I was in Year 7. I had just told my youth leader what had happened. It's like I had forgotten everything until I was standing at the altar at one of our youth rallies and suddenly received a multitude of flashbacks, unexpected and out of nowhere. I felt everything, I saw everything, and I heard everything. Probably one of the only times I hated the privilege of experiencing the senses.

We walked out of the auditorium—well, my youth leader walked out with me hanging over her left shoulder. My best friend was there too; she didn't know what was going on, but she stayed with me. I hung over her right shoulder. The three of us walked out of the auditorium and into a quiet and secluded place. We sat down on the old, red swivel chairs placed in the middle of the room. Here I knew I had to begin to explain everything I didn't want to talk about.

I thought opening up about a faded memory was the only thing I needed to do to feel better. I guess I thought healing would be complete when, in reality, the journey to overcoming was just beginning.

After a few months I had more conversations about what happened with the people closest to me. Ashamed and afraid of judgement, I spoke of my experience. I didn't want to but, apparently, I had to.

Overcoming is exactly that. A word still in action, still in attaining, a verb—still being or having to be done. It's still happening. It hasn't finished and when it feels as though I have overcome, I'm at the beginning of a new overcoming. It's never-ending. Layer upon layer is healing upon healing and with healing resides the overcoming. And I am still overcoming.

The year 2020 poured through our fingers like sand when you pick it up on a hot day at the beach. Now, it seems 2021 is a direct replica. No more free trial, folks, we've bought the subscription. In the beginning, I thought 2021 would be a year of answered prayers and dreams fulfilled. Instead, it has become a cliché: a year of wishful thinking.

* * *

At the start, I was hopeful and ready. I had made my peace with overcoming and I was prepared to take cautionary steps. I was ready to start over in my new layer of overcoming. It was as if I was at the starting point of a race, in position, ready to run at the sound of the starter pistol. But as unyielding restrictions persisted, the stretches and determination began to wear off.

I can't face the daily routine and expectations the way I used to. My capacity changed; it aged decades. I didn't keep stretching and preparing for the race ahead of me because I thought the off-season would last forever. I feel tired, worn out and overwhelmed at the demands I must cater to, which weren't as hard for me before the pandemic. Everyone else is at the starting line, ready to run the race, but I'm still trying to get my running shoes on.

I am at the beginning of yet another overcoming.

As I've grown, from a child, into adolescence and now into adulthood, when I peel back the layers of healing, I find there is more to overcome. You slay one head of a hydra and an additional two grow right back. Granted, there have been many things to overcome—a myriad of extended family dramas and ended friendships are the decorations and the icing on the cake. But issues like my childhood trauma and a global pandemic are the things that created the cake. And, although it looks damn good, you best believe it was the hardest thing to bake.

It's the paradox of listening to your feelings while also keeping strong and hoping for the best. It's the collision of great uncertainty and a longing to trust that there *truly is more*. It's the willingness to continue and the determination to preserve such trials. It's the self-control not to quit but to stay the path and walk alongside the One who has walked this very road. All things must be considered because when you opt for the easy or quick fix road, that action is always destructive.

Overcoming is hard; it is mentally strenuous and physically exhausting. But it is also beautiful. It can bring sweetness to what is bitter. It promotes life in dire situations. It commands character development and abolishes childish tendencies. It demands change for the price of time and promotes fortitude and maturity. I'm scared of the overcomings that are to come. But I am thankful for the ones that have passed.

I'm twenty-two years old and I have learnt that to become, I must overcome. And in the overcoming, I will be renewed and redefined in ways unfathomable and unattainable on my own. So, as we continue living in these dire times, hope remains. And it will be by grace and through faith that I will again overcome. It is hard and tiresome, but most things that are turn out to be worth it.

JESS DI GIACOMO is a blogger and editor. She focuses her writing on opinion and nonfiction pieces exploring themes of self-development, growth and faith. She is currently working on a collection of personal essays unpacking the meaning of life.

A Very Nice Day

Aimee Clarence

Lola sighed. The day felt longer than others. Not that it wasn't a nice day. The weather was actually very nice. The sun was warm against her face, and a light breeze would occasionally wake itself up enough to tussle her golden hair whenever it got too warm. Not to forget the grass, still lush with the remnants of spring, and that the swooping birds had let up for the time being. It was, in fact, a very nice day.

The problem with today was that it was a very *boring* day. Every day was a boring day, it seemed. Absolutely nothing happened. Her life had condensed to this one point on her porch on which she had spent most of her time since the weather had warmed.

Her gaze, as it often did, rested on the locked garden fence at the end of the grass-cracked path. It had been six days since it opened. It was a measly thing, really, that kept the outside world away. Lola longed to see the gate open, to wander through and discover all the curiosities the world had to offer. But not without Josie. Lola gave another heavy sigh. Josie barely moved from her bed most days now. Perhaps she should find Josie and bring her out here to sit with her? A nice day like this was bound to make her feel better.

Lola perked up when she heard a muffled voice from a few metres away and craned her neck to get a good view of the two new elements on the scene. The first was a middle-aged woman who seemed to be searching for something. It wasn't uncommon. Everyone seemed to be doing it now. Searching. Lola assumed they were searching for another person, needing to make contact—any kind of contact—even if it was prolonged and uncomfortable eye contact with a stranger ... Or maybe people kept getting masks confused with sunglasses and didn't think the other person would notice being blatantly stared at.

The second element was a cute dog. A very cute dog, Lola decided. He could have been a show dog. He walked with a poise that came only with practice and good bone structure. His fur was brushed to a sheen, and even from here Lola could make out the scent of a fresh wash. The dog glanced at her as he passed, wagging his tail. Lola's heart thumped faster in her chest.

Lola watched the woman search. The woman narrowed her eyes at her, and Lola assumed the woman was smiling beneath the mask. Or maybe the woman had poor eyesight and was trying to ascertain that Lola was actually there and not just some figment of her imagination or a lawn ornamentation. Lola *was* pretty small. Or perhaps was surprised to see Lola staring back at her. The woman was searching for her pack—after all, we are all essentially animals at the end of the day—and Lola had already found hers. She had Josie.

Lola watched until the two passed entirely out of sight, before once again sighing and laying her head down and bathing in the early spring sunlight. This was her life now: guessing the true nature of strangers' expressions and waiting for cute dogs to walk past. Her eyes blinked themselves closed slowly.

* * *

Lola didn't really see the importance of time: if the sun was up and still warm, that was good enough for her. So she wasn't sure how long had passed before she heard the car. She opened her eyes to watch and hoped the car would slow down. Would it be a man with food? If it *was* food, who was it for? What type of food was it? If it was food for her neighbour on the right, she would bet her left foot it was fish and chips. Lola was sure she had smelt fish and chips from his house at least once a week for a month. Josie ordered fish and chips sometimes. She always shared; she understood what love was. Even the smell of fish and chips was enough to wake Lola's stomach and fill her head with swirls of love and hunger and memory.

The car did not slow down. Or stop. Okay, it definitely wasn't delivering food. Lola sighed. So much for that. She lay back down, lifting her eyes to the cloudless sky and breathing in the smell of roses. They were overgrown in her little patch of the world. Josie used to tend to them every week. But Josie was still in bed. As always.

A bird landed on the lawn a few metres from her, and Lola, dark thoughts temporarily put aside, watched it with rapt attention. She didn't know what type of bird it was; it was a black-and-white one, but smaller than the ones that swooped you when you got too close. Lola watched it for a long time. It was almost as interesting as ignoring strangers' privacy and—depending on the weather—watching them from either the front porch or window. When the bird flew away, Lola wondered what it was like in the sky. A gate isn't in your way if you have wings.

* * *

The sun passed behind a cloud. The wind didn't feel as playful as it had earlier. There was a bite to it, a chill that Lola did not like. The darkening grey hues looked more sinister than inviting. Lola considered a moment before heaving herself up off the still-warm wood. She craned her neck to look down the long hallway behind her. Josie was still in bed. Lola trotted inside.

Lola stopped when she was halfway down the hall and sat down. She watched the road from there. The sun reappeared and her spot was just as inviting as it ever was. She didn't go back. That would look ridiculous. Lola sighed and began walking towards the living room slowly, considering her options. Getting food seemed like a lot of effort and begging was beneath her. And she just wasn't in the mood to bat around a toy. But she had napped plenty already. Lola was extroverted and affectionate, and she had reached her limit.

Footsteps thudded down the stairs.

'Lola!' A voice sung.

Lola looked up.

'Lola baby!'

It was Josie. *Her* Josie.

Lola stood up on the couch in rapt attention.

'Lola, walkies!'

That was it for Lola. That was by far more interesting than birdwatching or standing vigil at the front porch. She would go for a *walk*. And it would be *beyond* the gate. With Josie!

In a flash, Lola was sitting impatiently by the door. Josie strode to the table with a determined expression. She wanted to go beyond the gate just as badly as Lola did. If not more. Josie clipped a leash to the collar around Lola's throat. The leash still kind of grated on her. It wasn't very dignified. But it *did* mean she was going for a walk.

Josie's grin was huge when she bent beside Lola and scratched her behind the ears. 'Look who's sitting all *pretty*! You are very *very pretty* Lola! Yes, you *are*. Are you *excited*?'

Lola couldn't help the whine that escaped her chest as she responded to the tone, her tail wagging. To hell with dignity. She *was* excited.

AIMEE CLARENCE is a 5'1" ball of daydreams in high-heeled boots. Most of her time is spent talking to strangers and writing in cafes. She plans on directing all that energy into novel-writing and doing what she can in the arts.

Estelle

Lisa Kate Moule

Estelle is an extract from a larger work,
Motherhood and other Calamities.

Estelle combed the shelves of Greengully Bookshop. When she found *Parenting Girls*, recommendations from the mums at the school gate came back in echoes. She went home to make chai and brought Sigmond Petowski, parenting guru, to the sofa.

The sofa was hidden in a jungle of items: the rates bill, a magic wand, a doll's blanket covering a packet of Rizlas, a hair crimper, an extended family of Rewards cards and a Beeny Boo with crimped hair. The narrative in each object had the power to thieve her time and ensnare her in its treacle: just like the aggressive spruikers in Westfield with their sugary grins. She voiced her calming yogic mantra aloud, 'Sthiram Sukham Asanam' (strong, steady and stable), as she placed them on the floor.

She mindfully exhaled, then opened *Parenting Girls* and flicked through the chapters: 'Let's connect with consent', 'She is not you', before arriving at 'Fashion constraints'. Harmony was obsessed with all things glittery, garish and gaudy. She rested her head on the arm of the sofa next to an apple with a single Harmony-sized bite taken from it. She placed it on the floor next to Pete's jeans with the belt still in its loops and a long and bedraggled bandage—Harmony often exploited its theatricality. She went back to 'Fashion constraints'.

Fashion is for the catwalk, not for kindergarten. Childhood should be messy and not about 'being good.' Trade in the frills and the flounces for track pants and second-hand sneakers. It's heartbreaking watching a child become stifled by frilly dresses.

Estelle laughed. 'Pete, you have to read this.' Frilly dresses were Harmony's wind and fire, they were valued over love and honesty—to be fair, honesty didn't rate highly. She pulled one of those annoyingly squishy, therapy-landfill-toys from under her hip and threw it in with the mess on the floor. Who on earth would be happy wearing trackies and sneakers? Apart from PE teachers, of course. And the part about sitting and being good? If Harmony could do that, Estelle wouldn't be reading this shit.

In the kitchen she heard Pete scrape the burn from his toast into the bin. She called out to him from the adjoining lounge. 'Listen to this Pete …' She read from the book. 'Modest surroundings are best. A few things on a soft rug, leaves room for her developing imagination. Mindfully hide her least favourite toys.'

'Righto,' said Pete absent-mindedly.

She felt a choking sensation. She recognised this suffocation—this was oppression. She gazed around her small lounge room at the piles of paper, the sad disarray of their home; there was nothing simple here. She pulled false teeth out from under her leg. This book was triggering. Estelle began to wonder about Sigmond Petowski. Does he do the cleaning in his own house so that he can legitimately write this stuff? Or does he just make money advising other people to tidy their rooms—women who weren't getting paid?

She googled him on Harmony's iPad. He had been Father of the Year in 2015. The fact that there was such a thing, such a competition—to confuse fathering with a competitive sport—was idiotic. Even Harmony recognised that 'Student of the Week' was hackneyed.

Several of Sigmond's quotes came up in Google. One in particular caught her eye: 'Toxic body language has the power to erode the glue in a family unit'. She instantly had a visual image of his miserable wife, cleaning their house in trackie daks, rolling her eyes in torment. There was also a workshop: 'Cleanse your toxic female body language in a three-day mother and daughter workshop'.

Estelle began Nadi Shodhan from yoga. There must have been a new moon in Taurus because she couldn't find her sattva against the elevating rage at this man who wrote a book for mothers of daughters but criticised women—his wife, most likely—for toxic body language. This was murky; he was a toxic pseudo-feminist mansplainer—there was no award for this so far—*and* he might have the answers she needed for Harmony. It was a bitter pill.

She wanted—needed—to ring one of the school mums, but they wouldn't get it. Their kids were much more … normal than Harmony. Except Jenny. Valentino was always in trouble—he was a bit of an arsehole, really.

Pete strolled into the lounge, ready to leave. 'Bye, I'm off.' He saw the tears of frustration in her eyes. 'Are you alright?' He was off to taekwondo; he taught in the evening but always went into the studio to practise (escape) during the day.

'You need to be a part of this.' Estelle moved from the sofa and took the book and the iPad to the kitchen table. 'Have a look. "Anxious tension creates apprehension."'

He scanned the text. 'Yes … interesting.' He flicked through the pages until he got to the chapter 'Developing the pre-frontal cortex'. They read the page together.

'Here,' she said, running her finger along the lines. 'Wired up for panic … fight or flight … caveman times … crying baby would be first to be rescued, yada, yada … Harmony has *never* calmed herself down. She can't.'

'Or won't.'

'Her pre-frontal cortex is completely fucked.'

Pete stepped away from the book, 'I just don't remember kids ever being so disrespectful when I was growing up.' He was speaking as if he had no part in it.

'Then do something about it. You and Sigmond could clean up Harmony's room together.' There was no smile. Estelle sighed. 'No, we weren't that disrespectful, but remember what her psychologist said? Harmony needs more agency than we had, it makes them … unencumbered, less guilt driven … all the stuff that we weren't … in touch with their emotions, able to define boundaries. We grew up in a time of bogan parenting, caveman-like … you know the reason we have a redundant anxiety riddled system of fight-or-flight. To flee all those sexist, racist and homophobic comments of the 80s.'

Pete flicked through the book again further up the age scale. 'Harmony should be doing chores. Look here, "Even chores teach you to be an adult."'

Estelle rolled her eyes and looked pointedly at the jeans and belt on the floor. 'Can you imagine Harmony doing anything like a chore? Honestly, be reasonable …'

'So, it's up to you to decide what parts of the book we follow and what parts we don't? Chores were something I had to do for my parents.' Pete stood up away from the table.

'Your parents are wankers, they didn't give a shit about you. I am choosing these elements of parenting based on the degree of difficulty with the subject, our daughter.'

'They did care—do care.'

'They bought you a paper shredder for your birthday.'

'They're worried about identity theft.'

'Well, there's a fucken irony, because it's *my* identity that's been stolen!'

'Feel free to use the shredder then.'

Estelle froze in electric rage. Pete's chest inflated. His mouth crinkled at the corners in a near smile.

Estelle chanted, 'Sthiram Sukham …' In one violent thunderous sweep she cleared the table of its contents. 'Asanam', she bellowed. The Himalayan salt-shaker burst open and salt flakes skidded across the floorboards. The Mother's Day Camp Barista Coffee dripper lay smashed on the floor, its coffee dripping down the wall. The miniature Zen Garden lay upturned, the tiny rake on its back. The remaining chaos seamlessly absorbed into the daily clutter at the room's periphery. Her fingers clenched around Petowski and ripped out his 'Developing the prefrontal cortex' chapter. Her hands shook, her lungs heaved; her eyes were not rolling, but gleaning. She caught her breath. Then she remembered the weed. Her face softened imperceptibly. His eyes read her.

'No,' he said.

She got there first, to the back door, to the sofa, to the bowl underneath. He grabbed her arm, she took the last of it in her other hand, pungent and sticky.

'Give it …'

She put it in her mouth, before he could taekwondo it out of her hand, and swallowed.

'Estelle … you're completely insane.' He let go of her arm.

'Okay, when did you last check the school app?' She dusted off her hands.

'Um.' He shook his head, his eyes bulged with incredulity.

'I just can't do it anymore,' she said thinly, sharply, like an incision.

'And so, what? What are you going to do now? Give up?' His arm gestures became stormy and erratic.

'You know I'm at the fucken end here. AT. THE. END.' She broke off, the words caught in her throat. Something inside her chest broke and she steadied herself against the old sofa. 'I'm going out for a while. I'm going for a drive, and I won't be back for pick up.' There was no response. Then through gritted teeth she added, 'And I'm taking the iPad.'

His eyes focused hard on her as he shook his head in self-righteous betrayal. 'I would never do that to you.'

LISA MOULE is an actor and writer. She has performed in theatre and as a voice over artist in London, Ireland and Australia. She has studied at Melbourne University and École Internationale de Théâtre Jacques Lecoq, Paris. Lisa is currently writing *Motherhood and other Calamities* and has published a short story 'Estelle' (Swoop Books). lisakatemoule.net

Weeping Willow

Jasmine Mahon

Growing up I completely believed my mother's take on me: 'Soldier, you don't fit into this unit.' My mother had several husbands who also didn't fit in. Each one—in their time—was like an extra child and each time she would eventually realise she had a prize drongo on her hands. She hated heavy drinking, but she chose three big drinkers in a row. Her early death at forty-nine told of a hard life in abusive relationships.

I remember my parents having outrageous parties in the late 60s. These are some of my earliest memories. On these nights, the adults got ridiculously sauced while the kids ran wild through the streets in pyjamas, overly excited from the night air and the lack of watchful eyes.

One morning-after memory remains clear—the odour of stale beer and cigarettes, my goldfish floating belly-up in her bowl (which had been topped up with beer) and my uncle flaked out on the couch next to a woman who was not my aunty.

When there were no parties, it was the pub by the creek on Friday nights. My brother and I sat in the car. It was torturous—we had nothing to entertain us as we waited out the night. Sometimes there were other kids sitting in cars too, and then we had comrades for the night.

The creek banks were thick with weeping willows, and we were scared witless by them. The delicate swaying branches reached out to snatch us; the long quivering leaves seemed like bony, grasping fingers. We always bolted past them, chasing the other kids or racing up to the beer garden. The band's 'Hey good looking, what you got cooking?' floated out into the night. My mother was almost always dancing. She would have been in her twenties. My brother and I were entranced as we watched our mother dancing, her face aglow.

When I was ten, my baby sister, Jane, arrived. When Jane was two, she followed me up the street after I'd left for school. Feeling something behind me, I turned to see her toddling toward me, arms reaching up to me. I scooped her up and held her tight. I felt a fierce need to protect her as I took her back to the house.

My brother, Stephen, was two years older than me. My mother had always favoured men and he twigged onto this advantage early on. Regardless of what he got up to, he was always number one. His charm was lost on me. He smashed streetlights and bullied vulnerable kids at school. Once he held a boy three years younger than him down on a bull ant's nest until he was covered in stinging bites. Yet my mother adored him. Her lack of boundaries, along with her quiet glee for his exploits, ensured he was never held accountable for his actions.

One evening when Stephen was fifteen, he and a school friend took my mother's car. His friend was driving and he ploughed the car into a pole in the next street from our house. I heard the incredible boom and then the wail of sirens. My brother went through the windscreen and suffered brain damage. His friend's spleen was crushed by the steering wheel. He died five hours later in hospital.

My brother was not quite the same person after his rehabilitation. He would remain fifteen forever. Four years later he fell from a motorcycle and his fragile skull could not take the impact. 'Just trickles of blood from his ears ... not a scratch on him,' my mother said with red swollen eyes.

Mum had a plaque made and placed it in the front yard: 'To the world he was one, but to us he was the world, our son.' Yet there was no 'our', because my stepfather and brother had been locked in an alpha-male battle from day one. My stepfather's insincere, solemn grief at my brother's funeral was hard to stomach. Whenever I passed the plaque in the yard, my teenage contempt welled up. *Mum, REALLY ... a plaque in the front YARD?* And then feeling bad, I'd flip it around, saying to myself, *He's dead, he can have a plaque at least ... right?*

My mother's lack of interest in any of my successes continued to raise the bar for me—who I was and what I achieved was never enough. Why had my brother been so much on a pedestal, and why had I been under a rigid regime while he was free as a bird?

We were starved for stimulation. Our entertainment was the television and the only books in the house were my mother's trashy novels. None of us did particularly well at school. I sang in school concerts and remembered my matter-of-fact child's confidence. My mother finally sat up and took notice after I won a talent quest, *Stairway to the Stars*. Live TV was exciting stuff for a girl and her mother from bogan central.

I was fifteen when I joined a band. The other band members were horrified that I was a pop music fan, and they introduced me to the world of Neil Young, Led Zeppelin and Bob Dylan. A few years later, I set up house with the keyboard player. We had glorious summers in the old Queenslander house we rented. The rest of them were dope heads, but it wasn't for me—why smoke something that resulted in bingeing an entire packet of biscuits and then passing out?

My last stepfather was physically violent towards my mother. I witnessed this far too often and was always fearful of the next time it would happen. I cooked up various ways of doing away with this bully. A thwack to the back of the head with a brick was on the cards (the danger that man was in). I'd practise my responses to the police interrogation in my head, explaining how I hadn't intended to kill him but just wanted to protect my mother. I once jumped him from behind and attempted a double eye gouge that I'd seen on TV wrestling. After he shook me off, I ran to get my mother's friend, Gloria. Bless that woman: no questions asked, she flew down the road in her nightdress with me bringing up the rear, holding up my pyjama pants with the elastic gone.

Later, living in Melbourne in my twenties, I went back to Brisbane for Christmas. I'd escaped it all. It was behind us, and we could all move on. I could go home for Christmas like an ordinary person ... or so I thought. Only a few days in, my mother had clocked up an array of putdowns towards my sister. Suddenly I was ten years old again. I stood stock-still in the hall listening to the exchange and I realised. It wasn't me my mother particularly disliked—it was *all* women, and it was playing out the same way for my sister. I couldn't let it continue.

At twelve, Jane had at least another five years of this ahead of her. I explained misogyny to her and that our Mum was a misogynist; no matter what we did or who we were, we were never going to be enough for her. I didn't want Jane to think it was her fault, like I had for so long. Tears filled her eyes because she finally had an answer.

My sister and I knew what we had gained: a strong sense of fair play, loads of ability to bounce back and a keen eye for the underdog. We forged ahead despite anxiety and pervading self-doubt and created for ourselves the things we thought we didn't deserve. Our mother did many things to undermine our connection with her, but our drive to love her remained.

My sister loves to hear about the times before she was born: the wild parties, my poor goldfish (Goldie I and Goldie II met the same fate) and those nights when my brother and I ran past the creepy weeping willows to watch our mother glowing with delight as she danced the night away.

JASMINE MAHON is a jazz singer, writer and editor, and has also worked in corporate communications. She is currently interning with Brightside Story Studio whose services include fiction and memoir editorial and mentoring services for authors, as well as conducting author interviews for the Brightside Story Studio blog.

Imaginary String

Megan Payne

Excerpt from *Joanie*

Ramona sat in the car and searched for two details to notice. This was the first step in the game of self-soothing that their grandmother used to play with them. They looked at the empty road ahead without really seeing it. The game, an exercise in grounding, wasn't working so well this time. Ramona's thoughts were back where they had left Joanie … in the dining room, packed with small tables, four residents to each, wheelchairs in front of bowls of blended pea soup. Most of the other residents in the facility had blank stares, but as Ramona said goodbye to Joanie, holding her bony frame close, they noticed a turbulence in her cloudy blue eyes—pleading with them not to leave. At the door, as Ramona entered the keycode, they glanced back and saw the nurse holding the spoon up to Joanie's pursed lips, while Joanie lent forward with as much power as she could muster.

This image comforted Ramona through a long drive, which may have otherwise seen them buckle at the waist, slack-bodied and teary, each time they stopped at traffic lights. Instead, they drove with straight elbows, hands pressed into the steering wheel, spine flush with the car seat.

Now with the car parked, they slouched. Their T-shirt peeled from the leather seat cover. Every cell in their body wanted to remain in the car, or maybe flop onto the grassy verge, but as usual their emotions inhibited them rather than spurring them into action—even for a small action like a flop.

Ramona did feel guilty for leaving Joanie behind—though they hadn't actually been allowed to stay for lunch, and they knew they would return again soon, maybe tomorrow. Where else would they take their wallowing heart? But what they mostly felt guilty for was using the visit as a distraction.

They had called their grandmother Joanie since they were little. Being on a first-name basis, and in the business of secret sharing and keeping, theirs had been a non-hierarchical relationship—except when Ramona required a grandparent.

Ramona confided in Joanie whenever they were anxious over a decision: whether to return the friend's teddy bear they had stolen, dob on the school bully, or ask a girl, not a boy, to their high school ball.

While Joanie didn't hand Ramona answers, she used games to soothe and pull Ramona's focus towards what was important.

But, earlier in the year, when Ramona told Joanie they couldn't see a clear future with their boyfriend, Joanie had been the one incapable of focusing. Her memory was slipping. Ramona left their uncertainties about their boyfriend alone, took no action, and in the end the boyfriend left all by himself.

It had come as a shock.

Walking in the spring wind would help Ramona untangle their feelings.

They shook off their inhibitions, opened the car door and headed to the footpath at the top of the limestone cliffs. Leaving the path for the adjacent sand and scrub meant taking care near the cliff edge, which crumbled into the river below. At this time of year and at this height, the river and the sky appeared equally close, with the river flowing and swirling back upon itself and the sky full with fluttering clouds.

The river's bodies and tributaries reflected the weather patterns above. It saw more than Ramona could.

The footpath skirted one of the river's many bellies; a bay, of sorts. In the distance Ramona saw the crowds of houses and trees crinkling into the horizon. But this land-across was also close enough to be squinted at, and in certain parts, it was intimately familiar. Ramona could make out slate roof tiles and could have sworn that within the pink washes of bougainvillea they could see petals.

If only they could flow like the river, into many places at once, or better yet—be the all-seeing sky, able to hold the river in its sight all at once. Perhaps then they would gain enough perspective for the rest of their life.

Ramona walked at an easy pace and admired one ripple moving across the water. Small steps, one after the other.

'Are you going to Chicken rock?' said a high voice. A little girl in a tiny wetsuit had appeared with her parents and school-aged sibling.

To be polite, Ramona nodded. But when the girl and her family were merely a silhouette in the distance, they wondered if it was an honest reply.

As a teenager, Ramona had gone to Chicken rock many times with friends, always cringing at the suggestion to go, but unable to object and hell-bent on going with the flow, they went along with the preparations. They dreaded the moment where they would have to decide, again, not to join in. Too afraid of putting a foot wrong, of botching the jump and not surviving.

Chicken rock wasn't visible from this distance but already it was calling to Ramona. It would mock them if, again, they chose not to jump.

Ramona continued walking, not setting a sure course, but not turning around either. Instead, they turned their mind to Joanie. It seemed easier to focus on someone at the end of her life, or at least beyond the period of living where you need to make decisions for yourself. Ramona wasn't sure what kind of decisions Joanie had had to make, or what she had desired most. Ramona could no longer ask Joanie about this. But they knew what they really desired. Closeness.

Ramona sat down on a bench under a large peppermint tree, keeping to one side even though there was no one there to join them.

The river below ruffled in the wind that blew the leaves beside their ears, against and away from one another. Leaves change a lot within a season, and even within a day. Peppermint leaves smell amazing though, and fresh scents help make for clearer thoughts.

A broken spider's web waved between two branches. Further along on one branch, framed by some twigs, crouched a little black tree spider. Was it struggling against the wind or resting? Impossible to tell. But the spider reminded Ramona of the game Joanie had first taught them when they were small, having a small tantrum. Joanie had pointed to an orb spider, building its web outside the kitchen window. 'Look at how she spins her web.'

'Where does her web come from?'

'From inside of her.'

The game went like this: you selected one detail, in this case the orb spider, and then you found a second. Ramona had chosen their belly button.

Then, in your mind, between the two details you drew an imaginary line, making a string. The beauty of the game, Joanie had said, was that the details to which the string was fastened were not harmed by the game.

In the morning the web was gone.

'She's packed it away for the day,' said Joanie.

'Where is she?'

'Resting, re-fuelling.'

Ramona watched the spider in the peppermint tree. They tied an imaginary bow around its body and ran the string through the air out along the cliffs and sideways over some rocks. They spotted the family from earlier. Hovered the string above their heads. Then dipped the string to their level and tied a bow around the youngest girl's waist. The string didn't bother her; in fact, she helped to lengthen it as she walked out over the cliffs. Small, sure-footed strides. She set a bolder pace than the rest of her family. She stopped, swivelled around to face her sister, mum and dad, held out her hand to halt them, and just as abruptly, turned back, and kept walking. The dad cupped his hands to his mouth, called out and walked after her. The girl turned back around and held out two hands in front of her. Shook her wrists to halt her family. Stretched her arms overhead, then dropped them by her sides. She made two angry little fists in a theatrical rejection of a parental request. Shook her arms and pounded the air. The girl pointed to where the cliff cracked and became Chicken rock, became the final landmass before the river took over, and then she bellowed her chest, screamed a command and made the halting gesture with her hands again.

The imaginary string was still intact, but it thrashed in the wind like a giant skipping rope. Ramona attempted to wind it in. Although the girl looked confident, and Chicken rock wasn't as big as some of the other spots, the girl was only small. The parents called out again and she replied with a furious shake of her head and more wild fist throws. But as her family began to approach her, shortening the gap, the mum got something out of her bag and held it up. The girl stopped shaking. A pink tutu. The mum bent down and stretched the tutu's elastic band wide in an oval. It worked. The tutu had hooked the girl's attention. She approached. Even held onto her mum's shoulder for balance. Stepping inside the tutu's circle and pushing her mum's helping hands away, she pulled it up over her wetsuit all by herself. The parents now addressed both girls, the dad mimed a jumping action, and the little girl followed along with head nods as enthusiastic as her fist shakes had been. The mum put the little girl's hand in her older sister's, motioned for the two girls to go on ahead, and together the sisters stepped onto the very edge of Chicken rock.

The string wobbled and stretched, then the two sisters disappeared.

The mum and dad cheered. They approached the edge quickly and jumped into the river to join their children.

The imaginary string floated up and reeled back through the air before disappearing entirely.

Behind them, Ramona found the spider unharmed, safe and refuelling in the twigs.

Ramona used to think they would be able to reach the end of their life unharmed, without regrets. Had Joanie once thought this too?

Ramona stood up and continued walking along the path in the same direction as before.

Perhaps with enough distance, in time Ramona's heart would heal, and in time Ramona would place some value in its breaking. Because once Ramona was old, their every choice would have been formed from the pieces of something broken.

The water washed and the leaves blew, and these sounds sketched Ramona's feelings in ways they couldn't express yet, and Joanie couldn't anymore, not as well as she used to.

Up ahead, Ramona reached a clearing in the scrub. They knew what they wanted to do. Sidestepping the vegetation pushing through, as the track sloped ever so slightly Ramona pressed into the balls of their shoes with bent knees.

Some way down, the track opened out before the top of the rock. A boulder that had come away from the cliff face. Ramona stepped over the crevice, stood on Chicken rock.

The free fall was lengthy enough to give a jumper pause but short enough to splash the watcher. Not dangerous, but it had the feel of a risk.

Without taking off their clothes or shoes, without treading to the edge and peering down, breathing in and out, wasting precious seconds before fear caught up with their plan, caught up with their pursuit of a giddy feeling, a stomach in a throat, which like the feelings of hurt and break were also in pursuit of a home within; without any of this deliberation, Ramona ran—

right leg   left leg,   together,

and
jumped

through the
air,
breaking
the water
sharp
and then
smooth
cool bubbles,
bobbed their head
up

to finally breathe
and
see how impressive Chicken rock looked from the river.

MEGAN PAYNE is a dancer, choreographer and writer. Their poetry and fiction can be read in publications including by Perimeter Books, Visible Ink and #EnbyLife. Currently, Megan is working on a literary/fantasy/mystery novel and is interning with *The Suburban Review*'s editorial team.

Mia Fora Thymamai

Daniel T Car

'... mia forá thymámai m' agapoúses ...'
'... once upon a time you loved me ...'

The record spins beneath the needle: a muted plucking. Romani music, wagon wheels, tents, drying mud, grey skies. The scent of oak and straw and impending rain. Beneath me, a polished hardwood floor and a woven Turkish rug, musky and dusty and authentic. A roof above my head and a slowly rotating fan stirring the Melbourne summer heat. Or maybe it's the room that's spinning and the fan is staying true; the thought sends my nervous and digestive systems into a miniature rebellion. I close my eyes tight, place my palms flat against the floor, take a deep breath, then open my eyes.

The fan is spinning. I'm lying still.

'... tha me lipithí tha me xekhási ...'
'... morning will be sad of me, it will forget me ...'

Beside my head is a stack of half-read books. Their dog-eared pages are tabbed with curling sticky-notes, branded with semi-legible scribbled notations in every shade of red and blue ink available. *'Ariel'*. *'Lolita'*. *'The Crane Wife'*. *'Rumi'*. The title of the book on top is hidden from me where I lie, but it's a paperback and I can see and hear the pages ruffle, lift and lower with the light air current. Trying to speak? A million words beneath these pages, and I can't bear to read a single one.

> *'... Níkhta vrokherí ádhio to khéri ...'*
> *'... a rainy night, an empty hand ...'*

At a deceptively soulful Alexanderplatz, street merchants peddled fez hats and revolutionary symbols branded on badges or sewn into patches; skull rings, pointedly un-German soviet flags and red-starred leather caps. I was told the time in multiple cities from multiple time zones all at a glance and, behind me, the Fernsehturm pierced the sky. The Friendship Fountain, with its levels of overflowing copper basins, played host to a group of students; to mothers with their children; to who I guessed to be tourists (like me); to one guitar-playing busker (that was you).

You had short hair at the time, and that's what made you approachable; embarrassingly, I thought you were a guy until I had your attention and you stopped playing.

> *'... mia forá thymámai mou miloúses ...'*
> *'... once upon a time you talked to me ...'*

The bar was underground—literally, rather than the figuratively Berlin is famous for. The sign on the street read 'Get the fuck down', so we did. A bunch of mismatched nooks and mirrored booths, dark corners and scarce deep-blue or purple lighting. A golden skull. A black newt. Exposed brick and peeling wallpaper and low, unframed concrete doorways. A perfectly mischievous little den.

After four apology cocktails, the rain outside had stopped. Your hair was dried, but your jacket still stank of wet dog. You spoke to me about music. I talked about literature and poetry. We both swooned over Morrissey and Leonard Cohen. I read from the book I had with me while you gently ran your fingers through my long hair. You said you made the grand move from Leipzig to Berlin in search of adventure. I was travelling the world looking for inspiration.

'... psákhni na se vri ma dhen ... tha se vri ...'
'... looking for you but doesn't know where it can find you ...'

Three hours later we were in Leipzig, in a park whose name I can't ever remember. You'd tell me when I'd ask, and every time I would almost immediately forget. I do remember walking in the near-pitch black along a high gravel ledge, heading deeper and deeper into the forest-like parklands. That and, of course, I remember the shaky tower.

You told me the local guys brought their dates here and the shaking would make the girls scream. But it only made me laugh. By then the clouds were scarce, and the light pollution was minimal. After rocking the tower to demonstrate where its name came from, we threw down our sleeping bags and lay side by side, watching the stars and the satellites and the occasional meteor—'die schnuppe' as you'd say, and you'd gasp like a child. You'd sight down your arm like your point of view was also mine, like, by the time I looked, it definitely wouldn't be gone. Moments and memories, all just shooting stars.

> *'... tha 'rthi to proí kai tha perási ...'*
> *'... morning will come and pass ...'*

We stayed there and watched the sunrise: cold, orange, and expansive. The silent trek back through the park seemed to have only taken a minute. I walked behind you and I think the only thing that kept me moving forward through my fatigue was the hypnotising sway of your plaid skirt. We took an ICE train back to Berlin and had to fight sleep the whole way, or else we'd miss our stop and end up who knows where.

Your apartment was tiny, full of polaroids pegged and hung on strings, dangling scarves and materials that brushed my head as I walked through. And fairy lights. Your turntable and record collection were a lazy reach away from your mattress on the floor. I immediately recognised the record you put on as the song you were playing when I met you only the day before in that massive, mostly vacant Alexanderplatz. You lit a candle and set it to slowly burn a clearing essential oil. Then you ran a shower.

When I left, you gave me that record as a gift and I gave you my book.

> *'... mia forá thymámai m' agapoúses ...'*
> *'... once upon a time you loved me ...'*

That record spins now, beneath the needle; a muted plucking, Romani music sung with a slight German accent. Images of bicycle wheels and cobblestone puddles and grey skies and plaid. The scent of peppermint and soggy leather. The feeling of impending departure. A roof high above my head and a slowly rotating fan to stir around the Melbourne summer heat. Beneath me, a hardwood floor and a woven Turkish rug, musky and dusty and authentic. Another tear trickles down to my ear and then drops into a small pond to join its family. I close my eyes tight, put my palms flat against the floor, then open my eyes.

The world keeps spinning. I am lying still.

The turntable clicks and whirrs and sets to playing the record once more. I reach and pour myself another glass of dry red wine.

'… Níkhta vrokherí ádhio to khéri …'
'… a rainy night, an empty hand …'

DANIEL T CAR is an editor and writer who is currently on a horror bender, scarfing down Junji Ito manga and HP Lovecraft stories like he were dying in a snowy mountain range and they were force-fed to him by a giant anthropomorphic blackbird.

Hidden Tracks

Coming to terms
with a love of steam trains

Patrick Hornidge

When I was a kid, I used to climb on an old train in Bayswater Park. It was red, so naturally it was called James—*Thomas the Tank Engine* still had an obvious influence. I climbed up the back of it, through the tender, slid down the coal chute and then climbed again across the top of it. I played with the levers in the cab, pushing them in all directions, pretending to be a driver. It's a weird fantasy for small boys to have, driving trains—I wonder if many still do.

The train is still in the park, but it can't be climbed on anymore. OH&S has seen an end to that. Now it stands as a static monument, not just to carefree childhoods, but to the era of steam itself.

* * *

In April 2017, Steamrail, the main steam heritage group in Victoria, ran a double-header from Melbourne to Ballarat. Two engines pulling twenty or so carriages on a main line; it was a rare occasion.

I chased it.

I drove up back-roads that run right along the edge of the rail line, across old rotting timber bridges and along bush tracks that could barely be called roads. All in the name of getting good photos of these 'greyhounds of the rail'. But when I parked, I remained in my car, hidden, pointing my camera out the window like a paparazzi, almost like I was doing something illegal or immoral. I justified this by telling myself that this was the best way to get the photos I wanted.

But the real reason was that I wanted my interest to remain hidden. Anytime I talk of liking something I consider childish, like trains, I feel embarrassment rising inside me like steam rising in a boiler. The fascination is something I should have outgrown. Therefore, no one could know about it.

I still love the smell of coal smoke and of steam. It's hypnotising; a guilty pleasure.

I don't think car enthusiasts have to go through this same sense of guilt. Cars are cool and modern. I've seen men at the Grand Prix in Melbourne sprint to get the perfect picture of an F1 car without any fear of judgement. They are fuelled by the smell of petrol, just as I'm fuelled by steam.

Steam train enthusiasts don't have the same luxury. These trains are old relics of a nearly forgotten past. They are not cool.

In 1952, C Hamilton Ellis called steam railways 'one of the most beautiful things man has ever made'. I'm inclined to agree with him. Steam engines are beautiful. I have seen steam mingle with mist on the coldest winter mornings, and witnessed smoke reflect off iron rails that shine like a mirror in the summer twilight. Photo competitions are filled with pictures of steam railways. Countless novels and films are set in the carriages behind a steam engine. No other form of transport has this kind of *romance* behind it. You can't set a murder mystery on a short-haul passenger plane! Just think about the names that trains have been given over the years: *Flying Scotsman, Orient Express* and, closer to home, the once mighty *Spirit of Progress.*

There's something in that last name that speaks to me. Steam trains, despite being a rustic antique, still represent progress; humanity's control over its own destiny.

But the *Spirit of Progress* no longer runs and the name itself is nearly forgotten. Maybe the whole idea of progress itself has stalled and lies unremembered, like so much else from the steam era.

* * *

I walk over the Sandridge rail bridge to cross the Yarra a lot. Of course, it's not a rail bridge anymore, and Sandridge is now called Port Melbourne. The history that was here has long since gone. Just as the railway that was here destroyed the country that was here before it. It's all a cycle I suppose—creation and destruction.

Sometimes I try to imagine a train rattling and roaring its way over this bridge, as the first locomotive to run in Australia did in September 1854.

In Britain, the first passenger steam train ran over and killed a politician. Squeezed his leg 'almost to a jelly' apparently. As usual, Australia didn't have the same drama. Instead, Australia's first train broke down on its maiden voyage. There is something uniquely Australian about that.

I've walked along the route it took that day (now replaced by tram route 109) and imagined what it was like. The cheering of the crowd being drowned out by the train. This new technology being shown off in a new city already bloated on gold.

There would have been small boys in the crowd that day, watching the fastest thing they'd ever seen, not knowing how much that train would change the country over their lifetime.

But theirs was a fascination of the future. Mine is the fascination of the past—a sickness of nostalgia.

I know how the story goes: the locomotive would conquer this country. It would fascinate generations of small boys like me. Boys who didn't realise how much darkness was lurking behind this fascination.

I discovered just how much darkness there was behind my childish wonder in an almost forgotten Tasmanian town.

* * *

On Tasmania's west coast, the Queen River runs red; the colour of rusted blood. It is called a dead river, and it's the blood of the surrounding hills that flows down it. Those hills around Queenstown were a moonscape when I saw them—rock that was devoid of trees, shrubs, even grass. The football oval is moist gravel. All the results of acid rain. Here, the locomotive was directly responsible for this disaster. Copper was discovered here in 1892, but this valley is so inaccessible that it was a useless discovery. But the human mind and locomotive conquered. They pushed a railway through some of the wildest country on the planet. They dominated rainforest, rivers, mountains and metres of rain and managed to connect the pristine valley to the outside world. The mine operated, filling the Queen River with 100 million tonnes of poisoned runoff, and the air with unknowable amounts of unbreathable gas. All over town, 'Remember to boil water' signs can still be seen, and need to be followed.

None of this destruction could have happened without the railway.

But when I rode this railway, I forgot this. The rebranded West Coast Wilderness Railway is a ride into a prehistoric world. I could hear the almost 150-year-old loco tire itself climbing the near vertical hills, struggling to pull itself up and over the mountains through its own sheer will. But the fresh, Huon pine smells of the rainforest air made me forget about the deadness of Queenstown, and the danger of the drinking water just a few kilometres away.

This is a dilemma. Steam represents one thing I love and one thing I hate. The advent of the railways made freedom possible for so many while also destroying the natural world. It is freedom against destruction, liberty against industry, my desire to explore against my love of the natural.

On the other side of Tasmania, near the Huon River, I encountered the rusting remains of a once-mighty engine. It had been left there to die after its final trip many decades ago. The tracks it was still sitting on disappeared into the rainforest, just as the era of steam disappeared as cars and diesels took over.

Horses are put down at the end of their life; iron horses are left to rot and rust. Some were saved from this fate, either to be climbed on by children or given a new life as a tourist attraction.

The slow return to the earth, and the rebirth into new life; both things are romantic in a way.

The ones that survived though, they are now a relic—the fascinations of old men who have lost their vigour. Or younger men with no social skills. At least that's the stereotype.

* * *

In March 2020 I travelled to Newport. The old railway workshops were having an open day and as I had never seen them, I thought it would be interesting. I had expected a small crowd of that certain type of people, so I was very surprised when I could not get a parking spot within about half a kilometre of the entrance.

I had a sense of foreboding before heading in. I had always avoided places and events like this for fear of being judged. Going to the workshops felt like I was finally coming to terms with the part of myself that still likes the sound, smell and sight of these steamers. But the people I saw there—men and women of all ages, and of seemingly all classes—revealed something that I didn't think it would.

I can enjoy what I enjoy, without worrying about what other people think.

I also realised something else. Whenever I see a steam locomotive pass through a station (which happens more often than expected), people immediately reach for their phones to take pictures. The fascination with these beasts evidently still runs deep.

Why do I care about any of this? When I started writing this, it was going to be an exploration into why steam trains could be blamed for the current poor state of the world. And by the end, I would perhaps realise, deep down, that I hate steam.

But this has hasn't happened. My story has changed.

I love steam still; I probably always will. And it's not something I need to hide.

* * *

When I was a kid, I used to walk along the Puffing Billy tracks near Emerald, jumping out of the way if I heard a train approaching. It was a different time, just over quarter of a century ago. Now you can't even hang your legs out of the carriages, as people had been doing for over a century, and official signs warn of 'Penalties for trespassing on the railway'.

When I recently walked in the shadow of the yellowed-cream paintwork of the Nobelius Packing Shed—a century old, heritage listed, two-story remnant of what was once Victoria's largest plant nursery on Emerald's outskirts—I hoped to have a revelation to end this story, or maybe encounter something to move me on from my childish love of steam.

Instead, walking along the line brought me an inner peace that I hadn't felt in years. My footsteps on the sleepers matched the rhythm of a train and when my view transferred from the rusted tracks to the blue-green hills and mountains in the distance, I saw beauty.

I felt myself smile.

Maybe this is my revelation—don't hide what makes you embarrassed. Embrace it. It's what makes you unique.

I think much of my life will still be fuelled by steam. And I will continue to chase it. I might even get out of my car to do it next time.

PATRICK HORNIDGE is a nonfiction writer, very amateur photographer and an unashamed history nerd. He also dabbles in sports writing and historical fiction. He is currently investigating the impact that sporting crowds have had on his life and on Australian society. For more, visit pathornidge.me.

Out of Touch

Senaai Chapple

Out of Touch is an extract from a larger work.

Yesterday had no stakes; today is different.

The room still feels cold, despite now being full of people. Some of them I recognise. All of them are wearing the same charcoal uniform, with coloured badges decorating their breast pockets. They stand along the green walls, and I catch my father's eye, standing next to the General. He gives me a small smile, and I wish I could tell if it was real.

Hobb is waiting inside, dressed in his army regalia. 'Aria!' His smile is too wide, his demeanour too chirpy. It doesn't match the green-grey of the room, the metal chairs either side of the slate desk, the strange dampness seeping in through the walls. He steps aside, gesturing elaborately to one of the chairs.

This is it. I nod, and the room seems to collectively exhale. I head towards my seat while my father is ushered with the others into the adjoining observation room. I search for his outline in the two-way mirror, but I only see the pale face of someone utterly unprepared. I turn away and scoot my chair in closer, the metal legs screeching against the concrete.

The room spins into action. Someone puts a bottle of water in front of me and stabs an earpiece into my ear, someone else says, 'One two, one two,' and I nod. I self-consciously glance up at the cameras. Almost as suddenly as they appeared, everyone leaves, and it's just me and Hobb in an expanse of silence.

My heart catches, and I steady myself. *You can do this. Same as before.*

Hobb fidgets with his tie. 'We'll start small. Are you ready?'

I glance over to where I imagine my father is in the observation room, wishing I could see his nod of encouragement.

The bars of the chair are digging into my back, so I sit up straighter, but it doesn't help. I turn back to Hobb and nod.

He opens the heavy metal door to the right. 'We're ready for the first.'

Two guards usher a man into the room. He's handcuffed. His face is gruff and unshaven. They ease him into the chair opposite me and link his handcuffs to a bar on the desk, and retreat to the corner of the room, like vultures looking on.

Hobb takes his place behind me.

'Aria. Can you hear me?'

I recognise Harrison's voice in my earpiece, and exhale. I nod, knowing he'd see it on the camera feed.

'Bit of a crowd, hey?'

I give a small smile, grateful for his attempt to put me at ease.

'Alright. We'll start off simple: name.'

You know how to do this. I place my hand palm-down on top of the desk and look up at the resident. It feels wrong not to ask, at least.

'May I touch you?'

His frown deepens and I think there might be a language barrier.

I lift my arm up and place my hand against it, so he can see. Slowly, I reach towards his arm and touch my fingers just above the handcuff.

'What's your name?'

He stays silent.

Hobb leans over me. 'Name,' he says gruffly.

The resident lets out a huff before reluctantly answering, 'Arash Rahimi.'

I wait for the feeling.

Nothing.

I knew it. This is it. It was all in my head.

'Aria?' Hobb and Harrison speak at the same time, pulling me out of my head.

'Just give me a minute,' I snap. Everything's abuzz and I can't figure out the present from the feelings.

'Should you do something else?' Hobb asks.

I shake my head. 'I just need a minute.' I close my eyes and concentrate until I feel it, a clear, ringing sense. 'True.'

'Correct. You're doing great.' Harrison's voice echoes in my ear and I relax my shoulders. 'Okay, did he steal two rations of bread last week?'

A shoplifter? This was what they had brought me? I guess this is what Hobb meant by starting small. My hand was still on his arm.

'Did you steal two rations of bread last week?' I ask.

The answer comes swiftly this time. 'No.'

I smile at him, trying to be comforting. 'You don't need to speak.' I close my eyes.

There's a hunger in my stomach. I see myself handing over coupons, getting a loaf in return. No more.

I shake my head. 'He didn't.'

Hobb exhales loudly. 'Well done, Aria! Truly, incredible.' He's beaming and I can see the gold glint of a tooth filling. 'Let's get the next one in, hey?'

The guards approach and uncuff Arash. His eyes bore into mine as he's ushered away.

'Thank you,' I say to him, and everyone turns to me quizzically. I didn't know how else to end it. I brush down my skirt, wiping off my sweaty palms.

It's only a moment before another resident is brought in. This one is burlier, angrier. He strains against the handcuffs and tries to shrug off the guards. His hair is blond and dirty, his mouth permanently downturned. I meet his eyes and I feel the hairs rise on my neck.

He's cuffed to the bar in the same fashion.

Harrison's voice crackles through the earpiece. 'Name again.'

I try to make my voice as nice as possible. 'What's your name?'

'John Smith.' His mouth turns up at the corners and he leans back in his chair. They warned me some of the residents might be uncooperative.

I reach out and touch his arm, but I don't need to. I know it's a lie.

'One more try?' Harrison asks.

I take a breath. 'Your name, please.' I try to sound authoritative.

The resident sighs. 'Justin Waters.'

Another moment of clarity, and I know it's the truth. I nod towards Hobb.

'You're doing great.' Harrison's voice doesn't calm me this time.

I get a tingling at the back of my neck. *This one feels different.*

'Ask him about the events of the night of the twenty-fifth of March,' Harrison says.

'Where were you on the twenty-fifth of March?'

I wait. Nothing.

Hobb leans over me. 'Answer.'

Justin stares daggers at Hobb and I can feel what he's thinking. My limbs flow with adrenaline and I get the urge to swing a right hook.

I take my hand off his arm.

I turn to Hobb. 'Can you give us a minute?'

His eyes narrow. 'I need to supervise.'

'You can supervise from in there.' I nod my head towards the mirror. 'Just one minute, please. I can't get a clear read.'

He glances above my head, his brow furrowing. After a moment, he nods reluctantly and heads towards the observation room.

When I hear the soft click of the door latch, I turn back to Justin and reach forward again, my fingertips brushing the hair against his arm.

'Night of the twenty-fifth of March.'

He sighs, resigning himself. 'Home.'

True.

I repeat Harrison's questions. 'Home address?'

'25 Wylie Road.' *True.*

'Were you with Dexter Thomas?'

'Yes.' *True.*

'Did an altercation occur?'

He sits up a little straighter and understanding crosses his face. 'I didn't do it.'

I pull my hand back as his voice rings out crystal clear, in stark contrast to his gruff attitude. His eyes are deep, pleading.

I want to believe him.

'Night of the twenty-fifth,' I repeat.

Blood floods my limbs. I feel adrenaline pump my heart faster, nails clawing at my face. I can hear the screams of someone I love being held in the room next door. I know what they're doing to her. There's a searing heat in my stomach as a blade lodges itself, knocking the breath out of me. I feel the recoil of a shotgun against my shoulder.

I snatch my hand away from him.

'Aria?' There's concern in Harrison's voice.

'I … I don't know.'

There's a pause. 'Do you need to touch him again?'

I shake my head. 'No.' *I can't feel that again.*

There's a shuffle, and Hobb's voice is on the line. 'Aria?'

'I don't know, okay?'

The resident bows his head, away from my gaze, seemingly resigned.

'What do you mean you don't know? Did he kill the guy or not?' I can hear frustration in Hobb's voice.

'It's … complicated.'

'Complicated? What do you mean it's complicated?'

'He … there were other factors.' *This is all moving too fast. What have I gotten myself into?*

'Aria! Did he shoot the gun that killed Dexter Thomas?' Hobb bangs his fist on the desk.

I pause and close my eyes for a moment. *You felt it. You know. Tell the truth.* 'Yes,' I whisper.

'No!' The wail echoes around the room as Justin pulls back against his cuffs. The guards approach and start to release him from the table. His eyes pierce mine. 'No, please! I didn't do it! You have to listen!'

I shake my head helplessly, rising from my chair.

'Please! You need to help me!' He starts to cry, straining away from the guards as they drag him to the door that they brought him through.

'Wait …' I get up, but they're moving quickly, Justin's shoes scraping against the concrete floor. 'Wait, no. I … I think I made a mistake,' I plea. I look around the empty room for help.

'Aria!' Harrison screams into my ear. I tear out the earpiece.

'Wait.' It's all I can think to say. I reach the door moments after the guards close it, and I yank against the cold metal handle, pulling with all my weight and open the door.

I only have a second to take it in: Justin is pushed to his knees, hessian sack over his head, a pistol pointed against it. I hear the click before it happens.

The guards turn to me in slow motion as Justin's body slumps. My legs turn to stone as hands I vaguely recognise as Hobb's grab me, pulling me back into the room. The door closes with a thundering boom and the room plunges into silence.

After a moment, I tune in to muffled yelling from behind the glass. I know it's Dad, even though I can't hear what he's saying.

'Aria …' Hobb is standing in front of me, pinching his brow.

'I …' My throat constricts. 'How …' Tears start to leak down my face.

'Aria,' he repeats carefully.

The door to the observation room opens long enough for the General to slip in.

He addresses Hobb. 'Sit her down.'

'Wait, can someone just …' I stammer.

'Sit her down!'

Hobb takes a step towards me, but he doesn't need to. I slump into the chair.

There's salt in my mouth and I watch as tears fall onto the wool of my skirt, creating little wet dots. I wipe my cheeks angrily.

I replay Hobb's words from just a few days ago: 'The thought that someone is imprisoned for a crime they did not commit … it's heartbreaking.'

I can't shake Hobb's pitch when they came to me. 'What a gift you have, Aria,' he said. 'You could help people.' He was nothing more than a snake oil salesman.

I narrow my eyes at him now, watching as he wipes a hand down his face.

How did I not see it? My stomach turns and I start to retch.

'Aria.' The General's voice rings through the room. 'I understand this is difficult to grasp for someone your age.'

Fury rises in me.

He folds his arms across his chest. 'But this is better than the alternative.'

'Better than the alternative? What are you even talking about? They just—'

He walks towards me. 'That man committed an atrocity. You saw it—or, felt it—I don't know …' He waves his hand dismissively and drops into the chair opposite me. 'He made his own choices. It is nothing to do with you.'

'Nothing to do with me?' I finally found my voice. 'Without me you wouldn't have done that! You wouldn't have—he wouldn't have—I …' I turn to Hobb for help, but I can tell by his face that it's no use.

Hobb's voice is quiet, 'He got the punishment he deserved.'

I close my eyes and feel the welled-up tears stream down my cheeks. *You did this. You.*

'I want to go home.' It comes out as a whisper.

The General stands slowly and adjusts his jacket before turning to Hobb.

'Bring in the next one.'

The door to the observation room opens again as he leaves. I see enough to know my father isn't inside.

'Hobb, please.' I look up at him again.

He rubs a hand through his hair, before walking towards the door.

I feel the boldness rise inside me. 'I won't do it.'

He pauses, his hand on the handle. 'You will.'

I shake my head, surer now. 'I won't. There's nothing you can do to make me participate in this ... slaughter. I'm done. Find someone else. I want my father.'

He looks up at me, coldness in his eyes. 'And where do you think he is, Aria?'

Before I can answer he has disappeared through the door, ready to bring in the next resident.

SENAAI CHAPPLE is a writer, editor and podcaster from Brisbane who occasionally has something semi-intelligent to say about film analysis. She is currently interning at *Metro Magazine* and is one half of the film review podcast, *I Only Like You and Movies*. You can follow her on Twitter: @senaaileigh.

Hacking the House

Beatrice Paull

This excerpt is from the manuscript, *Hacking the House:*
a sixteen-year-old with secrets is drawn into the
intoxicating and turbulent world of activist-hackers.

I wait until it's dark. I'd told Mum and Nana Lil that I wasn't feeling well and had to go to bed early. It was kinda true. I hadn't eaten any dinner, which they took as a sign of near death. I can't remember the last time I'd skipped a meal, but tonight the pizza had just got stuck in my throat and wouldn't go down.

I sneak out the back door and collect my bike—a RacerGirl 500—from the garden.

Fifteen minutes of peddling and I'm in front of his house, the armpits of my t-shirt damp with sweat.

I'd gotten the address from Nana Lil—she knows everything. 44 Primrose St is in North Franklin, and it shows. It's a large block with an elegant, red brick home and carefully clipped lawns. Wisteria twists around the front porch and a well-behaved golden retriever peers at me through the white picket fence. No wonder Kit's family left our street to come here.

I remember being eleven and sitting on Kit's floor watching him put his ninja turtles into a box. I thought then that North Franklin and his new fancy school were *worlds away*. And when he never talked to me again after they moved, well, he might as well have moved to Siberia, not North Franklin.

And now here I am. Fifteen minutes across town, staring up at the quiet house of an old friend.

There's a light on in almost every room. It's just past dinner time and there are two cars in the driveway. Shit, his mum might be home. I didn't think about that. Why didn't I think about that? I smack a palm to my forehead, then immediately regret it. I probably have a red mark now. Great.

I lean my bike against a big elm tree and walk slowly around the house. The Haywoods are a trusting lot—I'm surprised that there are no fences to stop me from squeezing through the ornamental side hedges and into their backyard. The golden retriever pads next to me, nosing its head into my hand. I pat her and pray she stays quiet.

I peek through some of the windows, and bob down quickly when I see Kit's mum through one of them. She leans heavily against the kitchen bench, one hand covering her face. Her shoulders shake.

I swallow. Time to find Kit. It's really, really time to find him. I can't see him through any of the downstairs windows and I pause, chewing a fingernail. I was afraid it would come to this. He's somewhere upstairs. I look up and count four windows. Three have a light on. My phone is dead, and I don't have a rock and a steady arm, so there's no way of knowing which room is his. I get inventive.

Right next to the house is a big, sprawling oak. Its branches have grooves in them like Nana Lil's face, and it grows all the way past the house. Past, in fact, two of the lit-up windows.

I hoist a leg over the first branch and drag myself up. I pause to catch my breath. I'm only a metre off the ground, congratulations me. The dog sits down under the tree and watches me with her head tilted. I grip onto the next branch up and get my legs around it until I look like a sloth, hanging on for dear life. I grunt and swing myself up, and then up to the next branch and the next, accumulating splinters and scratches as I go. I'm almost level with the second-storey windows when my foot slips and I crash down, my knee colliding with hard wood, my fingers clutching at air. I let out a squeak before my hands grab onto a skinny branch.

The second from the left window is flung open and Kit pokes his head out into the night air.

'Lucy?' His eyes go as round as gobstoppers as he sees me dangling.

I hang on for dear life. Do not look down, Luce. Oh my god, this is maybe the worst thing to ever happen to me. My top is hitched up, showing my stomach and an embarrassing beige bra, and I've lost a shoe.

'Hi Kit. Can you ... pull me up?' The branch is bending ominously.

Strong hands grip my forearms and hoist me up over the windowsill. I tumble headfirst into the room and land in a pile on the carpet.

'We have a front door.'

Kit is standing, hands on hips, looking at me like I'm a Christmas present from Grandma that he's working out how to politely reject. He's shirtless, a pair of track pants low over his hips and headphones circling his neck. It's a good look for him.

Flat stomach. Trail of hair snaking beneath his waistband. Skin. So much boy skin. He should come to school like that. I'd be more likely to be on time for IT class.

I swallow and look away. 'Sorry. Guess I should have knocked.' But that would have meant talking to his sobbing mum.

'Were you … spying on me or something?' His cheeks are turning a surprising shade of pink.

'What? No!' I stand up and my left leg buckles. Sharp pain shoots through my ankle and I stumble. Kit reaches out for my arm.

'You twisted something didn't you?' He shakes his head and helps me over to sit on his unmade bed.

'Ankle,' I say, rubbing it gently. My faithful sock and flats combo is not made for tree climbing. Why didn't I wear those white Adidas sneakers Cammie bought me?

Kit's room is cool. Undeniably cool. There are giant posters covering the wall above his bed: The Strokes, The Arctic Monkeys, Toploader and one of a skinny dark-haired girl with her hip jutted out enticing you to watch *Pulp Fiction*. A split in her black dress reveals a perfect, tanned leg: a leg that ends just near Kit's pillow. His double bed is a mess of white sheets and burgundy blankets. There's an intimidating set of speakers on his bedside table, next to acne cream and a tissue box. No clothes litter the floor, and his desk is against the wall with an enormous desktop computer and some textbooks neatly lined up.

There's a corkboard behind the computer, with concert ticket stubs and a big photo of his dad, his mouth open mid-laugh. He looks like I remember him, glowing and warm. That must have been before the chemo started.

I'm about to drag my gaze away when it snags on a slip of crumpled drawing paper, half tucked under the other things on the board. It's a sketch of three kids and a cat, roughly done in coloured pencil. The boy has a basketball for a head. I stare at it. I remember drawing that, years ago when Kit had gone outside to play ball instead of drinking Milo and drawing with me and Harper. I'd scrunched up my picture and thrown it at him in a fit of anger. He'd just smiled and put it in his shorts pocket. He must have kept it, all this time.

As I look at that faded, childish drawing, something shifts inside me. I would never, in a million years, have thought he would keep that.

Kit pulls on a loose grey t-shirt, rolls his desk chair over and sits in front of me. 'So. What's up Luce?' The side of his mouth tugs up uncertainly. 'I thought you were planning to never speak to me again.'

'That *was* the plan.' I pull my ankle up to the bed and cradle it in my hands.

'Do you want some ice for that foot? Antiseptic?'

I pull the foot closer to me, so the bleeding scratches don't stain his sheets. 'I'm good.'

A silence stretches out. Kit waits, watching me carefully. 'Are you?'

Yes.

'I'm in.' I say, hearing the words leave my mouth before I've even decided to say them. 'I'm one hundred per cent in. Helping your sister. I'll help you get in contact with Congressman Hoff.'

The words hang in the air between us. I can't take them back. I sit on my shaking hands. I don't want to take them back. Not really. Mostly not. Like, I'm at least fifty per cent certain I don't.

'Are you serious?' Kit is a mix of confusion and bright hope. 'What changed your mind?'

I take a deep breath. 'I've been thinking a lot about Harper. What's happening to her isn't right. The CIA shouldn't be allowed to do that to a fifteen-year-old girl.' I look up at the ceiling. 'And you're right—Hoff might be able to help through the House Intelligence Committee. Their whole job is to have oversight of the intelligence agencies, to make sure they are following the law. The committee can access classified information too and launch an investigation if they think the CIA is abusing their powers.' I chew on my lip. 'So, I'll help.'

A grin stretches wide across Kit's face. 'Really? That's awesome, honestly. With you, we'd be much more likely to be able to talk to him and convince him that what's happening to Harper is completely unfair … and also illegal.'

'There's just one thing.' I interrupt him. 'I'll help you, but I don't want Hoff to know I have anything to do with this.' My stomach churns. 'And there's something important I want you to help me with in exchange.' I clench my hands into fists in my lap. I've been thinking about this all day. What I want. What I need to try to do.

Kit frowns. 'What is it?'

I say the words slowly, choosing each word with care. 'I want him to lose the election. I want to absolutely *destroy* his reputation.'

He blinks at the bitter anger in my voice. 'Must not have liked your internship very much …'

'It's not about that.' I grind my teeth together. How am I going to explain this to him? 'Everyone thinks they know Hoff. They think he's the charming family man, a star politician on the rise who never puts a foot wrong. But people don't know the real him.'

The real Hoff is a man I never want to be near again. A man who ran his hands over my skin and smelled my hair when he leaned close. Then threatened me to keep me quiet.

I'm not staying quiet anymore.

Kit is looking at me strangely.

'I mean,' I add quickly, 'he's one of the people in charge of making sure the CIA and the intelligence community don't go rogue. And now, under his watch, they've taken Harper and others and are keeping them who knows where!'

Kit is nodding. He seems convinced, enough.

'A man like that shouldn't be re-elected. You use your hacking skills, and I'll use my knowledge of him. Together, there might be a chance, even a small chance, that we could stop him getting re-elected, and ruin him.'

I know there's a million reasons why I shouldn't get involved in the world of hacking: the world of Kit, Sam, Harper and the Swarm. But Hoff has given me no choice. It's not right that he can do what he did to me and face no consequences. It's not right that he's going to win another election because he's tricking a whole country into thinking he's someone he's not. None of that is right—so I have to do *something* about it. And this is the only plan I've got.

Kit sits back down and leans forward, his elbows propped against his knees. 'This is a huge deal ... what you're suggesting we do.' He hesitates. 'You sure there isn't any other reason you're suddenly keen to destroy a congressman?'

BEATRICE PAULL is a lawyer by day and a writer by early morning. Nights are not her thing. She has degrees in law, philosophy and French, and studied international cyberlaw in Europe. She has published essays and book reviews in the *Herald Sun*, and in magazines *Right Now* and *Good Reading*.

Loss

Andie Rodriguez Awad

I'm at a funeral. For no other reason other than moral support and, I guess, appearances. I didn't know the dearly departed, but I know her daughter, Lucy, a colleague I barely mix with because we work in different departments. The boss made me represent the firm, while he's off playing golf.

Heads hang low all around me, accompanied by occasional soft crying. The small church is bursting with mourners—this lady couldn't have known this many people, could she?—dressed in their best black attire. Death draining life, and everyone in it, from any colour.

The air is stifling, and I wish I was wearing my casual red linen dress and flat gold sandals. Instead, I'm draped in the only adequate black dress I could find in my closet this morning, matched with the only black shoes I own—a pair of merciless high heels.

Between the quiet sobbing, I sit wringing my hands on my lap. Before long, I pretend that I'm attending my mother's funeral. An icy shiver runs down my back as I realise I feel, well, nothing. Stone cold. Not even an ounce of sadness.

My chest tightens, and I shift uncomfortably in my seat. The only emotion that washes over me is relief. Relieved, she is finally gone. I teeter on the edge of reality as I squeeze my eyes shut, hang my head and pinch myself. It works and a prickle stings my eyes.

Without warning, I'm eight years old again and stuck in the bathroom cupboard, crying, begging. *Let me out. Let me out, Mummy. I promise I'll be good.* The back of my legs sting as welts rise, the skin broken and red where the willow tree branch slashed like a whip.

Someone places a hand on my arm and I startle back to the present. An elderly lady is offering me a tissue, her expression pained and empathetic all at once. My face is wet, and it takes all my strength not to recoil in horror. I take the tissue and mouth a thank you while giving silent thanks Lucy can't see me. She'd surely think me weird for crying.

I dry my face, take a deep breath, and open my eyes wide, ensuring I don't get caught off guard again.

Everyone here seems so sad about this woman's passing. Their loss makes me sad. Empathy at its best. At least I possess that, and that has to count for something, right? Trying to empathise with my inconsolable colleague by imagining what it would be like to lose a mother. I'm failing miserably.

My tears were not empathetic. They were the pathetic pity tears of a victim. That's what my mother would say. My sadness doesn't count, not today. Not ever.

Unfortunately for me, mother is still alive and kicking and frustrating as ever. I straighten my back and breathe out. I only realise how loud I exhaled when a woman turns to frown at me. *Eyes front, lady, mind your own.*

The decadent white flowers on the coffin, the grief, the

eulogy—a reprieve from the sombre, with certain memories il-luminating the space with soft laughter—all demand entrance to my heart; access to my soul. But that portal is firmly closed when I think about my mother. My throat thickens and heat rises to my cheeks.

My stomach churns as I realise this is not how I want to feel when her day arrives. Empty, or worse, grateful for her loss. I want to feel heartbreak, not relief. It's what makes us decent human beings, fragile and kind. Isn't it? Or am I allowed to say *Screw it! She was cruel and I'm glad she's finally gone!*

Of course I'm allowed.

But it's not me. Well, part of it is, but I don't want to be that side of my twisted self. I need to bury that part deep down. Together with the memories, the mental scars.

Many would surely scoff at the suffering inflicted by my mother's hands compared to their atrocities.

What do they know? It's not a competition.

Is your suffering more than mine?

Or do we all end up in the same therapy room?

Is our pain quantifiable depending on the type of torture inflicted on us as children?

Do physical scars trump mental abuse? Vice versa?

Authoritarian was the flavour of the day when I was grow-ing up. Children should be seen, not heard, the favourite tune played. And in my house, my mother took any means necessary to ensure the tune was well played. A lump rises to my throat. *Get a grip, woman. No victims here.*

From the look on Lucy's tear-stained face, it was not the mu-sic played at her house.

So unfair. *You got what you deserved,* that little voice reminds me. Her voice. Heat flushes through my body, and I have an overpowering desire to run away. But that would be inappropriate.

I'm at a funeral.

ANDIE RODRIGUEZ AWAD has lived in Melbourne since immigrating from Argentina in 1979. To enhance her English literacy skills, she read voraciously and soon after began penning her own stories. In 2019 she started an Associate Degree in Professional Writing and Editing at RMIT University and is currently working on her first novel.

Without a Trace

Marie Jiménez

L iving in a trance. Making the motions. Living in a dream. I look back to what I consider the reality—to the past, to my childhood. To when life was family. Sunday lunches at Nan's, my loving grandmother. She was the matriarch. The eldest of twenty grandchildren, I was doted on. Nan was my soulmate.

I pass the property where I grew up, off St Kilda Road in inner Melbourne. The stately mansion, Kildimo, built by my maternal grandfather for his beloved wife, my Nan. There they reared their children. When I was growing up, our family gathered on the lawn every Sunday for lunch; three uncles, their wives and children, and my gentle, bachelor uncle. We enjoyed tennis, croquet and good food, in the company of family members and their dogs who also loved the afternoons.

The property covered three blocks—35, 37 and 39. A graceful home on each. One was for my great-grandparents. Another, a boarding house, where occupants lived out their lives, almost like family. And, tucked in between, our family home.

I remember those happy years. My widowed mother, always smiling, helping her mother and pandering to her siblings. The market garden, tended by the Italian gardener for over fifty years. The gravel drive, with the curved, tiled border. The canopied section, leading from the red front gate to the garages across the rear of the property where horses and jinkers were housed. The stables, used for the motor car when it came to Melbourne. The rickety wooden gate to the rear lane, with the large steel bolt, that I found difficult to open. The chicken house, where the chooks lived out their lives, well past their egg-laying days. Nan's pets, never for the pot.

The house was flanked by the *en-tout-cas* tennis court. The manual roller was pushed with great effort to prepare the court for our fiercely-fought tennis matches. No whites. Just the ping of the ball, the roar of the watching family as aces threw dust into the air. All fun. The gracious peppercorn tree overseeing all, the family playing below its protective arms on the finely manicured grass. The large aviary, abuzz with birdsong, fronted by the granite bust of my grandfather, that had been sculpted by Paul Montford, the renowned stonemason of the Shrine of Remembrance. The initials DEV carved into the stone.

* * *

After Nan died, we sold the property. I went to the auction to say goodbye to the old home. I was taken aback. Open to the public, crowds of bargain hunters and stickybeaks poured through. The timber panelling, the floorboards, the skirting boards, the stained-glass windows and doors fought over by the scavengers. These people had no right to treat our home like this. There was no respect shown to the family or the lives that had been lived there. I had to say farewell to the gracious lady, so full of memories. To me, it was not a grand old mansion. To me, it was home and family.

I had a fortunate childhood. To this day, I have not replicated that life of love and caring. Did the old home contribute to this? I think so. Built with love: destroyed for greed.

* * *

I wonder what happened to the spirits. My great-grandparents. The boarders, who were evicted without mercy at the end? Nan, who spent her last moments of life there? Her home-birthed children? Or her sister-in-law, who lived in the upstairs back bedroom, until the age of ninety-six?

From time to time, I walk down that street, now crowded with parking meters. The palm trees that line the curb are still standing. They know. They watch everything. They remember us. I touch their fronds. They reply. I look up into their heights. They are survivors.

The property is up for sale and redevelopment again. The family that bought our property during the market downturn did not appreciate its history, nor the elegance of the homes. The wreckers had a field day.

Now, not a living trace, of Nan, nor her children. Nor her home.

Gone. Not a trace. But etched into my memory.

MARIE JIMÉNEZ is a Melbourne-based writer and book lover. Marie loves travel, the outdoors and observing the lives of others. Marie is currently writing her first memoir based on her life in Chile as a foreign wife, mother and tourism operator. Marie is published in *Mosaic*, Boroondara Writers Inc, Tablo, 2019.

The Last Party

MK Kuch

Nothing visited the farm anymore.

Once it was a place full of native wildlife, but now it was just one of the many forgotten fields that lined the side of a deserted highway. The only humans who visited were the ones who lived there, and the only animals to be found were feral cats and snakes. The colourful birds that once came around every day to eat the flowers or seeds from the trees hadn't been seen in almost a year, the same amount of time it had been since the last apple tree on Tali's farm had stopped fruiting. Bees and other pollinating animals couldn't survive the rising radiation, so the only fruiting trees Tali had left were a few cherries, two lemons, an apricot and four peach trees, all of which self-pollinate.

Tali had made a deal with a nearby Christmas tree farmer two winters into the collapse. He would give her wood to burn when the months got cold, in exchange for any goods she could make with her remaining fruit. She remembered happier times, going to a farm just like it as a kid; her parents would let her and her brother pick out whatever tree they wanted, then the farmer would cut it down and help her father tie it to the roof of their car. No need for Christmas trees anymore, since there was nothing to celebrate.

Before this deal, Tali had been forced to cut down most of the trees on her property, leaving only the tall Japanese maple that sat a few metres from her backdoor. In autumn, on those rare occasions when the haze of nuclear winter cleared, the sun would shine through its turning leaves, causing her living room to be bathed in gold-orange light for the afternoon. On those days she would pretend she was a kid again, back when things were normal. She would read on the ancient tweed couch that was made up of ugly greens and browns, and love it because her mother had loved it. These days reminded her of before.

Five years ago—two months before the world turned on itself—Tali had bought the small house and the hundred acres it sat on. The land was littered with dozens of fruiting trees. She filled the house with the furniture from her childhood home and planned to live there with her brother, Eli. They would make jam and farm and try to forget everything that had happened to them. They wouldn't need to worry about making a living, after all, the death of their parents meant they had enough money to ensure they would never have to get a job if they didn't want one. Their pockets full but their hearts drained.

Money meant nothing now. When the economy crashed, their bank accounts may as well have been filled with shirt buttons. Although, those might actually be worth something. The currency of the broken world was trade and barter, and Tali didn't have much left to trade. Most of those beautiful trees that scattered the property and produced sweet aromas in spring were gone. The animals were gone. Eli was gone.

'I'm gonna join the fight,' Eli had said over breakfast one morning.

'What?' Tali replid, choking on her tea. She didn't know where it came from. They had talked countless times about government corruption and how pointless this war was. How they were using innocent people as pawns in their selfish game of chess on a global scale. She was about to remind Eli of all this, but he pre-emptively put his hand up to silence her.

'I know you don't agree, but I've already signed up. I'm leaving next week and arguing won't change anything.'

All the fight left her before she could even try. She knew that once Eli had decided something, nothing would stop him. Arguing about it would only have ruined their last week together.

The night before he left, Tali threw him a going-away party. It was just the two of them now, so they opened a bottle of homemade peach liqueur to share. Alcohol was technically illegal, but so was growing your own produce. The government had made it very clear that any fruit or vegetable grown in untreated soil would likely be contaminated, and that the only safe foods to consume were ones produced by Verified Venders®. Tali thought it was all bullshit, that they just wanted to stop people from being able to sustain themselves and keep them under the thumb of the government. Eli wasn't sure and didn't eat their fruit unless it had been processed first.

They partied late into the night. Singing their favourite songs and talking about absolutely everything that wasn't Eli's impending departure.

If there was a lull in conversation, Tali would say something like, 'Do you remember Suzie, our old neighbour?' then leap into a story of how she used to try and steal their childhood cat by putting food out to lure her over the fence. They kept this up until the bottle was empty and their well of stories had run just as dry.

When Tali returned from the kitchen after putting their empty glasses in the sink, Eli looked at her, and she knew the conversation was finally going to take a turn.

'Tali,' Eli said in a tone he hadn't used since telling her about their parents' accident six years ago. 'If I don't make it back, I …' His voice started to crack, and Tali didn't want to hear anymore.

'You'll make it back!' She said—barely stopping herself from screaming at her brother. 'And when you do, you can tell me then, okay?'

Tali stared at him until he backed down and changed the topic to something she could stomach. She suggested they sleep on the couches in the living room that night, like they used to when they were kids. When they had family movie nights and both of them would fall asleep on the couch. Tali was grateful when he agreed. As much as she didn't want to admit it, she was scared this would be their final night together as a family.

She went to get pillows and blankets from her room down the hall. Only when she was a room away, where Eli couldn't see her, did she let a single tear fall down her cheek.

* * *

The next morning, she woke to the sharp pain of a hangover, the kind you start getting in your mid-twenties that reminds you that you can no longer drink yourself into a stupor the night before important meetings. But there were no meetings, not anymore.

Tali and Eli spent the morning cleaning up from the night before. When he asked her for help shaving his head, she almost broke, but just nodded and went to grab the scissors and razor.

The truck came for Eli at noon. His heavy canvas bag and too-big uniform made him look like a kid on his first day of primary school. He told Tali that his training would help him grow muscle, so he needed the bigger uniform.

'I love you,' Tali said, holding Eli tight. 'Stay safe.'

'I'll see you soon Tali. Save me some cherry vodka, won't you?'

He kissed her on the forehead and climbed into the truck. She tried to keep her face stoic. She couldn't let Eli see what she really thought. That he was leaving her just like their parents, just like everyone else had after the war began.

He's doing what he thinks is right, Tali told herself over and over again, until the truck had turned back onto the road that would take him to the closest airport. When it was finally out of sight, she couldn't keep her legs from failing her anymore, and fell to the ground in a heap.

With her hands in the dirt, she thought how nice it would be to be a tree instead. Her tears would be rain drops, seeping through the soil to her parched roots. She could wait it out, weathering the storms as they came, and hoping to survive until his return.

MK 'MINNIE' KUCH is a writer and lover of all things fantasy. They enjoy getting lost in a podcast and reading queer stories. They can either be found on their hammock drinking cold coffee, or on Twitter: @minnie_kuch.

Muddy Plains

Hanna Begic

'Identity becomes a prison-house. We are locked in with only those who are deemed our own for company. It is the prison-house of our own imaginations—these fictions, these stories carefully woven from collective memories, memories that are not even one's own, but we are convinced are more real because of that.'
—Stan Grant, *On Identity*

Following a moment of silence, two women with white ochre on their foreheads sing a mourning song while the crowd beat their chest in time with clapping sticks. The loud thump of hands pounding over flesh is heard through the persistent rain. A sea of black, red and yellow floods the Wurundjeri land. An Aboriginal Gumbaynggirr man—the activist by the name of Uncle Gary Foley—breaks the trance with a voice that could raise the dead.

'We still don't have justice, but we've got a better opportunity now, at this moment to bring about change. It gives old blokes like me a little bit of heart,' he yells.

Thousands of people with face masks hold signs and wear the colours of the Aboriginal flag. *Always Was, Always Will Be.* The gravity of the earth has shifted, exuding unfathomable sorrow and generational rage. Glancing around at the different groups of people, this is the first time I have ever felt connected to Australia.

* * *

'What does it mean to be Australian?' I asked my partner casually one morning. I didn't realise I'd never asked anyone that question. Yet it is a question I'd been asking myself for years.

'Comradery and sport, I guess?' he replied as he tilted his head to one side.

Earlier that week we'd watched an IQ2 racism debate where Stan Grant argued that the Australian dream had been left to rot. We'd heard words of 'having a fair go, classlessness, stoicism, egalitarianism and mateship.' These words rang hollow. All I had known of Australia's history was plagued by the ethnocentric teachings of a misguided government. Australian historian Richard White wrote that 'there is no real Australia waiting to be uncovered; a national identity is an invention.' If this is true, then why does our national identity depend upon a white male viewpoint?

The national identity was birthed in Australia's infancy. Sara Cousins, a research fellow at the National Centre for Australian Studies at Monash University, explains how it was forged from the gold rush of the 1880s. The white settler male was regarded as adaptable, independent and sport loving. He was egalitarian and valued mateship above authority. This Australian stereotype was crafted from the cultural suppression of Aboriginals, Torres

Strait Islanders, and other minorities. It served to colonise the landscape, suppress frontier violence and establish legitimacy based on the exploitation of natural resources and First Nations peoples.

If personal identity is deeply rooted in culture, what does this say about me? Maybe one of the reasons I've struggled with my identity is that these myths created by power-hungry politicians still shape our imagining of what it means to be Australian. An 'us' and 'them' mentality begins to form when emphasising a national identity like this.

Growing up, I listened to people closest to me justify their hatred for refugees based on the belief that people seeking asylum were more likely to be aggressive than those who were not. They argued that people who came from war-torn countries would vent their anger on local communities. I could hear the fear as they spoke. Fear that a hijab would compromise their national identity, their way of life. If this came from the people closest to me, who knew me and my family's history, how many others felt the same way?

* * *

In the summer of 2018, I found out I wasn't an Australian citizen. I had applied for an Australian passport for my upcoming trip to Japan when I got the call. A customer service representative told me I needed to apply for citizenship. It didn't make any sense. I was born in Melbourne's north-western suburbs, had a HECS loan, a bank loan and paid taxes. It was bullshit.

I argued with the rep for close to half an hour till I said, as politely as possible, 'Fuck this'. I threw my phone at the floor and punched at my computer keys frantically, hoping she was wrong. She wasn't. Being born in Australia doesn't make you an Australian citizen.

The automatic birthright to citizenship ended on 20 August 1986, under section 12 of the *Australian Citizenship Act 2007.* Children born in Australia after that date are only citizens if one of their parents is a citizen at the time of birth. My parents were on refugee visas; therefore, I wasn't a citizen. To this day, I have an immigration account.

As I peel away the layers of contempt and frustration I feel towards the government's immigration policies, I finally understand the gravity of the piece of paper that Mum likes to keep with her. It's one that many people, now more than ever, would and have died for. But when my friends ask me why I don't feel Australian, it's because of this: deep down, I know that the policy that denied me a citizenship was just one cog in a broken system that decides who is and isn't Australian.

* * *

In a few months, I will be the same age Mum was when she fled Yugoslavia. She left behind everything. At twenty-seven, all she had to her name was a tattered suitcase with two pairs of underwear, a few clothing items, and a handful of sentimental pieces that were easy to carry: jewellery, photos and odd bits of fabric. It's been years since she told me her story—a story of bullet-ridden buildings and burnt-out windows.

Most of the details I had forgotten; others probably warped after revisiting them as often as I did. I tried to stitch together the stories Mum told me during my childhood. At times I had to confirm with Gran if they were true. As I near twenty-seven, it becomes harder to imagine.

The early days of April 1992 would become one of the most significant modern wars of ethnic cleansing, massacres and genocide. A civil war had broken out that resulted in over 140,000 deaths, 2 million internally displaced persons, 2.4 million refugees, and ultimately, the separation of the Yugoslav Federation. The Bosnian Genocide was the first European crime to be formally classified as such since World War II, with mass graves still being found to this day.

In July 1992, Mum would leave her father and brother because the man she fell in love with would be hunted and slaughtered based on his religious background—Muslim. If they didn't leave, his body would be among the thousands of others rotting in the stench-ridden soil or decomposing at the bottom of a lake. Little did she know that when her father smuggled them out, it would be the last time she would ever see him again.

* * *

I've procrastinated about writing this piece more times than I care to admit. I'm scared of saying the wrong thing or offending people that I have an abundance of love and respect for. I understand and acknowledge the privileges I have in a country that fetishises whiteness. But not writing this essay because it makes me uncomfortable isn't a good enough excuse anymore.

I've tried to piece together the frayed fabrics of my family's past, left buried in earth and dirt far from here. Mum always said there are some stones better left unturned. But what happens when we choose to ignore horrors that scare us to our core? We forget those who came before us and were sacrificed in the process. Some stones have to be ripped from the depths of the earth. I dialled Mum's number.

'Did you want to leave Yugoslavia?' I asked her bluntly.

'Of course not. But people were disappearing overnight. They were killed or put in concentration camps. Bodies were found in lakes. That's just what happened.'

'How did you and Dad get out?'

'No one could get in or out, Bosnia was surrounded by the Serbian army. My father was in the military and faked our papers. Our papers said I needed to have surgery in Belgrade. That was the only way out. Your grandmother had to wait to come later when more refugees were leaving,' she replied calmly in her thick accent.

'Was religion a big part of everyone's lives back then?'

'Not really. We were Catholic-Orthodox. For fifty years after World War II, the communist party had banned religion. Afterwards, you could have your faith but back then no one made a big deal out of it. Everyone got along. We celebrated everything in my family. But then politicians began using religion to get power. Neighbours would report neighbours. And people would just disappear,' she said, very matter-of-factly.

'Did anyone protest or try to fight back?!'

'How could you? The army was strong. People were afraid to say anything. Especially now. There are still war criminals in power today. Everyone who could get out, got out and the people that stayed said, "Could be worse".'

My chest starts to tighten the more we speak.

'Do you miss it at all?'

'There was always doubt until I went back there. People who are still there are religiously orientated and not the people I had grown up with. Their way of thinking is very different. No freedom of speech.'

'Do you feel Australian?' I paused. 'Do you feel like you belong here?'

'I would say about ninety-five percent, yes. I don't belong to that place anymore. It's dead to me. I don't want to have anything to do with that country. Nothing. I hate it.'

This wasn't the place I had dreamt about.

'Best thing to do is to be ignorant. Don't write about this. Don't talk about this. Be stupid. There's a lot of religious expats in Australia from the war. I walked into someone's house here and saw a framed photo of a war criminal on their wall. Be ignorant about this and deal with it.' Her voice never broke, tongue razor sharp.

The stories we tell ourselves are the hardest ones to confront. Until that phone conversation, I didn't realise how much of my own identity was ingrained into a culture that my mother passionately denies.

I have always been proud to be the daughter of refugees—that will never change.

But a part of me grasped onto a romanticised narrative of overseas uncles and cousins sitting at a round wooden table, food from my childhood covering stained lace cloths. I dreamt about walking barefoot down cobbled stones and swimming in thunderous waterfalls, finding parts of myself from that culture that would make me whole. I thought that if I walked on the land my ancestors carved, I would find the missing piece. But Mum was right; that place didn't exist. Because what is a place without its people?

'What does it mean to be Australian?' I ask myself, walking past trees older than man, the smell of eucalyptus stinging my nose.

I think about Stan Grant's beautifully articulate words, woven out of a deep love for this country's muddy plains, furrowed fields, and elders past and present. In his book, *On Identity*, he writes, 'The soul eroding, stifling expectations of identity demand that you will be this and no other. You will exist only in opposites—difference will define you.' He is right.

I think back to the two women with white ochre on their foreheads, singing a mourning song while the crowd beat their chest in time with clapping sticks. I remember feeling, for the first time, a sliver of belonging. It is their land that I walk on. Their land that keeps me alive. And our differences that define us.

HANNA BEGIC is an Australian writer and editor residing in sunny Melbourne. She avidly engages in independent publishing communities that advocate for counter-culture movements and marginalised peoples. You can find her at the local pub listening to live music and losing at a game of pool.

Mother of the World

Alivia Mantel

I hear her broken voice
in the city noise,
feel her touch in the wind
and her pull in the water.
A lover,
a mother,
a leader,
a daughter.

I'm sorry for what we've done to your heart.

So many of us
wanted no part
in this,
but here we are.
We see the scars,
we are fools
with no sense and no plan
and no virtues.

It's hard to believe you're still with us.

Battered and bruised,
she doesn't ask for much.
We still see her rain
wash away
all we've done wrong.

Does a butcher deserve a birdsong?

I'm sorry for what we've done to your veins.

In moonlight
and in sunbeams,
I'll forever be lost for words.
Beauty incomprehensible,
ancient and wild.

Do not mistake kindness for weakness.

She does not need us.
On the contrary,
she would be better off without.

I'm sorry for what we've done to your lungs.

I will never blame the victim
for shedding every trace of her oppressor.
I cannot blame you,
Mother of the world,
for what you may do
to survive.
We are living on borrowed time.

ALIVIA MANTEL is a writer, musician and model with a passion for storytelling and performance. She is currently working on an elemental fantasy novel, inspired by her love for nature, and experimenting with video game writing and narrative design. You can find her on Twitter at @AliviaMantel.

Finding Under Difficult Circumstances

Pam Swanborough

B y the time you read this anything might have happened. She might have fallen in love by the time you read this. By the time you read this she might be dead. For that's just how it works. Don't feel bad for reading. It's just how things work.

* * *

All the old people had already died. Boomers. They had gone 'boom' as they hit the ground, or the car bonnet, something like that.

'No,' said Mother—before she died—'that's not why the word.'

But it worked, so who cared. Fuck them. They died—killed themselves—some from shame, and some from guilt and regret and, eventually, some from being the last ones left. None of them had died from doing something when something was still possible, so who cared? Dead, done, over.

Only it didn't stop at the old people. Forget the new diseases and toxic spills and weather chaos; bleakness went viral.

Mother, friends, strangers just died because they didn't want to be alive anymore. Just, that's how it works. Apparently.

And here we are, she thought. The Few. Or is it the Phew?

It was shit being the Few.

She lived behind a sign that said: 'Mad Old Cat Woman Lives Here'. She wasn't mad, or old. And they weren't exactly cats. Or words: 🐱💩😊🐱🐱👉🏠

And she didn't live *Here*, but a bit further into the cul-de-sac. But it was a good sign, in blood, and it kept the marketeers away from the garage door. Garages were a good place to live; the only solid remnants of those shit housing estates that covered the hills like lichen on rock, like street rubbish after rain—how many people *were* there, once?—the garages still standing while the dumb glossy houses they were attached to had slid into heaps of cheap rubble and sodden cardboard. And who had a car anymore … and was there anywhere to go that was less shit than here?

She wasn't beautiful but then who was? She had all her arms and legs, which was a good start. She grew a bit of this 'n' that in the big windows of the rubble houses, traded a bit of this 'n' that at the crossroads, in the dawn or dusk, like everyone did. She made string and baskets to trade, and was better off than mere foragers. She had never been in love, but intended to be, one day. She surely wasn't in love with the engineer.

She'd found the place time back. And then less time back, she'd found the engineer and they had worked together towards this one amazing day. A few safe people had joined them. She had made sure they were safe: she'd followed them to see where they lived.

Anyone who holed up in the old market in the centre of town—*a marketeer*—wasn't safe. She could usually tell because they smelt of what they ate: death. If a marketeer picked their rotten teeth, they might be dislodging a bit of your grandmother's gristle, or your old pet dog's skin. So it was always better to check.

This was too important.

The pool. It had been her favourite place as a kid, just before she learnt how shit everything was going to be. Just before she learnt that no matter how awful she felt on any given day, she'd never feel that good again. That the story books were all fairytale: the stories of having a home with electricity and birthday parties; the stories that said, 'If Tommy has five apples and he gives one to his sister, how many apples … '; stories called *Mediterranean Cooking*, *Lonely Planet Travel Guide*, *Daisy Visits the Dentist*, *The Rights of Man* … all fucking fairy tales. Apples didn't grow any more, winters were too hot. Most things didn't grow any more.

Fucking boomers. They died and so all the good stuff stopped. Or. All the good stuff stopped and so they died. Who cared!

Actually, she cared. She cared that there weren't enough people left to look after things, or places, or each other. She cared that the only organisation was in the murderous gangs. Everyone else: everyone for themselves. She cared that she didn't know what to tell the few little kids she met, how to help them feed themselves or stay safe, or even dry. Stuff that people had figured out like thousands of years ago. Stuff that dogs and … well … 'cats'… could do with no trouble, people were just shit at now. Now they were sitting in the dark and looking at/eating/sleeping on/breathing in all the crap rubbish that generations had left behind. Hiding from the sky and the wind and the sun. Hiding from all the best bits of the fairytales.

The pool. They'd worked like … she didn't know what they'd worked like. Like someone in a story, probably. And here they were, these few, these skinny, scrofulous, rickety Few. In crumbling swimming clothes picked from the ruins of the shop. Laughing and scared and hugging each other just to feel the heat of scabby skin against scabby, lousy skin, this one uncertain, hopeful time.

The place was huge—*how many people, once?* The glass roof was dense with vines and moss; some fallen panels left gapes that sagged inwards with creeping growths. Giant tubes wormed through the air above them, except where they drooped into the near-empty scummy pools. The windows were clouded by mould, the floor littered like a forest. From outside it looked like a giant compost heap. Inside, it was like sitting in a leaf: dank, herbaceous. All that growth and nothing edible; it really annoyed her.

But the pool itself: amazing. She ignored the bigger pools reaching out from the cavernous shadows, and instead concentrated on this one: small and manageable. She'd scrubbed every filthy inch of it with old chemicals that made her dizzy, until the tiles gleamed clean and white. While she'd cleaned upstairs, the engineer had done engineering things downstairs: dragged in bits and wires and tins of stuff, mumbled and cursed, and banged and yelped. The newcomers had helped her gather rainwater, and fill the pool 'til it shifted and gleamed like … language escaped her again. Was it like some wet ocean animal in the dimness? She had never even seen clean open water, for fuck's sake, let alone an ocean. How could she describe this thing before her other than with only these rubbish words the dead had left behind? When things disappear, their words also go extinct. The water in the pool shifted like water. There, that's the best she could do, and fuck you if you don't like it.

This night, the engineer was doing something below ground, and she was holding the candles for light, and it was taking ages. She was jiggling with excitement. She was jiggling with impatience. She was jiggling with boredom and running out of candles when it happened: light and noise and vibration. Fire, storm, sun, none of these lights were good things anymore, but this, wow, this!

The rooms lit up. She saw how manky she was, and how beautiful the engineer's grubby smile. The floor was shaking, and people were shouting upstairs. But not an earthquake; machinery was doing something all around them. She ran upstairs behind the engineer, grinning at the bony arse in front of her.

Water was heating up, moving and bubbling in its tiled bowl. They all jumped in and it was unbelievable: hot and clean over these poor neglected arms and legs, heads and backs. For a moment everyone stood still, gazing at each other. Then the engineer did a thing with one hand, and a huge piece of water flew up, fell over her head, stole her breath. She, she ...

She did the same thing, stabbing the pool with her hand like a blade, and the water flew over the engineer's head, stealing the engineer's breath. For one breath's beat.

Then everyone went crazy at once. Water everywhere, bodies in it and under it and through it, drinking it and scrubbing their heads and feet and each other, limbs and bums and bellies all in a heap, laughing and gasping and crying and laughing some more.

After a time, the floating happened. They stretched out and lay back, all soft and clean like babies in mothers' bellies. Some linked hands and smiled at each other, drifting.

She linked the fingers of her hand—the good one, with all the fingers—with the engineer's clever hand and smiled.

Maybe at the engineer. It was hard to say with her eyes closed. They breathed, in and out, slowly. They rolled their shoulders. They stretched their spines. They dropped their guard.

It might have been the light or the noise that drew them like a yell in the night: marketeers. Their necrotic stink slid into the clean air.

The fight was hopeless, one-sided: weaponised hunger against clean damp happiness.

A mechanical cough, a bitter burning smell over the sharp blood smell, and the lights failed. Black silence and the marketeers were gone, taking swimmers with them. Dragged feet left muddy trails on the floor.

She wasn't dead. It occurred to her that being alive or being dead was just how things were. But the engineer lay still, cooling in her arms, not floating any more. She remembered the fading smile as the engineer tried to shelter her, and felt something fall, collapse, break inside her. So then, like everything, she had arrived at love when it was too late? And so then love too was going to be shit?

She was struggling to pull the wet body out of the pool, for no reason other than she couldn't leave it in the water to rot, when a mechanical cough and the lights flashed on again; a human cough and the engineer was smiling weakly up at her. Raising her head with the effort of lifting her friend, she caught a flash of light on the small red curve of something across the dark space.

In the moist glass-roofed shade, way off in a corner mess of rubbish bins and litter, was a funny little group of funny little trees, their roots snaking across the floor to another small pool. With at least one red apple, maybe even five. The lights went out for good, but she was electric with ideas.

Whatever the fuck *five* was, she felt sure the engineer would teach her …

PAM SWANBOROUGH lives in rural Victoria, having worked in Australia and Europe; her interests include almost everything. Her writing explores the psychology of power imbalance and innocence, human failings and global uncertainty, through literary fiction and magical realism. Samples of her work can be found at pamswanborough. com.

Creature of the Night

Katrina Burge

The strings of the balalaika rang out through the grand ball-room, men and women spinning hand in hand. Red and blue dresses swept along the floor in wide circles. Sweat ran down the men's foreheads onto their bushy brows. Andrei took Yelena's hand, husband and wife bowing as the song ended. She leaned in close to his ear and spoke. His fingers slowly curled into a fist and Yelena turned as pale as her flowing, white dress.

He struck his wife, the *thwack* masked by the cheering crowd. She fell to the floor. Men and women around the couple stood and watched as she clutched her cheek; her brown, plaited hair fell across her face. Andrei's dress shoes clicked across the ball-room's ceramic tiles and toward the stage. As the band launched into their next song, he signalled for them to stop.

'Thank you all for coming.' His booming voice bounced off the walls. 'You will find your way out the same way you came in. Please accept my apologies for cutting the night short. My wife is feeling rather ill.' He paused, looking down at his wife. A smile curled under his heavy brown beard. '*Za Zdarovje!*' he cried out.

The guests raised their wine glasses to the stage. '*Za Zdarovje!*'

* * *

The creature returned to his usual space in the stove. He wiped his tears with a furry, clawed paw and smashed his head against the inside of the oven door.

Bang.

Bang.

Bang.

Yelena sobbed silently in bed, wincing with each *bang* from downstairs. Andrei snored loudly next to her. She dared not wake him.

Hours later, when the weeping had ceased, the creature's claws scratched against the metal door as he pulled himself out of the stove. Cutlery and leftover napkins from previous dinner parties in better times were strewn around the kitchen. Dust gathered on the unused pots and pans stacked upon the stove. On the floor, one saucepan tainted crimson with blood lay among the dirt and grime. The creature sat next to the saucepan and let out a shrieking howl. The bad man was going to pay.

* * *

Yelena lifted the red cushioned lid of her golden jewellery box, revealing her collection of shimmering rings. She opened the compartments and drew out a fine silver bracelet. As she fastened the clasp around her slim wrist, she looked to where her husband still slept. A flashback danced across her mind: Andrei embracing her in the morning, his beard tickling her forehead. Admiring her from bed as she selected her jewellery for the day. Helping her fasten her necklace and saying, '*Ya obozhaju tebya, Yelena.*' I adore you, Yelena.

He rolled over, a hairy buttock poking out from under the satin covers. It was almost funny—this regal room and bed and Andrei, a giant in his slumber, waiting to unleash his wrath upon whoever dared wake him.

She admired her bracelet as it glinted in the morning sun, before slipping through the bedroom door. Each footstep down the stairs synced with the growing beating of her heart. It had been loud last night.

The kitchen was as decrepit as ever, but nothing seemed out of place. Breathing a sigh of relief, Yelena went about her usual routine: moving the stacks of pots and pans out of the way, drawing open the curtains, and laying Andrei's plate and cutlery on the supper table in the dining room. But when she went to pick up the saucepan, it was missing. It had fallen against the stone floor with a clatter yesterday, after Andrei had beaten it over her head.

Perhaps he had picked it up before the party, not wanting any drunken guests to stumble into the wrong room and find a bloodied saucepan. She laughed to herself. In this mess, who would notice such a thing? And even if they had, would they have cared? The men and women had seen Yelena around the streets of Moscow, bruises and burns on her face and body, whispering as she passed by.

Hugging her arms around herself, she made her way to the coolroom to grab two eggs, but could find only one. Yelena could already feel the white-hot strike of his fist against her face after placing a single egg in front of Andrei. Her stomach swirled. Knowing that he would still be asleep in his hungover stupor for another hour or so, she grabbed her shawl and made her way into town.

Yelena didn't need a mirror. Her bruises were reflected on every face she passed by. Some didn't even try to hide the shock.

Others gave her a sympathetic glance. Those were worse. Mr Kuznetsov eyed her as she entered his grocery store. She stared at his thick moustache as she spoke. 'Eggs, please.'

He passed them over the counter, giving her the same remark he always did. 'Stay safe, Yelena.'

The snow had started coming down hard, covering the dirty streets. She stopped to pull her thin shawl tighter around her shoulders. Beside her was the warmth of Ms Morozova's bookshop, dull candlelight glowing through the frosted windows. Knowing that there would be a warm cup of tea waiting inside for her, Yelena opened the door.

The little tinkle of a bell rang out. The smell of woody incense caressed her nose. A husky voice called out from the back of the store, 'Just one second!', then there was the jingling of necklaces as her large figure appeared through the beaded doorway.

'Yelena!' she cried, nearly suffocating her in her massive bosom. She placed a polished purple finger under Yelena's chin, examining her face and clicking her tongue in disapproval. 'My dear, my dear. I'll get the tea.' She gestured for Yelena to sit down in front of the table covered with a red and gold cloth that surely cost thousands of roubles. She reached under the cloth and bought out a beautiful silver samovar, etchings of leaves crafted into its sides. First opening the lid to place the tea leaves inside, she then placed charcoal down the chimney and left the water to boil.

'Ms Morozova, may I talk to you about something?'

'Anything, my dear.'

'There have been … strange happenings in my house.' She chose her words carefully. Ms Morozova was a kind woman, but if she too suspected Yelena was going crazy … she shuddered at the thought.

She leaned in closer, barely audible over the sound of the water beginning to boil.

'Finding things in a different place to where I left them. Strange noises in the middle of the night. Sometimes objects disappear completely.' Her voice shook as she spoke, as much as she willed it to stop. 'I think there is a spirit in the house, and it wants to kill my husband.'

'What kind of spirit?'

It was so nonchalant, so casual. The words began to tumble from Yelena's mouth in a rush. 'It all began a few years ago. When we got pregnant, Andrei could not contain his excitement. He'd bring me flowers home and tell me, "Yelena, you must be the best cook in Moscow". I'm sure you heard what happened next.'

'After my miscarriage we were both heartbroken. Andrei grew distant—working late as I slaved away in the kitchen all day. He scoffed down his food with only a belch in gratitude. It all became too much for me.' Yelena fiddled with the bracelet on her thin, pale wrist. 'I begged him to let us hire some servants to help out. That was the first time he struck me. Certainly not the last.'

Ms Morozova nodded, pouring the tea.

'That night, I heard crying downstairs. Like a howling dog. I woke Andrei, who snores like a boar. He could hear nothing. He told me I was crazy. And that's how it's gone on. Whenever he hurts me, come night I will hear howling, or pots and pans smashing. I have gone downstairs to find broken plates the next morning, and I hurry to clean it before Andrei wakes, lest he think it was me.'

Ms Morozova stared intently at Yelena. She leaned forward, her necklaces swinging back and forth. 'Have you seen the spirit?' Her voice was an enthusiastic whisper, her brown eyes like liquid caramel, lit up by the candles between them.

'Never. I am afraid to go downstairs when it is happening.'

Ms Morozova stood, her sandals shuffling against the red carpet as she disappeared through the beaded doorway.

Yelena wondered if she was going to return. Perhaps she had gone out to call the lunatic asylum and have them pick her up. She was a polite woman like that; she wouldn't have called them in front of Yelena and embarrassed her. But she shuffled back into the room, clutching an ancient-looking book. She placed it on the table, a cloud of dust lifting from the red cover. *History of the Domovoy* was printed in thick, gold letters.

'This book contains the first known mention of the domovoy. Drink your tea, my dear, and I will explain.' She clasped her hands together, resting them on her large belly.

'My mother first gave me this book many years ago. We lived on a farm just past Ukraine. We had lots of fine livestock. The neighbour was very jealous; his animals were sickly and thin. We weren't a rich family, but we had such good fortune.'

Her purple eyeshadow glimmered as she watched her own memories as if they were dancing through the bookshop itself.

'Papa became suspicious. "Why us? Do we not feed our animals the same meals?" he wondered. Mother told him to just leave it be. But Papa did not listen, typical man he was.' She laughed. 'He hid in the barn one night where he saw a small creature feeding our horses. Papa said the only part that wasn't covered in fur were its eyes. They shone in the moonlight like dark beads. He was disgusted that such a dirty creature was contaminating our horses' food. Papa drilled a hole in the feeding trough so the creature could no longer fill it.'

Yelena rubbed a finger over the bruise on her wrist, her cold tea forgotten.

'The next morning, our animals were dead. The stable was smashed to pieces. Of course, we knew it was the creature. But we could not say anything to Papa. After that, we had no more good fortune in our house. Things went missing and got moved around.' A shadow passed over her eyes, no longer liquid caramel but dark, deep brown.

'One morning a broom was left on the floor. Papa tripped on it and broke his arm. I think it was the stress that eventually killed him. Heart attack, my dear. Mother told me then that a domovoy inhabited our house. An ancestral spirit of the household. She called him Grandfather. "Grandfather is here to protect us," she would say. "He lives in the stove, and we must not anger him as Papa did." We asked Grandfather for forgiveness for what Papa had done. Our good fortune returned.'

She opened the dusty old book, turning to a page filled with sketchings of a small creature covered in fur with the face of an old man.

'This, my dear, is what inhabits your home too. He seems to have taken a liking to you. But he will continue to get more aggressive until something is done. You never know when he will turn on you too.' She waggled a wrinkled finger. 'Yelena, you must choose. Your husband or the domovoy. If you wish to live on, you must eradicate one.'

KATRINA BURGE is a Melbourne-based published author with several years of experience writing for videogames in Ireland. She spends her time developing her manuscripts and copyediting for publishing houses. Katrina plans to further her career in narrative design while continuing her journey as an author.

Heat

Caroline Arnoul

Heat is an extract from a larger work.

C at thinks of herself as a good person. Someone who believes in the universe and karma—who gives back to the world, who understands we are all connected. Someone who lives in the moment because the past isn't something she wants to remember.

As the sun rises over the hinterland, she sits cross-legged in her yoga studio, reflecting on these thoughts.

It's what she believes and what she lives by—generate positive energy and receive positive energy in return.

Cat loves the energy of her morning yoga class. Her regulars. There's never much said between them. The 6.30am yoga devotees aren't known for being chatty—not at this time of the morning.

It's a time for introspection and reflection, for gentle stretching to open up the body and prepare it for the day, for making sure that body and soul are aligned.

She opens her eyes and draws the class out of the corpse pose. Her voice is calm and measured. 'When you're ready, gently roll onto your side and open your eyes.'

She takes a long inhale. 'Slowly come up into a sitting position.'

She waits a couple of beats until the class is all in position. Some of the older ones take a little longer and she doesn't want them to feel pressured.

She brings her hands together in the prayer position and bows her head, her scarred right hand a reminder of all she has to be grateful for. 'Namaste.'

'Namaste,' the group murmurs in soft reply.

She stands up, shaking her legs out and then lifting up her yoga mat. 'Have a great day,' she says brightly, as the class roll up their mats and push their bare feet into coloured rubber thongs.

There was a new person in class today, someone she doesn't recognise. Cat moves forward to welcome her, but the woman puts her head down, turns away and slips out the door before Cat can reach her.

After the last class members leave, Cat pads around the studio—straightening the pile of blue blocks, re-rolling mats, untangling the ropes hanging from the side wall, turning off the essential oil diffuser.

Then, as she always does, she stops for a moment before the full-length window at the front of the studio and gives thanks. For this place, for this magnificent view.

Today already feels like one of the days the area is famous for. Golden light dapples through the trees and the sky is a brilliant blue, with the promise of heat even at this hour. There's a clear view down along the ridge of gums to the sparkling sapphire coast, and in the distance the lighthouse gleams white on the headland.

She is so lucky. Truly, *truly* lucky.

Cat leans her bike against the wall of the Sunshine Café. It's almost full already, but she knows Adam will have saved a table. She pushes open the door and is thrown into a bright world of buzz and chatter—fresh with just-squeezed orange juice, the smell of coffee and the sound of the coffee grinder. She waves at Adam over the counter.

'Hiya,' he says as he froths milk at the coffee machine. He points towards her favourite table in the corner.

'Awesome, thanks,' she calls out. 'Jeannie here yet?'

He shakes his head. 'Haven't seen her.'

Cat picks the local paper up from a rack near the front door and takes it to the table, hoping Jeannie won't be too long. Jeannie's never been one for punctuality, so she's not holding her breath.

As she sits down, Adam appears with her regular order, a turmeric latte.

'There are benefits to sleeping with the barista,' she says. He flicks her with his tea towel in mock embarrassment, but his eyes are smiling.

'I hope there are more benefits than that.'

'Of course,' she replies with a laugh.

'You left early this morning.'

'I couldn't sleep,' she says, stirring her latte. 'So, I headed to the studio early.'

'You still okay to help tonight?' he asks.

She nods, licking the foam from her lips.

'Absolutely. But I've got to get through beach yoga with the influencers first. Believe me, that's the hard part of my day.'

Adam laughs. 'Good luck with that.'

Cat looks around the café at the mix of locals and canny tourists who know to head into the hinterland for a respite from the chaos of the beach. Hawkes Bay, with its backpackers and Instagrammers is where people want to be seen. Churchill, with its one street containing a café, a yoga studio and a general store, is the antithesis of that. It's more like the place people come to when they want to hide away from the world.

She pushes the finished latte to one side, checks there's still no sign of Jeannie and turns over the paper with a sigh.

The front-page story catches her eye. A house fire down in town—a young family saved by a passer-by. There's a photo of the hero who saved the children. It's the type of story the local paper loves—a fire, a dramatic rescue and an unidentified hero. He's standing outside the front of the house, with a toddler in one arm, holding the hand of an older child. He's looking straight into the camera and Cat's blood runs cold.

Because she knows the man in the photo. She knows him very well. And the photo is an impossibility—it has to be—because the man in the photo has been dead for six years.

CAROLINE ARNOUL is a writer and editor living on the Mornington Peninsula. By day, she runs Purple Frog, a Melbourne-based media and communications agency. By night, she writes psychological thrillers for YA and adults with the hope that one day, one of her manuscripts will make it into print.

Down Here Alone

Ayden A Carter

One soul travelling the road that night wouldn't make its destination; you brought me back to see how it happened.

The rain pelted the asphalt chaotically. You sat beside me on the roadside, fur soaked, your paws sitting in puddles that reflected the harsh headlights. It was coming for us. Through squinted eyes I couldn't tell how fast it was travelling; I couldn't see the driver, yet I felt a connection to them. I came to, feeling the chill of the cold rain trace down my back.

The car came straight at us. I scooped you up, hugged you to my chest, and rolled out of the way. The car swerved and I felt the close swoosh as it passed. We fell down the incline, rolling through the muck and underbrush. Wood and stone stabbed into my back as we skidded down the valley, my feet kicking off the stumps and trunks, my arms clutching you tight to keep you from slipping out of my grasp. Even with the cracks and scraps that filled my ears, I heard the tyres hiss and the car spin off the road—collecting branches and dirt as it ricocheted off the trees and gravel. It crumpled and crashed into a steaming heap not far from us.

You unfurled yourself and sniffed at the air, catching glimpses of the headlight beams bouncing off the broken glass in the grass and mud. You wished I hadn't hurt myself so badly trying to protect you, but you knew I'd do anything to keep you safe. I cradled my wounds, wincing in pain. You nestled by my side and put a paw on my arm and when my wary eyes met yours, you healed my wounds.

It was breathtaking. I don't know how you did it, but my cuts and bruises dulled and then vanished from my body. We gingerly stepped under the shade of a nearby oak, creeping under its protruding roots and using its leaves as a shield from the rain. We stayed with the wreck for as long as the rain held, but we couldn't have known that the rain would never stop.

I was with Dad when he heard the news, or rather, he was with me. Sitting on the end of the hospital bed, he wept as the doctor told him that Mum had crashed the night before, while he had been stuck with me. He had been stuck with me for so many nights, something like this was bound to happen. After the doctor left, Dad searched the web on his phone and found the report. There was no chance she had survived, but he couldn't understand what she was doing in the middle of the day on the road to Foster. *There's nothing out there for her*, you explained to my sister, Susie. You both cried away from me, you didn't try to hide Mum's death from me like you hid all the others—like you hid Gomez's.

I wanted one of you to hug me, but neither of you seemed to want to touch me anymore. I wished I could've mourned Mum like you did, but I didn't miss her. It had been so long since she had visited that I couldn't remember what she looked like.

You and I walked through the glade. It was much greener than the farmland around it. The hills and meadows were all brown and musty; the clay soil gave the grass a darker hue. Not that it wasn't nice to look at, but it couldn't compare to the green glade, or even the forest.

Was this where my mum was driving to? Why had no one ever mentioned it to me? They should've known that I was going to find it.

We didn't step to any beat, we didn't aim in any direction, you had just brought me out here for some tranquillity. I was sad that it took Mum's death for you to bring me here. I asked you your name, and you told me it was Gomez. I knew it was and I had always known it was you. I always liked your name; it suited your black fur and pale green eyes.

I was expecting a grand journey from you when you came for me. I thought you would've taken me away from the hospital, away from my family. But you didn't. You told me you couldn't, and I believed you. You just wanted to give me a chance to feel something—to feel free.

You wanted me to know that I wasn't down here alone, but ever since you left it's only been me.

'Fourteen years comes down to this?' Susie said, her arms folded and face red.

'One year comes to this,' Dad replied, his cheeks flushed and wet from tears.

'Don't do this to him, he can hear you. He's been fighting for you, me and Mum for this past year. Don't let his effort go in vain,' she said, resting a palm on my arm. I tried to speak to her, but the best I could muster was a groan. Her eyes looked to mine, and I knew she felt the smile I couldn't show.

'I can't keep coming here Suze, and you can't either.'

Dad turned and faced the window. He could try as hard as he liked, but the window wouldn't take him away. I'd already tried.

'Dad, he's your son.'

'He's my burden now,' he snapped back at Susie.

'Dad, you can't say that!' Her hand flew to her mouth.

'You should've heard your mother talk about him. *I don't wanna hold him, I don't wanna see him*, is the first thing she said when she had him.'

'No, no, she loved him,' Susie trailed off. Dad spun, jabbing a finger at her.

'Don't give me that bullshit, Suze. You didn't stop us from sending him away and you only cared when he got worse.'

You popped up on the end of my bed, your tail swaying from side to side as you came to rub against my chin. Their fight turned into an argument, and you put your paws on my eyes and started to purr into my ear.

I opened my eyes, and I wasn't in bed.

I wasn't in the room.

I was sitting on the outside windowsill, gazing at the city view. My butt barely fit on the ledge and my legs dangled towards the courtyard of the hospital seven storeys below. You were right next to me.

You laid a paw out for me, and I put my hand in it. They wouldn't know about this. How could they? Maybe if they did, they'd change their minds.

'It's okay, we know what your dad is going to do.' I nodded.

'You can do it before he does if you want to.'

I thought about it.

'And it'll be okay.' I smiled.

'You'll be with me again after it's done.'
I was.

AYDEN A CARTER earned himself an acquired brain injury at fourteen. From there, he's been producing art in whatever chaotic form it may take. From novels, to shows, to hosting events, and acting as ghosts in a dating game. Follow @AydenACarter on Twitter to see what chaos forms next.

The Apology

Rosie Watts

Frank thought he'd never feel the dying up there. But he did. It was in the air, and the water too. He felt it in the lifeless way the waves lapped the shores and the wind's despairing breaths and howling cries. Its relentless chill seized his bones in the winter and its stench sweated from his pores in the summer. He was trapped in the dying up there, beholden to the mood swings of their angered mother. Her warnings: they all heard but listened too late.

There were still times Frank woke at four in the morning, sprung upward all sweaty-backed and dry-mouthed. If sleep didn't free him, he'd scramble to slip on his weather-worn pants and squelch his feet into his still-damp boots—muscle memory from a time before, like a fish's tail fin still flopping after it's been severed from all it knew. Fishing: that was what Frank knew. It was the fear of keeping old mates waiting on the dock, breathing into their hands and rubbing them together, looking for Frank, cursing him for being late; it was knowing just how much time it took to get all the nets and the boat ready, and the way fingers move slower in the cold, stiff and blistered—those were the ropes that hoisted Frank out of bed.

The worst mornings were when he made it as far as the kitchen. The wooden steps creaked underfoot, he'd duck the low beam at the bottom and then, when the dog Jesse didn't rise, run up to him and stretch, he knew. No work. No work no more, except for the secret kind, of course.

Jesse watched, her head still, eyes moving under her brow, as Frank fumbled for a mug and then the coffee. He came to her because there was no one else to come to so early. No one. No one no more.

But today wasn't one of those days. Frank was woken without need. A charcoal grey resided outside the blind-less window; it was not light that had woken him, but sound. Little feet shuffling below, murmured thoughts. A clatter of spoons and crockery that sounded like it was trying to be quiet, as much as it was failing. Frank could see his grandson Sam in his mind's eye. He could see Sam stretching upwards, balancing on the balls of his feet to reach for a mug and then the coffee. He could see him opening the fridge, and the slosh of the milk overboard as he missed the cup's edge.

Frank rubbed his hands over his eyes. The skin of his palms was rough like a rocky beach, his stubble beard like sand itself. He sat up and swung his feet over the bedside. His gut rested upon his thighs, his back was soft and rounded, naturally hunched from the years of dragging nets and working the boat.

He smiled at the photo of Peggy on the bed stand, remembering how, when Sam had seen it, he asked what it was, picked up the frame and looked at the back for more, an 'on' button, a screen, anything. There had to be more.

The floorboards announced Frank's arrival.

'Oh, you're awake,' Sam said. 'I was going to bring you breakfast.'

Frank smiled. 'Were you now? Well, why don't we eat at the table, together?'

The table was by the window, which looked out over what was once a sprawling green that dropped into a white stone cliff face and ended with rocks upon which the pale salt water thrashed. Now the end of the green was ever nearing—erosion accelerated by rising temperatures and other reactions the climate scientists were always warning of. Frank didn't need their warnings. He could see them, unlike most, and that was worse than any set of numbers or scientific words.

Frank helped Sam cook some more toast and even found some old cocoa in the back of the cupboard that he mixed with sugar and microwaved milk.

Sam's eyes lit up. 'You can make hot chocolate just like that?'

Frank nodded. 'Sure can.'

They sat across from one another at the table: past and future meeting.

'You like it up here?' Frank asked through a mouthful of toast and jam. Sam, Frank's only child's only child, was staying with him for the summer.

Sam nodded. 'Yeah. I like the way it smells here.' He took a bite of toast.

Frank grunted. 'Your mum thought it'd be good for ya, the fresh air and all. How's about a walk later?' He washed down paps of chewed toast and crumbs with the coffee Sam made.

'Too sweet?' Sam asked.

Frank laughed. His face must have given him away. 'Just a tad.'

* * *

The wind was stronger on the clifftops than Sam had expected. And the air was suffocatingly clean. He was glad Grandad had made him wear the beanie that covered his cheeks and tied up at the chin, even if it was from the olden days and smelt funny. Grandad gripped his hand tightly and then loosely, as if he'd forgotten how to hold a hand. Sam looked up at him. Salt encrusted his beard and dried out his blistered lips; there were wind-tears in his eyes, but he was smiling. And so was Sam.

They reached the cliff's edge in well under forty minutes, a far shorter trek than when Grandad was young. Sam tightened his grip on Grandad's hand as they stood metres from the drop. Grandad looked like he was straight out of one of Mum's old photos, his boot resting on a rock, tears pooling at the corner of his eyes, cheeks pink like jam on white toast.

Sam looked out over the blood red sea that expanded for miles until it merged with the grey sky, where the clouds skimmed the water's surface. He followed Grandad towards a set of narrow steps that had been carved into the cliff face decades ago. He had to let go of Grandad's hand, pressing both his palms into the rough of the cliff rock as they made their way down. At the bottom, the pebbles on the shore felt like safety underfoot, even though they were a far cry from the pavement he was used to in the city and moved and crunched beneath his weight.

The whirring of the wind dissipated, replaced by the ocean's song.

Grandad waved his hand to the sea. 'This used to be full of fish.'

'Didn't you used to be a fisherman?' asked Sam.

'I was, yes.' Grandad stopped and turned to face the water.

Sam remembered a photo Mum showed him, of Grandad on the boat, proud and happy. 'Why did you stop fishing? You liked it, didn't you?'

Grandad's eyes were red around the edges and Sam wasn't sure if it was what he'd said or the salt air that stung them. 'There was hardly any fish left; none worth fishing anyway. And then they made it illegal.'

Sam nodded, but he wasn't sure who 'they' were. 'Is that why the water's this colour?' Sam had learnt enough about the time before to know that the oceans were usually green or blue.

'Yes,' Grandad said. 'That's overgrown algae. We didn't know then how bad it would get. I mean, they said, but what else were we to do? There was no jobs.'

They. Sam thought of the man Mum had been listening to, the one who spoke about a plan to make more fish. He told Grandad, but he wasn't as pleased as Mum had been.

'It's not the natural way, Sam. They'll see. Some people just don't want to admit it.'

'Admit what?'

'Defeat.' Grandad's gaze dropped to his feet and he set off along the shore again.

* * *

Sam's legs were tiring, his shoulders drooping, when he saw it. The flash of orange in the big rocks up ahead. Adrenaline coursed through him at the sight, evaporating the tiredness in his limbs.

'Look,' he said into the wind, and started running. To his surprise, Grandad ran too. He'd never seen an old man run before. Sam ran fast and neared the rocks in seconds.

'Is it, is it just plastic?' Grandad called.

The wind carried his cry to Sam, who cried back, 'It's a fish! It's a fish!' He knelt, the wet rockface grazing his knee. The fish was trapped between two rocks, tail in the water but unable to submerge and swim away. Sam had never seen a fish in real life before. It was slimy and its mouth kept gaping, gasping for air. It seemed to only have one eye, as far as Sam could tell, which was wide-open and pointed straight at him. Sam froze, unsure what to do, relieved to feel Grandad's leg beside him seconds later.

'Here, fill this with water.' Grandad pulled a container from his parka pocket.

Sam wondered why he had it but didn't stop to ask. He scrambled to the edge where the water was deeper and dipped the container down.

Grandad was kneeling now, his hands, un-gloved, reaching for the dying fish. He scooped it from the wedge of rock and algae, then placed it in the container.

Sam watched as the fish relaxed and moved the funny bits on its sides and tail.

Grandad put the lid on the container and took it from Sam's hands. 'C'mon,' he said. 'We need to get out of here.'

* * *

It had been almost a year since his last find. Frank couldn't believe the boy had spotted that speck of orange. He must have the eye for it. Those two bastards would be at the house soon. They had to hurry, to beat them.

'I can't walk this fast,' Sam cried.

'The fish won't last long in that container,' Frank shouted.

It wasn't strictly true, but there was no time for the truth, to explain that the government officials who lived in town, a pair of scientists, biologists, whatever, were part of that fish-making program. They had sensors all over the ocean and would've spotted that fish, no doubt. They'd want it. They'd manhandle it in their labs, trying to reproduce a natural wonder. That's where most of the last fish had wound up—bin bags of mutilated, mangled miracles.

There was no black car out front when the house finally came into view. Frank could barely catch breath in his lungs, but there was no way those bastards were getting that fish.

Frank huffed. 'Right.' He placed the tub on the table and thudded down the hall. Frank had said to never go down there, so Sam stayed put.

A screeching of tires made Sam jump. A black car with tinted windows was making tracks towards the house. 'A car!' he yelled.

Jesse barked and growled.

Frank reappeared with a set of keys in his hand. 'Damn. Down girl.' He picked up the fish and thrust it into Sam's hands. 'Go to the room at the end of the hall, shut the door behind you and don't open it for anyone. I've got a key. I'll be there soon.'

The thudding on the front door came seconds later. Frank watched as Sam slipped into the darkness of the hallway. He waited to hear the click of the lock. The thudding came again, louder.

'Alright, alright,' Frank yelled, thrusting the door open.

The pair of 'em stood shoulder to shoulder in the doorway, both in smug suits with expressions to match.

'Afternoon Frank,' the blond one smiled, shades still on.

They flashed their tags hanging from their lanyards to justify their presence.

Frank grunted. He already knew what they said: some fancy titles, chief operations somebody or others for the National Fish Replenishment Scheme.

'One of our sensors detected a fish this morning not far from here,' the one with hair like slicked black seaweed chimed in. 'Now there's no sight of it. Vanished. We know you like walking, thought we'd check in, see if you've seen anything.'

Frank shook his head. 'Nup, nothing.'

Seaweed nodded. 'Funny that. It's also funny that this isn't the first time. Don't you think?'

'I don't know, maybe your sensors are bust.'

'Nah,' Blondie said, 'That's not it.'

'Well, sorry fellas. I can't help ya, not a science man like you two, bit beyond me a mystery like this.'

Seaweed chuckled. 'Alright, Frank.' He leant in till Frank could smell his morning coffee staling on his breath. 'Just know we're onto you. Whatever it is, we'll find out.'

They left in a flurry of dust.

Frank shut the door. 'Pricks.'

* * *

Sam was standing frozen in the aquarium, clutching his container, when Frank clambered down the metal stairs. Sam didn't turn to look. His eyes were fixed on the glass that arched above them, a single layer separating them from a seemingly endless blue water, the bluest Sam had ever seen. He felt as if he was standing on the ocean floor. Schools of fishes swam by him and above him, pinks and oranges and yellows. The light behind the glass reflected waves of green along his cheeks and across his eyes.

'What is this?' he whispered.

'It's sorry,' said Grandad.

ROSIE WATTS is a marcomms professional in the for-purpose sector and a freelance nonfiction writer. She writes speculative short stories with feminist, social and environmental themes (sometimes, all in one) and is currently writing an adult sci-fi novel that explores the social ramifications of tech-focused solutions to the climate crisis.

16.07.1918

CJ Cleghorn

There's blood on my hands. I don't know when it got there, or how. We were the ones shooting; how am I covered in blood? The volunteer privates loaded the bodies, but I'm *still* covered in blood.

'You alright?' Yurovsky grunts, his eyes narrowed on the dark road ahead.

I take a deep drag from my cigarette and exhale through a slit in the window.

'Are you?'

He swallows hard. 'At least we're not in the back.'

My mind is blank. All I can focus on is the cigarette in my bloody, shaking hand.

'Where will we even go …?'

He says this more to himself than me, but it sends my head spiralling. What if someone comes upon us? What if some villager catches us and we have to 'take care of them'? What if no one finds us? What if no one finds *them*, and this is all just swept under the rug like nothing? It was *murder*.

I shake my head. I can't think like that. It was an order—

following orders. We're following orders. Orders from Lenin himself. He knows better than I do. He knows *why*. We don't need to question it. It isn't *murder*.

The frozen brakes screech as Yurovsky pulls into a dark copse of trees. He's spotted a patch of ground unburdened by snow. It'll be easy to dig. He yanks up the hand brake and turns to me, his hand outstretched. I pass over the slim cigarette and he sucks at it deeply, his cheeks pulled into his slender, bearded face. We sit in silence for a moment, listening to the creaky old truck cool down. When he's finished, he flicks the cigarette to the dirt-covered floor and secures his *ushanka* on his head. He looks at me and I do the same without hesitation.

We hop out of the truck and find the volunteer privates already leaping out of the back. Though the bodies are fresh, I feel like I can smell the beginning of rot, the yellowing of flesh, the pus and maggots. A private whose name I can't remember flicks on his torch, and I blink away the nightmares forming in the back of my mind.

'Dig,' I order.

They dig. I try to light another cigarette, but my hand is shaking. I give up and chuck the wasted butt in the dirt.

'We better unload.' Yurovsky's gruff voice is back, the unease I saw in the cab of the truck replaced with his hard, loyal military persona.

I close my eyes and nod. The first body I come to is the Tsar himself—Nicholai Alexandrovich Romanov. The most powerful man in Russia, now reduced to a sack of blood and bones and muscle and hair. I avoid his glassy eyes and drag him from the back of the truck, the corpse hitting the ground with a meaty thud.

'Strip 'em,' Yurovsky grunts.

I meet Yurovsky's gaze in question, but he stares me down, daring me to object. I nod obediently. I object, and I'm labelled a traitor. I object, and I've done all this for nothing. I object … and I end up like him.

I kneel beside the body and barely look as I unbutton Romanov's coat and shirt. I hesitate at the trousers, but I can feel Yurovsky watching me. So I detach. My rational brain, the person I am, leaves my body and I'm just another human, doing what I need to do.

In this state, I'm able to make short work of the Tsar and the doctor, Botkin. But when I reach the body of little Anastasia, tears threaten my eyes. She's just a girl. Only seventeen. She's just wearing her nightgown, the little frills flecked with her family's blood. When I move strands of long hair from her neck to remove her necklace, I notice a flutter. My heart plummets and I freeze.

There's no way.

Looking around for watchful eyes, I carefully place my fingers on the side of her throat. It's faint … but there's a heartbeat. My mind whirls. How can she not be dead?! Near twenty of us emptied our guns into them in that basement; she should be riddled with bullets.

Panic creeps up my neck and I quickly stand, taking out another cigarette.

'Comrade, what are you doing?' Yurovsky barks, and I jolt.

'Just need a smoke. It's cold.' I can't think of anything else to say; I'm too focused on the *alive* grand duchess at my feet.

I should say something. I should shoot her myself. After all, wouldn't it be a mercy? She's obviously injured: her white nightgown is caked with blood. But how much of it is hers? What if she could actually *live*?

I'm able to light the cigarette, but the tobacco does nothing to calm my nerves. It's a habit now—a social crutch I use when I don't know what else to do with myself. I lightly prod the grand duchess with my boot, wondering if she's faking or if she's actually unconscious. If it's the former, maybe I can convince her to run. She may not make it far, but it's a chance—which is more than we gave the rest of them.

Yurovsky's eyeing me now, as if he can smell my disloyalty. I toss my cigarette and kneel again. There's nothing I can do: I help her, I'm a traitor; I kill her, I'm a coward. At least with the latter I'd be praised, though I doubt I'd ever be able to live with myself.

I disrobe the child and catch some volunteers leering with interest at her naked, bloody body. I sneer at them with as much venom as I can muster, and they quickly return to their digging. They're almost done now, their pile of soil neighboured by a heap of ragged, regal clothing. Naked, the Romanov family is just like everyone else. Maybe that's what Lenin wanted: to equalise them. Dead, they're only human. Dead, they're not a threat. Dead, and the revolution is complete.

Anastasia stirs, and I step back. Yurovsky meets my eyes, then shoots her in the head.

Our job is done. We have saved Russia.

CJ CLEGHORN is an Australian writer, editor and learning designer. She thrives in an octopus-style writing environment, with pencils working on several different ideas at once: be they YA, historical fiction or fantasy. You can find all of her projects on her website: cjcleghorn.com.

Earth ... and Other Illusions

Matthew Goodrich

Earth ... and Other Illusions is an excerpt
from a larger work.

D ad insists I attend a party in the hills.
'I'm not invited,' I say.
'If your brother's invited, then you are too,' he says.
'Plus, you need the air.'

'The higher altitudes won't help.'

'Don't be a wise-arse!'

I sigh. 'Fine.'

As Dad taxis Forrest and I to the party, I gaze out the window, watching the neighbourhood whisk by. Kids race through sprinkler rain with the kind of laughing abandon seen in those who haven't had life happen to them yet. For them, the world remains enough.

Above the town, in the evening light, the pine-pricked mountains look like milk and blood, and as we draw nearer to them, they appear to triple in size like angry waves surging up. I jam my eyelids shut, unable to escape the impression that they're about to squash us like bugs, but when I open them again, the mountains are as they were, held in place by Newton's Laws of Motion.

As we pull up to the party, Dad says something to Forrest that I can't hear, and Forrest says, 'Don't worry. He'll be fine.'

Dad's worried about me: a few weeks ago, during vacation, I hurt myself attempting to crawl into a parallel mirror at the mall. It looked nice in there—alternate dimensions rolling away infinitely.

Dad thinks I have bats in my belfry—he said it a few days ago. I asked him what a belfry was, and he said he didn't know, and I said he shouldn't use the idiom then. He told me not to call him an idiot. And I said I didn't. And then I told him that, as far as he knows, belfry might be a made-up word, and that would make him equally as insane as the person who invented the expression in the first place. I held my tongue after that, because he looked like he was on the verge of an aneurysm. A later visit to my dictionary would reveal that belfry *is* a word. Though that wasn't my point. Truth be told, I'm not sure I had one …

When we arrive at the destination, Forrest turns to look at me from the front seat.

'Are you ready, Felix?'

'No,' I say, unable to escape the feeling that something terrible is about to happen.

'Well, you have to be,' he says.

I lurch out of the car and pull myself upright—immediately stunned by the size of the house. It's a mansion really, white as a wedding cake. It looks like it was designed by moviemakers—like that film where the protagonist sailed to the edge of the world and struck up against a paper horizon.

As I walk toward the door, I imagine myself an unwitting participant in a reality television show, and when we step inside, I ask Forrest whose party it is, but my voice is lost in the whomp of music—that or he chooses to ignore me.

He leans back against the benchtop in the kitchen, letting his crutches slip forward as a widening crowd of sycophants line up to sign his newly plastered leg.

Even with a spiral fracture of the tibia, he is *still* their reigning quarterback.

With eyes down, I weave my way to the living room where everyone spins the bottle and shoots pool and throws themselves into keg stands. I laugh when they laugh, and right when I'm about to forget about my woes, a passing girl loudly whispers that I've used make-up to hide my acne.

I haul myself into the backyard, frantically wiping away the evidence.

Fuck them, I tell myself. F U C K T H E M A L L!

When I think I've removed the make-up, I thrust my hands in my pockets. It's an awkward posture when you're standing alone, so I withdraw them, and let my arms hang loosely instead—but then I feel like a tumbleweed, as if I'll be whisked away in a tiny wind.

I need to use my hands. I'd be okay if I had a beer or a wine or a—

I suck in a large gulp of air, put on a grin larger than I feel, cross the yard, and ask an alpha with cauliflower hair if I can bum a Marlboro. He narrows his eyes at me, puts three cigarettes in his mouth, lights them up, pushes smoke at my face, and says, 'I'm out, man. Sorry.'

I want to tell him that the left and right hemispheres of his brain have migrated from his skull to his biceps, and that he might want to have a doctor look him over, but I'm far too intimidated, so instead, I retreat to the tree again, feeling like a leper.

Minutes later, that niggling sensation returns—the sense that an immense awfulness is afoot. I try to establish what I'm worried about, but I'm too preoccupied by the fact that the alpha is now rationing away half his cigarette pack to a throng of heartbreakers with large, round, fluttering eyes.

When they've picked him clean like vultures to a bone, they wobble through the yard, trailing the aroma of peach schnapps and tobacco. 'Did you smell his breath, Tory? I mean *puhleeease*! Hasn't he heard of mints?'

They laugh like witches, their teeth stained with lipstick, until a member of their group starts puking. And as I watch hot sausages of vomit sizzle across the lawn towards me, I wonder if this is what Dad meant by needing some air.

Fuck this!

I march back toward the house, bracing myself to ask Forrest the question I promised I wouldn't ask him—'Mind if we call it a night?'—only to stop halfway across the yard when I spot him through the living room window: he's eased himself into an armchair, an acoustic guitar hugged to chest, and everyone who is anyone is huddled around him in song, including a redhead with toothpaste teeth who's eyeballing him like she's seeing a rainbow for the first time.

Even from outside, I recognise the notes; he's playing 'Fake Plastic Trees' ... poorly. It doesn't matter, though—his thick, lumbering fingers make it seem like a badly plucked chord is essential to the composition, like it was always written that way.

Forrest—that hotshot of a human, enduringly talented at everything he sets his mind to, and everything he doesn't.

With jaw tensing, I make my way to a pool by the rearmost edge of the yard. Its surface is green and scummy with misuse. I tear off my Nikes, roll up my pants, and plunge my legs into its mossy surface, kicking holes in the algae—trying not to listen to people hissing at me with words like *FREAK* and *LOSER* and perhaps worst of all, 'that *PRICK* who ruined everything'.

They know then. Maybe Forrest told them everything—told them I'm to blame for his leg, told them I'm to blame for him missing play-offs.

When I resolve to look their way, all I can see are hot, red nicotine tips pointing at me threateningly. And right when I'm about to dive into the pool, or shout at them, or run the hell away, Forrest arrives and threatens them with an arse-whooping.

'Take a hike!' he yells.

As if by command, the nicotine tips tumble to the lawn like stars cut from strings, extinguishing themselves in the grass.

'Don't mind them,' he says, planting himself next to me and wrapping an arm around my shoulder. 'Losers all.'

I agree, silently. I know them from school. They've moved back inside now, casting sidelong glances at me through a window at the back of the house, finger-combing their hard, modelled hair. It's almost like they've stuck their heads in buckets of glue—to say nothing of their ridiculous spray-on tans; they look like oversized Oompa-Loompas.

All told though, if they're losers, what does that make me? Who, after all, has their legs in the swampy backyard pool?

I turn to Forrest. 'Why are you being so nice to me?'

'You're my brother,' he says, as if that explains it. 'Let's hit the road!'

Even though I'd like nothing more in the world, I tell him that the redhead with toothpaste teeth will probably want him around.

He laughs at that expression, and his laugh is loose and kind and triumphant, like a clown. 'Toothpaste teeth?'

I laugh too, not knowing why it's funny.

'You know what, Ef? You're the weirdest son of a bitch there is,' he says, leaping up and wrestling himself onto his crutches.

'Yeah.'

'It's no wonder they pick on you.'

'Yeah.'

'But I wouldn't have you any other way, kiddo!' he says, messing up my already tragic ten-dollar haircut.

'Thanks, Forrest.'

He shuffles down the side of the house—yells back. 'I'm ready when you are, Ef.'

I stand, tear my shoes on, and call out. 'Aren't we getting a cab?'

He keeps moving. 'Nah, we can walk it. It's a lovely night out anyway—no use wasting it.'

I race up to him. 'It's an hours walk, Forrest,' I say, a little uncertainly. 'And what about your leg?'

'What leg?' he asks, pushing his way down the side of the house. 'You mean this thing? It's not like I'm going to *walk* on it.'

As we move ahead, I catch sight of the redhead with toothpaste teeth propped up against a washing machine through the laundry window; she's French-ing the alpha with cauliflower hair.

I throw Forrest a private look, wondering if he's seen them. And that's when I notice it: something lonely passing through his face like a shadow. Is *this* why he wants to leave?

He crutches harder, out into the twisting mountain roads. And there is something victorious about him—a little too victorious, and again, the persistent instinct that shit is about to hit the proverbial fan spreads across my heart like a storm cloud.

I want to argue my case further, but when I catch up to him, his eyes are the kind you don't argue with—luminous and eager.

'What's the hurry?' I ask, when we've made it a few miles from the house.

He stops, opens his jacket, and yanks a bottle of expensive-looking wine from an interior pocket.

'*This* is the hurry,' he says, tearing the cap off, and taking a slug.

'Nice steal,' I say.

He hands me the wine. I have some. It's awful—but I don't show it, and when I hand it back to him, I tell him it's a 'lovely drop'. He doesn't believe me—takes a pull, and then returns it my way. I take another glug. And then another. And then even more. And it's nicer with every swig—the wine coursing through my marrow like hot magma.

'No more questions,' says Forrest. And then we're off again—him crutching, me walking, both of us drinking.

We pass the bottle back and forth again and again. And we know when to pass it—exactly when—with that rare instinct that brothers have for each other's thoughts. It's not surprising. We've always been glad at the same time, sad at the same time, manic at the same time, sick at the same time—we even have the same nightmares. I tell him how weird that is, and he smiles at me, and I smile back.

We talk about this and that, the minutes flying by—the hours maybe—and when I piss against a tree, I arc my yellow relief through the air in zigzags with a cracking grin, big as anything, thinking things I'd never think, laughing at things I'd never laugh at, my head thick with easiness.

This is it! To be alive! Now!

'You're a lightweight,' says Forrest.

'That I am,' I say. Zip. Hiccup. Hiccup. Hiccup. Happy, happy, happy again. No more storm cloud heart.

When I hand the bottle back, he pours the remainder of the wine over his head, tosses aside his crutches and tap-dances like a lunatic. And I'm laughing and laughing because even with a right leg in signed plaster he looks every bit the virtuoso, like he's a Hollywood star in technicolour, twirling across rooftops waving an umbrella in artificial rain. And I'm dancing too, almost against my will, feeling like I'm the last remaining human being on Earth.

We're drunk as anything now, not so much with wine, but with life itself—our shadows lengthening across the mountain path like giants, like gods.

To think I imagined these mountains could squash us like bugs. We ride the waves that are these mountains. We ride the waves that are our fear. And right as we are high and bright and forever, and right as we imagine ourselves invincible, and right when nothing at all could possibly go wrong …

—I
t
h
a
p
p
e
n
s.

That terrible thing that was coming up the tubes: Forrest makes a misstep, tilts horizontal, and vanishes, wheeling off the side of the mountain, leaving behind him nothing but a tornado of withered leaves.

* * *

It took Forrest eighteen years to die.

I wonder how long it will take me.

MATTHEW GOODRICH is a Melbourne-based writer with a love for all things YA. Matthew scripted a two-minute road-safety commercial for cinema distribution that has been recognised locally and overseas. Furthermore, two of his screenplays have found themselves included in films that have screened internationally: *Scission* and *Death Blooms*.

A Cold Season

Matthew Hooper

When I come in, Mama, who is not my real mama, is preparing kindling for the fire, squatting by the hearth with her back to me. All I can see are her curved brown hands cracking small bits of wood.

'You back already, Beth?' she says. Then, in the pale light, Mama turns. I hear her flat shoes slide on the wooden floor. 'Here child,' she says, and she looks across, one eye darker than the other. Then, as if it's something new—me learning to break up sticks—she says, 'Hold your hands together.' She holds her hands forward with the fists clamped around a bundle of small sticks. She looks at me. Turns her hands. I hear the wood creak. Then it snaps.

'Beth! Are you listening?' She glares, sucking breath between her teeth. 'You try.'

'Most of them snap pretty easy,' I say, cracking my second one, pulling it up against itself, tearing the bark away from its side.

'Is that right?' Mama says. We put the ones we've done in a pile, and soon we are not talking at all, but squatting side by side in the cold morning room, cracking small sticks, Mama and me, making a pile as big as a dog.

'Mama,' I say without thinking, 'when you think Owens is coming back?' She stands up and walks out into the hallway. I straightaway wish I had kept to just breaking sticks, cause my question makes Mama's face turn cruel. I move across to where she was, and I feel the weak sun on my back and watch my shadow moving on the dusty floor. Then Mama, who must have guessed how alone I was feeling, comes back and settles herself nice and close.

'Your father, Owens, is dead, Beth,' she says. 'I should have never let him go up that mountain after Samuel. We lost both of them. Now, please …' and I turn towards her and see her eyes for just a moment while she breathes out a sigh. 'Just stack that basket,' she says standing up again with her knees creaking, 'then you can come and help me with the chickens.'

With the shock of Mama's words going into my body I continue to break sticks. I hear her outside now, at the chicken house. She is raking out the dirty straw. The scritch of the rake makes me shudder because I know she is going to choose that young rust-coloured one for dinner and take its head off in the yard and serve it up to Wallace. My plan is to stay inside until it's done.

The pale sunlight livens up a bit, still coming through the window, and I break up more sticks and lay them on top of the pile in the basket. When the sticks are done I stand, and through the window I can see them chickens—in the yard now—and there's the sound of a shovel scraping on the ground. The room is so cold my ears hurt and I'm thinking I'll light the fire, even though Mama says I'm too young. I turn to the fireplace again, still with the weak sun on my back, and I set the sticks in the hearth. I squat again and take some leaves by the pile and I scrunch them and roll them into balls. They spike my palms but I keep rolling until I see the little leaf-skeletons they have inside themselves, all twisted and dry. I try not to think about what Mama is doing outside. I try not to think about what Mama said about Owens. I don't agree with her. I know he's alive. I can feel it. But I can't tell Mama that. It makes her angry. So, I just feel the rough leaves against my hands.

Crush and roll. Crush and roll. I put the skeleton balls on a curved piece of bark in the hearth: fill it up like a boat. I find some unbroken leaves and lay them on standing up. I think of Owens: that last time I saw him, standing at the tree line with the first rays of sun on his face. I think of his breath coming out in the cold grey air like wool. How it floated off and came apart. I think of my cousin, Samuel, too. His quiet voice reading to me at night-time. But that's all I can think about: just those two things, while I set the fire.

I lay some small sticks and light a match and push it right under the little gauze leaf-skeletons and they catch and turn in the tiny flame. I push the pile up on itself, and a wisp of smoke rises up—grey and pretty and like something all its own. And then the thin flame comes, crackling and spitting. I pick up some more sticks and put them on and soon the heat of the flame bulges against my hands and I know it's alive and I slide back on my haunches and feel the corrugated boards under my soft inside shoes.

Listening to the fire burn and being sucked up by the chimney, I hold my hands to it, warming them against the morning cold. I don't care what Mama's gonna say. Aching for Owens and Samuel has made me immune to Mama's little cruelties. I sit on my haunches and watch the yellow and orange flames and think about my father up the mountain looking for Samuel. I think about how every fire's got its own way of coming alive and making its shapes and sounds and progress. Mostly I think of the big ones with sticks lined high before they start and how Mama covers those ones in kerosene before she lights them, and they pounce up the chimney toward the night sky like a big orange cat.

This fire is full and round and slow. It is like a ball. I put on bigger sticks and one split log and then I get all the shoes from yesterday—what are wet and muddy—and put them up close and bring over Mama's washing and spread the cool wet things out over the two sticks what are resting on the back of chairs. Normally we swap them sticks over all morning so each one gets its turn looking at the fire and the steam lifts off and the curve in the sticks lifts as the weight of water leaves them clothes and they fill instead with the smell of wood-smoke.

After the clothes is up near the fire, I sit by the flames and put up a stick bridge for some fidgety ants. They is running up and down as if they all lost their eyes. But they don't like my bridge. So I go to flicking some off, the ones I can, and warming my hands and flicking some more off like that while I am still waiting for Mama to come back in with the dead chicken. But she doesn't.

I put the firescreen up and I stand looking out the window. All I see is the sand, the dust blowing against the dark cracked wood of the barn and I see the grey sky curling like a bad omen. I turn and move them wet shoes around and the room is full with heat and damp and my face is red and warm.

* * *

This year winter came late, and all at once, like it had been bunching up behind the hills before it arrived. That's what tricked Samuel. He wasn't ready for it. He got lost up the mountain and Owens went up after him. It's a long time to be up there. Almost two weeks. And the snow's deep now. We can see it from here and Mama says they is dead. But I know Mama is wrong. Mama is negative. The snow is not down here yet and I can feel Owens up there looking around. Staying in one of the little huts. He is not cold and still. Maybe Samuel is, but not Owens.

Where we are the valley swoops right up the mountain, and the winter brings mists what roll down: cold and thick and they turn and hover like clouds, and the trees and everything change colour to dark and glistening from them mists. What follows are colder nights and snow. Little Sasha—Samuel's twin brother, and ten years older than me, and is called little because he's so tall, like Samuel—he promised he would take me up there so we could look, too. Every day Little Sasha goes up to the edge of the trees to look at the weather. But each time he comes back saying it's closed out past the escarpment. I pestered him so much he took me up with him last week when Mama was in town. He knows she wouldn't allow it. Too dangerous, she says. No use losing good people after dead, she says. But we went up, slipping on leaves what's almost mud, past the tree line and into the damp shadows as far as the gravestones. We went up 'til we thought we could hear the river. But both times it started raining and Little Sasha made us turn back.

So I keep my hope by thinking of Owens, of him cooking fried eggs with dark beans at the table. I think of Owens showing me a blister on his heal the size of coin, the sun in his eyes and his squint, him sitting waiting on the bench outside the back door, him standing and shielding his eyes and scuffing the dirt on the path with his boot and smoking one of the small cigars he keeps loose in his top pocket. Walking back to the blossom grove he would pull ahead and I'd watch his limping gait and think of the war and how Samuel had told me that Owens had been a soldier. But I never believed that, cause Owens never told me about it, neither did my real mama.

The fire is bright now and the condensation on the windows—what's always there in the mornings—has almost gone. The pale sun lifts itself right out from behind the curtain of trees on the other side of the valley and I adjust the firescreen, shifting it gently on the hearthstones. Then I think I can hear Mama calling out and I turn with a jittery feeling in my stomach, hoping she's done with that chicken, but it's Little Sasha leaning on the doorway with a smile on his face.

'You lit the fire, Beth.'

'Mama lit it,' I say.

'Really?' says Little Sasha. 'She must've run pretty fast. Cause I can see her with the big rifle aiming at rabbits.' And he points with his finger, his thumb up to the ceiling. 'She's fast,' he says with a smile what lets me know he knows I'm lying and I move close to the window, away from the heat of the flames to see Mama way off in the distance lifting the rifle. The sound of it makes me jump. 'There,' says Little Sasha pointing again, 'that's half a rabbit.' He's talking soft but laughing at the same time. 'I don't know why she uses that big gun. It just blows everything to pieces.'

'She asked me to come help with a chicken,' I say.

'I guess she changed her mind,' says Little Sasha, and he's looking across the valley and up toward the mountain. And he's still. And I hear his breathing and he goes to say something and

I know it's about his brother, Samuel. But he stops, because we don't talk about that. I see his hands are fists in his pockets. He's warming them from his outside work, and it's like he's holding his worries, curled up and kept as small as he can make them.

MATTHEW HOOPER is a novel assessor and a creative writer. He worked as a novel assessor at Writers Victoria for ten years. He has degrees in Fine Art, Art History and Cinema Studies, and a Masters Degree in Creative Writing. He taught creative writing at the CAE and runs workshops in schools for teachers and students.

An Inventory of Public Toilets in Northern Spain

Alison Killick

The Camino de Santiago, an 800 kilometre pilgrimage walk across northern Spain, starts by crossing the Pyrenees, which are quite big, so you set out at dawn. The first stage, about twenty-five kilometres, goes up, then steeply up. I doubted I could do it, and people at home doubted more, yet here I stood at the first yellow arrow in Saint-Jean-Pied-de-Port and in four and a half weeks I hoped to see the towers of Santiago's Cathedral. Today we would walk for about seven hours seeing grass as green as a child's painting; wild hill ponies that I later learn are caught and used for meat; fresh, eager pilgrims; black-faced sheep; and a shepherd with his matted collie, but no public toilets. The Pyrenees don't have public toilets.

When you have chronic bowel disease, you learn several things early. The most important thing is to only go to places within twenty metres of a toilet. You learn that it's preferable if there is no one else in the toilet block when you go, and best-case scenario is if someone is jackhammering right outside the toilet block. You learn other things too, like drinking a couple of glasses of champagne means diarrhoea for two weeks and not to tell people about your disease because people don't like bowel-focused conversations. You learn that you are seen as faulty, and faulty in a dirty way. You sometimes can't control your shit, but we live in a society where your shit has to be under control. You learn to hide your condition.

The disease makes your gut as unpredictable and embarrassing as a father who walks into a party twenty minutes early to pick you up instead of waiting in the car like all the other parents. It makes you reluctant to try something new, reluctant to go out, reluctant to chase your dream of walking across Spain. You just don't know when it's going to bubble and seethe like the mud pools of Rotorua and require twenty-five trips to the toilet in a single morning.

Growing up, I learned from my parents that certain topics were off limits: sex and bodily functions, especially bowels. Farting was not allowed. My parents were religious, which meant you had to behave in a certain way. The man was the head of the home and girls were supposed to strive for prayerful sweetness and first prize in Sunday school attendance. Also, a lot of Christian country music was played on a suitcase-sized tape deck. There is no known cause of bowel disease, but being forced to listen to Christian country music should be considered a possible trigger.

When I was diagnosed with ulcerative colitis at nineteen, I didn't know how to tell my parents. How could I say *bloody stools, ulcerated colon* and *rectal examination* when even the word *fart* was considered distasteful? Sweetness and ulcerative colitis don't go together. So, on the rare times it had to be mentioned, I called it an *autoimmune disease* to sanitise it, easing the pressure on everyone.

When I first met my partner, I tried to conceal my condition, but it turns out that giving yourself an enema in a tent on your first camping trip with your new boyfriend makes it hard to hide. We had a two-person tent and a couple of those tiny hiking mattresses that take two puffs to blow up. After he'd gone to sleep, I got out one of the enemas I had to use every night. It's quite tricky when it's dark and you're in a confined space. I tried to be quiet, but there was a bit of rustling around involved. I looked over my shoulder. He was awake.

'What did I miss?' he asked.

'Um …' I ran through possible stories in my head that would make me seem less repulsive, but at 2am I was not at my most creative.

'I had to use an enema for my ulcerative colitis,' I blurted.

There was a short silence, which I expected to be broken at any second by the sound of him clawing through the tent walls to escape.

'Oh, okay,' he said and fell back to sleep.

It turns out he doesn't give a shit about shit. When he was growing up, he farted whenever he wanted.

Chronic bowel disease forces you to live a life that is less. You do less, you change plans, you stay home. If your job doesn't allow frequent toilet breaks, you have to stop working even if you don't want to. You become familiar with social isolation because you can't trust your bowel. If you go out, you might get into a situation where people find out that you are faulty. You might make someone feel uncomfortable. You learn to do things differently or to do different things. But it's always less than you want.

After a stint in hospital, I am put on new drugs that relieve some of my symptoms. I can think about emerging from isolation and rejoining life. I want to do something epic, something only fit, well, amazing people do. Something impossible for someone like me.

'Hey, I want to walk the Camino de Santiago,' I say to my partner.

'What's that?' he asks.

'It's an 800 kilometre walk in Spain.'

'What the hell! Why?'

I can't really give a coherent answer. Since medieval times, pilgrims have made their way to Santiago hoping for a miracle, or forgiveness, or spiritual credit. None of those things interest me; I want to go because I am sick of doing less than I want.

It doesn't take much to get him on board, even though he knows it will probably be an 800 kilometre toilet hunt. Maybe he's just glad to see me get out of the house. He starts checking flights. Friends and family ask, 'Are you sure that's a good idea? Why not just go to Noosa?'

We do eight months of training walks around Melbourne's suburbs that lengthen week by week, I swallow a trail mix of medication daily, and my pack is one-third prescription drugs. My partner, the eternal optimist, shrugs it off, but we both know that if my bowel decides to play up over there, I could be facing surgery in a hospital that may not have the required medical expertise.

But we go.

After the toilet-less Pyrenees, which meant I had to shit behind rocks and in ditches, villages spring up about every five kilometres and in the villages there are cafes, and in the cafes there are toilets. I still sometimes have to go behind a tree, but so does everyone else. Here, I am just like everyone else.

Not many dickheads do the Camino. They are not attracted to walking long distances alongside strangers, carrying a heavy pack, sharing food, wine and blister treatments. It's pretty much a dickhead-free four weeks. I'm still camouflaging my symptoms, because it's habitual, but it occurs to me that maybe I don't need to. Everyone out here has some ailment or another caused by relentless walking. Everyone supports each other. Maybe this is a safe environment to break free of the constraints I've placed on myself.

I decide to tell the little clan of people we have walked with for the past couple of weeks. People we have bonded with over coffee, fetid socks and the same intense desire for a glass or two of local wine at the end of each day's walk. Americans with perfect teeth, a man who has walked all the way from his front door in Berlin, a Danish lady who believes we must know Princess Mary. We have a common bond; we've moved beyond what separates us. We all have sore feet.

We are walking through an emerald tunnel of trees, as perfect as a movie set. Even though my heart is pounding, I say those words.

'I have ulcerative colitis.'

I'm watching for a hint of a cringe. I don't see any.

'Oh, okay. One of my best friends has Crohn's disease,' one says. 'That's similar right?'

'Yeah, similar,' I say.

'Well, it's great that you're out here,' he says.

I look over at Johanna, a super-fit American.

'Well done you! It's hard enough doing the Camino without that on top,' she says as she gives me a quick hug.

They all congratulate me on my effort. They think I'm an amazing person doing something epic. I'm stunned. Maybe the stigma I felt when I was nineteen need no longer apply. Maybe most people farted when they were growing up. Then my partner comes walking down the track naked because it's World Naked Hiking Day and bowels are forgotten.

Later that morning, we climb the last hill and see the towers of the cathedral in the distance. I will walk into Santiago this afternoon with my partner on our twenty-sixth anniversary. I have walked in clouds over mountains, seen poppies transform entire valleys red, avoided a rainstorm in a bar with a donkey, had a lapsed hipster from far Kew do Reiki on my feet, eaten cheese with an international model, held out my pilgrim passport to be stamped by a blind man in a Templar knight hospital and watched my toes turn into blistered mush. I walked 800 kilometres and only saw two public toilets. I told people about my disease, and they weren't repelled. I crammed every day with more. I did not live less.

ALISON KILLICK is a Melbourne-based writer and is currently working on her first novel. She has a degree in Visual Arts and a Master of Education. When not writing, she reads voraciously and plans long-distance walks in faraway places.

The industry in me

Mel Fulton

The industry in me
is furious and trigger-happy
High heels clacking,
flip phone clacking, too—
open and shut, open and shut, open and shut—
like sexy dentures
like expensive dogs
pencil-skirted, yapping, in tiled rooms:
'Cool meeting!' 'Great sex!'
The echo is damning

'Minute this, pool boy!'
I hurtle across the desk
in executive meeting rooms
I don't play by the norms
Below the line! Below the waist! Below the belt!
MANAGE ME BEFORE I MANAGE YOU

My blood percolates,
leaches from my ears
The ice in my soul is boiling
I'm moving forward
I'm in the coalface, in it!
I'm pillaging this purgatory list of actionable tasks
'Let me come back to you on that …'
in HELL

Broiled alive in this extra-collagen proto-enhanced
skin-tightening bone broth
'Great work on the press release!'
Teeth gnashing
I fog the mirror with my hot, wet meaninglessness
My network-based amphibious death croak
The alphabet smearing all around me
'I'll give you ten per cent of a hundred per cent of zero per cent!'

Eight hours photocopying the photocopies of the photocopies
of my arse
into pixelated crack infinity
and not even any of me
not the mask of my face
nor the raw meat of my spirit
not even a scrag of my DNA remains

That's my final offer
Sign the contract!
Chink the glasses
A dry martini with an eyeball floating in it
A pen scratching a sheet of blank, white, eternal paper—
You're fired …

MEL FULTON is a writer and editor. She has never held a corporate job.

About *Rise*

As you turn each page of this anthology, you are witness to the culmination of years of hard work by the students of RMIT's Associate Degree in Professional Writing and Editing. This anthology is a result of the 2021 Towards Publication course and for many students it is the full-stop in what has been an exciting, enlightening and assiduous journey.

Some of these students are specialists in creative writing, others are training to become editors, corporate writers and communications specialists, or to work in one of the many components of the publishing industry.

Exemplifying the industry-based, hands-on ethos of the Associate Degree, students have experienced the entire book-creation process. They have developed their writing through workshopping with peers and guidance from specialist writing teachers, and participated in writer–editor collaboration throughout the stages of structural editing, copyediting and proofreading for this anthology.

Each contributor submitted two pieces to our selection team—Rosie Watts, Mike Hills, Kelsie Harford and Jess

Di Giacomo—who selected one piece from each author to be put forward for publication.

Creative development and production of the anthology, including briefing our cover designer, Josh Durham, was overseen by our production team—Amanda Johnson, Dakota Stafford, Isabella Liistro, Jasmine Alavuk and Ysabel Kershaw.

Our editorial team—Daniel T Car, Hanna Begic, Jasmine Mahon, Senaai Chapple and Zach Garry—created an editorial style guide, answered our never-ending queries, and had the final word in all editorial and style issues.

The proofreading team—Ben Cumming, Emma Beckenham, Joshua Dabelstein, Pat Hornidge, and Senaai Chapple—were our last line of defence against any pesky stray commas or spelling mistakes, working tirelessly to ensure the anthology is error-free.

Finally, enlisting the writer of our introduction, Graeme Simsion, promoting the anthology to the rest of RMIT and organising the *Rise* launch was the work of the promotion team—Ayden A Carter, Aimee Clarence, Amy Bullow, Eden Taylor and Kelsie Harford.